THEY'RE STILL AT IT!

In the absence of any further collections recounting the adventures of the regulars in Callahan's Crosstime Saloon, many readers have given up. Apparently even Hugo-award winner Spider Robinson was finding *Callahan's* a hard act to follow.

BUT, they were wrong. To prove it, here's a whole 'nother quart(et) of stories from the backroad bar that's out of this world. And to make sure you believe what he says about Callahan's, the Spider has included some of his non-fiction, too.

Listen to the story of the loud-mouth time-traveler who tried to use a rip in the space-time continuum to make a fast buck.

Read about Ralph, the talking German Shepherd (but be warned: of all shaggy dog stories, shaggy dog stories about German Shepherds are the wurst).

You have to keep in mind that the good people of Callahan's have an inordinate love of the bad pun—the poorer, the better—a love almost as great as the love they have for each other and the myriad lost souls of this and any other world who should chance to fall among them. Wednesday night is a good night to be in Callahan's Crosstime Saloon—if you need it, you can find it. But remember—

STRICTLY CASH

TIME TRAVELERS STRICTLY CASH

BOOKS BY SPIDER ROBINSON:

Telempath
*Callahan's Crosstime Saloon** (collection)
Stardance (in collaboration with Jeanne Robinson)
Antinomy (collection)
The Best Of All Possible Worlds, V. I (ed.)*
*Time Travelers Strictly Cash (And Other Stories)** (collection)
Mindkiller

* —currently available in Ace paperback

TIME TRAVELERS STRICTLY CASH

SPIDER ROBINSON

SF

ACE BOOKS, NEW YORK

THE TRAVELERS STRICTLY CASH

An Ace Science Fiction Book/published by arrangement with
the author

PRINTING HISTORY
Ace edition / March 1981
Third printing / January 1983

ISBN: 0-441-81277-5

Ace Science Fiction Books are published by Charter Communications, Inc.
200 Madison Avenue, New York, New York 10016.
PRINTED IN THE UNITED STATES OF AMERICA

This one's for Jim Baen,
of course.

TABLE OF CONTENTS

FOREWORDS

TO NEW READERS:

If you have never heard of Callahan's Place before, a brief word of introduction should be offered—since four stories in this book take place there.

Don't worry! You're not late, nothing has started without you, there is no lengthy What-Has-Gone-Before to digest before you can begin. The Callahan stories have appeared in several different magazines, and so I've done my best to make each individual story self-contained. All you need to know going in is that Callahan's bar has a fireplace, and a chalk line on the floor about ten meters away, and that patrons who are willing to give up the change from their drink are welcome to toe that line, propose a toast, and eighty-six their empty glass in that fireplace. (Callahan gets a bulk discount on glasses.) As a result of this custom, a great many strange stories end up getting told in Callahan's Place, and you may, if you wish, skip now directly to the first one, "Fivesight."

TO FRIENDS OF CALLAHAN'S PLACE:

All right, I give up.

I tried; God knows I tried; you'd think a professional liar could have pulled it off. But you people are just too clever for me. My cover is blown; time to face the music and confess.

In the first collection of Callahan's bar stories, **Callahan's Crosstime Saloon** *(Ace paperback), I maintained flatly that there is no such tavern. "Callahan's Place," I said at that time, "exists only between (a) my ears, (b) assorted* **Analog** *and* **Vertex** *covers, and of course (c) the covers of this book. If there is in fact a Callahan's Place out there in the so-called real world, and you know where it is, I sincerely hope you'll tell* me.''

In a fit of craftiness, I even went so far as to insert a few subtle contradictions in the stories themselves. For example, on page 130 I stated that the Place is always crowded on holidays; on page 162 I said it is usually empty on holidays. By this brilliant ploy I hoped I could discredit myself, and appear to be an absent-minded fictioneer. Such details get noticed! I have a hundred letters from readers who spotted that discrepancy, each convinced that they are smarter than me.

Since it seemed to work so well, I continued the custom. To each of the Callahan yarns Jake has told me since that first book was closed up I have added a tiny inconsistency with the rest of the series (and an autographed cigar butt to the first reader who correctly names them all). By this means I believed I could maintain the hoax forever.

But there are five letters on my desk that say that the jig is up.

The first four are from people who found Callahan's Place. All four had needed to believe so badly that they ignored my disclaimer: they simply kept searching for the Place until they found it. I should have known it would happen. The Place is like that. But those letters caused me to reconsider the ethics of concealing the truth. How many people needed Callahan's, but gave up because I told them the quest was hopeless?

Look: there is no restaurant so good that it can survive Being Discovered. If you know a real nice place to hang out, the best thing you can do—for yourself and for the place—is to keep your mouth shut about it, at least publicly. Close friends can sometimes be tipped off—but even here care is required, as every friend has other close friends. It sounds selfish, but it's just pragmatic. If five hundred people try to share an apple, nobody benefits. Especially not the apple. So my inclination has been to play Callahan's Place close to the vest.

But there's that fifth letter I mentioned.

It is from Mike Callahan. Handwritten, of course; his pinkies are a typewriter-key-and-a-half in width. The penmanship is superb; some long-ago nun's stern discipline has triumphed over broken fingers and popped knuckles and a natural disposition to be easygoing in all things. The ink is green. The paper is wrinkled and beer-stained, and smells faintly of cigar smoke—very cheap cigar smoke.

Mike writes, in part:

> I appreciate your trying to keep the tourists and voyeurs out of our hair—if this Place gets too crowded, I can't let people smash their glasses in the fireplace. By all means keep our location under your hat, and keep your hat in a safe-deposit box. But I think you've gone just a bit too far in that direction. If folks think your stories are *fiction*, they're liable to get the idea that this Place is only imaginary, that a Place like this couldn't 'really' exist. They'll miss the point that *any* bar can be Callahan's Place, as soon as responsible people start hanging out there together. You'd be surprised how many sad sons of bitches believe people only care about each other in books.
>
> I don't think you've given too many clues to our location. 'Somewhere off Route 25A in Suffolk County, N.Y.' covers a lot of territory—anybody who can track us from that is either hurting bad enough to belong here, or resourceful enough to buy a round for the house.
>
> So let's go public.
>
> P.S.: When are you coming down for a visit? The Doc has a new stinker for you, and Jake and Eddie want to jam.

Which last brings me to a second confession:

This is NOT "just" a collection of Callahan's Place stories, and so it is not, strictly speaking, a sequel to Callahan's Crosstime Saloon.

It was supposed *to be; that's how the contract reads. Yet Callahan stories occupy a little less than half the total wordage, just over 60% of the fiction content. Why? Well, now that I've revealed the truth—that Callahan's Place really exists—I can explain. It's absurdly simple, really.*

I don't live in Suffolk County any more.

I had so much success transcribing Jake's yarns about Callahan's Place (somehow that way-out stuff never seems to happen while I'm there) that I was encouraged to try writing real science fiction on my own. It worked out rather well, and soon I decided I wanted to do it for a living. But the year I went freelance my annual income went from around ten thousand to around one thousand, and the next year it took a sharp drop—it speedily became apparent that I would have to live somewhere much less expensive than Suffolk County, Long Island. I chose the woods of Nova Scotia's great North Mountain, and eventually made that province my home. I haven't been back to Long Island but three or four quick visits since the first book of Callahan's stories was closed up. Each time I wormed another yarn out of Jake; each time I sold the results to a magazine (and my financial agreement with Jake is none of your business, thanks)—but the total wordage as of last week was only 28,000, somewhat less than half a book.

That's where matters stood when Jim Baen, then editor of Ace Books and my old chum, called up to remind me that it has been a long time since I contracted to supply a second Callahan's book.

(Hell, it's been a long time since the deadline.)

I had failed, you see, to anticipate just how popular Callahan's Place would become. Crosstime Saloon was published almost four years ago; here I sit at my desk wearing a Callahan's Place t-shirt (not my doing—an Ann Arbor entrepreneur saw a profit in them). On the desk is a Callahan's Christmas card (again, private enterprise), three different lyric sheets for songs written about the Place, and cassettes containing two more. Also on the desk is a copy of the new hardcover edition of Saloon (available from Ridley Enslow, 60 Crescent Place, Short Hills, NJ 07078), which exists because the paperback was named a Best Book For Young Adults in 1977 by the American Library Association. Funny stories almost never get nominated for Hugos, but "Dog Day Evening," herein reprinted, is one of about five to make it in the last ten years. In 1978 The Sydney (Australia) Science Fiction Foundation awarded me the Pat Terry

Memorial Award for Humorous Writing, for the Callahan stories. (It is one of the most practical awards I know: a silver-plated beer mug.) Television and movie rights to the book have been optioned, radio rights are being negotiated, I understand a tunnel in Boston has been named after Callahan . . .

In short, Baen had reason to believe he could sell another Callahan book. Furthermore, in law, he owned one, half paid for. "Where," he inquired politely, "is it?"

I explained the situation, and assured him that a trip to Long Island was simply not possible any time in the forseeable future.

He assured me that a trip to Sing Sing was inevitable if I didn't deliver.

So we compromised.

Herein be four stories from Callahan's Place. Herein also be four non-Callahan stories, all written within the last year (NOT, in other words, out-takes from my other story collection, Antinomy *[currently available from Dell Books], but newer, even better stuff.). Finally, this book contains three non-fiction pieces, two at the request of Jim Baen and one on my own initiative. The two Baen insisted on were the very first book review column I ever wrote (for reasons to be discussed later) and an essay I wrote for his superb bookazine* Destinies *concerning Robert A. Heinlein. The one I threw in is a speech I made at the 1978 Minneapolis Science Fiction Convention concerning the nature and value of fandom.*

Put it all together, wrap it up with commentary, and it approaches 80,000 words, a pretty good-sized book, of which I find that I am inordinately proud.

Now: there will, *some day, be a "second Callahan book," composed exclusively of Jake's yarns. Those contained in this book will form less than half of it. If you want to wait for it, by all means do so.*

But one thing that would hasten the day of its arrival would be for this book to make a bundle of money.

—Spider Robinson
Halifax, 1980

FIVESIGHT

I know what the exact date was, of course, but I can't see that it would matter to you. Say it was just another Saturday night at Callahan's Place.

Which is to say that the joint was merry as hell, as usual. Over in the corner Fast Eddie sat in joyous combat with Eubie Blake's old rag "Tricky Fingers," and a crowd had gathered around the piano to cheer him on. It is a demonically difficult rag, which Eubie wrote for the specific purpose of humiliating his competitors, and Eddie takes a crack at it maybe once or twice a year. He was playing it with his whole body, grinning like a murderer and spraying sweat in all directions. The onlookers fed him energy in the form of whoops and rebel yells, and one of the unlikely miracles about Callahan's Place is that no one claps along with Eddie's music who cannot keep time. All across the rest of the tavern people whirled and danced, laughing because they could not make their feet move one fourth as fast as Eddie's hands. Behind the bar Callahan danced with himself, and bottles danced with each other on the shelves behind him. I sat stock-still in front of the bar, clutched my third drink in fifteen minutes, and concentrated on not bursting into tears.

Doc Webster caught me at it. You would not think that a man navigating that much mass around a crowded room could spare attention for anything else; furthermore, he was dancing with Josie Bauer, who is enough to hold anyone's attention. She is very pretty and limber enough to kick a man standing behind her in the eye. But the Doc has a built-in compass for pain; when his eyes fell on mine, they stayed there.

His *other* professional gift is for tact and delicacy. He did not glance at the calendar, he did not pause in his dance, he did not so much as frown. But I knew that he knew.

Then the dance whirled him away. I spun my chair around to the bar and gulped whiskey. Eddie brought "Tricky Fingers" to a triumphant conclusion, hammering that final chord home with both hands, and his howl of pure glee was audible even over the roar of applause that rose from the whole crew at once. Many glasses hit the fireplace together, and happy conversation began everywhere. I finished my drink. For the hundredth time I was grateful that Callahan keeps no mirror behind his bar: Behind me, I knew, Doc Webster would be whispering in various ears, unobtrusively passing the word, and I didn't want to see it.

"Hit me again, Mike," I called out.

"Half a sec, Jake," Callahan boomed cheerily. He finished drawing a pitcher of beer, stuck a straw into it, and passed it across to Long-Drink McGonnigle, who ferried it to Eddie. The big barkeep ambled my way, running damp hands through his thinning red hair. "Beer?"

I produced a very authentic-looking grin. "Irish again."

Callahan looked ever so slightly pained and rubbed his big broken nose. "I'll have to have your keys, Jake."

The expression *one too many* has only a limited meaning at Callahan's Place. Mike operates on the assumption that his customers are grown-ups—he'll keep on serving you for as long as you can stand up and order 'em intelligibly. But no one drunk drives home from Callahan's. When he decides you've reached your limit, you have to surrender your car keys to keep on drinking, then let Pyotr—who drinks only ginger ale—drive you home when you fold.

"British constitution," I tried experimentally. "The lethal policeman dismisseth us. Peter Pepper packed his pipe with paraquat . . ."

Mike kept his big hand out for the keys. "I've heard you sing 'Shiny Stockings' blind drunk wouthout a single syllabobble, Jake."

"Damn it," I began, and stopped. "Make it a beer, Mike."

He nodded and brought me a Löwenbräu dark. "How about a toast?"

I glanced at him sharply. There was a toast that I urgently

wanted to make, to have behind me for another year.
"Maybe later."

"Sure. Hey, *Drink*! How about a toast around here?"

Long-Drink looked up from across the room. "I'm your
man." The conversation began to abate as he threaded his
way through the crowd to the chalk line on the floor and stood
facing the deep brick fireplace. He is considerably taller than
somewhat, and he towered over everyone. He waited until he
had our attention.

"Ladies and gentlemen and regular customers," he said
then, "you may find this difficult to believe, but in my youth
I was known far and wide as a jackass." This brought a
spirited response, which he endured stoically. "My only
passion in life, back in my college days, was grossing people
out. I considered it a holy mission, and I had a whole crew of
other jackasses to tell me I was just terrific. I would type long
letters onto a roll of toilet paper, smear mustard on the last
square, then roll it back up and mail it in a box. I kept a dead
mouse in my pocket at all times. I streaked Town Hall in
1952. I loved to see eyes glaze. And I regret to confess that I
concentrated mostly on ladies, because they were the easiest
to gross out. Foul Phil, they called me in them days. I'll tell
you what cured me." He wet his whistle, confident of our
attention.

"The only trouble with a reputation for crudeness is that
sooner or later you run short of unsuspecting victims. So you
look for new faces. One day I'm at a party off campus, and I
notice a young lady I've never seen before, a pretty little
thing in an off-the-shoulder blouse. *Oboy,* I sez to myself,
fresh blood! What'll I do? I've got the mouse in one pocket,
the rectal-thermometer swizzle stick in the other, but she
looks so virginal and innocent I decide the hell with subtlety,
I'll try a direct approach. So I walk over to where she's sittin'
talkin' to Petey LeFave on a little couch. I come up behind
her, like, upzip me trousers, out with me instrument, and lay
it across her shoulder."

There were some howls of outrage, from the men as much
as from the women, and some giggles, from the women as

much as from the men. "Well, I said I was a jackass," the Drink said, and we all applauded.

"No reaction whatsoever do I get from her," he went on, dropping into his fake brogue. "People grinnin' or growlin' all round the room just like here, Petey's eyes poppin', but this lady gives no sign that she's aware of me presence atall, atall. I kinda wiggle it a bit, and not a glance does she give me. Finally I can't stand it. 'Hey,' I sez, tappin, her other shoulder and pointing, 'what do you think *this* is?' And she takes a leisurely look. Then she looks me in the eye and says, 'It's something like a man's penis, only smaller.' "

An explosion of laughter and applause filled the room.

". . . wherefore," continued Long-Drink, "I propose a toast: to me youth, and may God save me from a relapse." And the cheers overcame the laughter as he gulped his drink and flung the glass into the fireplace. I nearly grinned myself.

"My turn," Tommy Janssen called out, and the Drink made way for him at the chalk line. Tommy's probably the youngest of the regulars; I'd put him at just about twenty-one. His hair is even longer than mine, but he keeps his face mowed.

"This happened to me just last week. I went into the city for a party, and I left it too late, and it was the *wrong* neighborhood of New York for a civilian to be in at that time of night, right? A dreadful error! Never been so scared in my life. I'm walking on tippy-toe, looking in every doorway I pass and trying to look insolvent, and the burning question in my mind is, 'Are the crosstown buses still running?' Because if they are, I can catch one a block away that'll take me to bright lights and safety—but I've forgotten how late the crosstown bus keeps running in this part of town. It's my only hope. I keep on walking, scared as hell. And when I get to the bus stop, there, leaning up against a mailbox, is the biggest, meanest-looking, ugliest, *blackest* man I have ever seen in my life. Head shaved, three days' worth of beard, big scar on his face, hands in his pockets."

Not a sound in the joint.

"So the essential thing is not to let them know you're

scared. I put a big grin on my face, and I walk right up to him, and I stammer, 'Uh . . . crosstown bus run all night long?' And the fella goes . . .'' Tommy mimed a ferocious-looking giant with his hands in his pockets. Then suddenly he yanked them out, clapped them rhythmically, and sang, ''*Doo*-dah, *doo*-dah!''

The whole bar dissolved in laughter.

''. . . fella whipped out a joint, and we both got high while we waited for the bus,'' he went on, and the laughter redoubled. Tommy finished his beer and cocked the empty. ''So my toast is to prejudice,'' he finished, and pegged the glass square into the hearth, and the laughter became a standing ovation. Isham Latimer, who is the exact color of recording tape, came over and gave Tommy a beer, a grin, and some skin.

Suddenly I thought I understood something, and it filled me with shame.

Perhaps in my self-involvement I was wrong. I had not seen the Doc communicate in any way with Long-Drink or Tommy, nor had the toasters seemed to notice me at all. But all at once it seemed suspicious that both men, both proud men, had picked tonight to stand up and uncharacteristically tell egg-on-my-face anecdotes. Damn Doc Webster! I had been trying so hard to keep my pain off my face, so determined to get my toast made and get home without bringing my friends down.

Or was I, with the egotism of the wounded, reading too much into a couple of good anecdotes well told? I wanted to hear the next toast. I turned around to set my beer down so I could prop my face up on both fists, and was stunned out of my self-involvement, and was further ashamed.

It was inconceivable that I could have sat next to her for a full fifteen minutes without noticing her—anywhere in the world, let alone at Callahan's Place.

I worked the night shift in a hospital once, pushing a broom. The only new faces you see are the ones they wheel into Emergency. There are two basic ways people react facially to mortal agony. The first kind smiles a lot, slightly apologetically, thanks everyone elaborately for small favors, extravagantly praises the hospital and its every employee. The face is animated, trying to ensure that the last impression it leaves before going under the knife is of a helluva nice person whom it would be a shame to lose. The second kind is absolutely blank-faced, so utterly wrapped up in wondering whether he's dying that he has no attention left for working the switches and levers of the face—or so *certain* of death that the perpetual dialogue people conduct with their faces has ceased to interest him. It's not the *total* deanimation of a corpse's face, but it's not far from it.

Her face was of the second type. I suppose it could have been cancer or some such, but somehow I knew her pain was not physical. I was just as sure that it might be fatal. I was so shocked I violated the prime rule of Callahan's Place without even thinking about it. "Good God, lady," I blurted, "What's the *matter*?"

Her head turned toward me with such elaborate care that I knew her car keys must be in the coffee can behind the bar. Her eyes took awhile focusing on me, but when they did, there was no one looking out of them. She enunciated her words.

"Is it to me to whom you are referring?"

She was not especially pretty, not particularly well dressed, her hair cut wrong for her face and in need of brushing. She was a normal person, in other words, save that her face was uninhabited, and somehow I could not take my eyes off her. It was not the pain—I *wanted* to take my eyes from that—it was something else.

It was necessary to get her attention. "Nothing, nothing, just wanted to tell you your hair's on fire."

She nodded. "Think nothing of it." She turned back to her screwdriver and started to take a sip and sprayed it all over the counter. She shrieked on the inhale, dropped the glass, and flung her hands at her hair.

Conversation stopped all over the house.

She whirled on me, ready to achieve total fury at the

slightest sign of a smile, and I debated giving her that release but decided she could not afford the energy it would cost her. "I'm truly, truly sorry," I said at once, "but a minute ago you weren't here and now you are, and that's the way I wanted it."

Callahan was there, his big knuckly hand resting light as lint on my shoulder. His expression was mournful. "Prying, Jake? You?"

"That's up to her, Mike," I said, holding her eyes.

"What you *talkin'* about?" she asked.

"Lady," I said, "there's so much pain on your face I just have to ask you, How come? If you don't want to tell me, then I'm prying."

She blinked. "And if you are?"

"The little guy with a face like a foot who has by now tiptoed up behind me will brush his blackjack across my occiput, and I'll wake up tomorrow with the same kind of head you're gonna have. Right, Eddie?"

"Dat's right, Jake," the piano man's voice came from just behind me.

She shook her head dizzily, then looked around at friendly, attentive faces. "What the *hell* kind of place is this?"

Usually we prefer to let newcomers figure that out for themselves, but I couldn't wait that long. "This is Callahan's. Most joints the barkeep listens to your troubles, but we happen to love this one so much that we all share his load. This is the place you found because you needed to." I gave it everything I had.

She looked around again, searching faces. I saw her look for the prurience of the accident spectator and not find it; then I saw her look again for compassion and find it. She turned back to me and looked me over carefully. I tried to look gentle, trust-worthy, understanding, wise, and strong. I wanted to be more than I was for her. "He's not prying, Eddie," she said at last. "Sure, I'll tell you people. You're not going to believe it anyway. Innkeeper, gimme coffee, light and sweet."

She picked somebody's empty from the bar, got down

unsteadily from her chair, and walked with great care to the chalk line. "You people like toasts? I'll give you a toast. To fivesight," she said, and whipped her glass so hard she nearly fell. It smashed in the geometrical center of the fireplace, and residual alcohol made the flames ripple through the spectrum.

I made a small sound.

By the time she had regained her balance, young Tommy was straightening up from the chair he had placed behind her, brushing his hair back over his shoulders. She sat gratefully. We formed a ragged half-circle in front of her, and Shorty Steinitz brought her the coffee. I sat at her feet and studied her as she sipped it. Her face was still not pretty, but now that the lights were back on in it, you could see that she was beautiful, and I'll take that any day. Go chase a pretty one and see what it gets you. The coffee seemed to help steady her.

"It starts out prosaic," she began. "Three years ago my first husband, Freddie, took off with a sculptress named, God help us, Kitten, leaving me with empty savings and checking, a mortgage I couldn't cut, and a seven-year-old son. Freddie was the life of the party. Lily of the valley. So I got myself a job on a specialist newspaper. Little businessmen's daily, average subscriber's median income fifty kay. The front-page story always happened to be about the firm that had bought the most ad space that week. Got the picture? I did a weekly Leisure Supplement, ten pages every Thursday, with a . . . you don't care about this crap. I don't care about this crap.

"So one day I'm sitting at my little steel desk. This place is a reconverted warehouse, one immense office, and the editorial department is six desks pushed together in the back, near the paste-up tables and the library and the wire. Everybody else is gone to lunch, and I'm just gonna leave myself when this guy from accounting comes over. I couldn't remember his name; he was one of those grim, stolid, fatalistic guys that accounting departments run to. He hands me two envelopes. 'This is for you,' he says, 'and this one's for Tom.' Tom was the hippie who put out the weekly Real Estate Supplement. So I start to open mine—it feels like there's candy in it—and he gives me this *look* and says, 'Oh *no*, not *now.*' I look at him like *huh*? and he says, 'Not until it's time. You'll know when,' and he leaves. *Okay*, I say to myself, and I put both envelopes in a drawer, and I go to lunch and forget it.

"About three o'clock I wrap up my work, and I get to thinking about how strange his face looked when he gave me those envelopes. So I take out mine and open it. Inside it are two very big downs—you know, powerful tranquilizers. I sit up straight. I open Tom's envelope, and if I hadn't worked in a drugstore once, I never would have recognized it. Demerol. Synthetic morphine, one of the most addictive drugs in the world.

"Now Tom is a hippie-looking guy, like I say, long hair and mustache, not long like yours, but long for a newspaper. So I figure this accounting guy is maybe his pusher and somehow he's got the idea I'm a potential customer. I was kind of fidgety and tense in those days. So I get mad as hell, and I'm just thinking about taking Tom into the darkroom and chewing him out good, and I look up, and the guy from accounting is staring at me from all the way across the room. No expression at all, he just looks. It gives me the heebie-jeebies.

"Now, overhead is this gigantic air-conditioning unit, from the old warehouse days, that's supposed to cool the whole building and never does. What it does is drip water on editorial and make so much goddamn noise you can't talk on the phone while it's on. And what it does, right at that moment, is rip loose and drop straight down, maybe eight hundred pounds. It crushes all the desks in editorial, and it kills Mabel and Art and Dolores and Phil and takes two toes off of Tom's right foot and misses me completely. A flying piece of wire snips off one of my ponytails.

"So I sit there with my mouth open, and in the silence I hear the publisher say, 'God *damn* it,' from the middle of the room, and I climb over the wreckage and get the Demerol into Tom, and then I make a tourniquet on his arch out of rubber bands and blue pencils, and then everybody's taking

me away and saying stupid things. I took those two tranquilizers and went home.''

She took a sip of her coffee and sat up a little straighter.
Her eyes were the color of sun-cured Hawaiian buds. ''They
shut the paper down for a week. The next day, when I woke
up, I got out my employee directory and looked this guy up.
While Bobby was in school, I went over to his house. It took
me hours to break him down, but I wouldn't take no answer
for an answer. Finally he gave up.

'' 'I've got fivesight,' he told me. 'Something just a little
bit better than foresight.' It was the only joke I ever heard him
make, then or since.''

I made the gasping sound again. ''Precognition,'' Doc
Webster breathed. Awkwardly, from my tailor's seat, I
worked my keys out of my pocket and tossed them to Callahan. He caught them in the coffee can he had ready and
started a shot of Bushmill's on its way to me without a word.

''You know the expression 'Bad news travels fast'?'' she
asked. ''For him it travels so fast it gets there before the
event. About three hours before, more or less. But only *bad*
news. Disasters, accidents, traumas large and small are all he
ever sees.''

''That sounds ideal,'' Doc Webster said thoughtfully.
''He doesn't have to lose the fun of *pleasant* surprises, but he
doesn't have to worry about unpleasant ones. That sounds
like the best way to . . .'' He shifted his immense bulk in his
chair. ''Damn it, what *is* the verb for precognition? *Precog-
nite*?''

''Ain't they the guys that sang that 'Jeremiah was a
bullfrog' song?'' Long-Drink murmured to Tommy, who
kicked him hard in the shins.

''That shows how much you know about it,'' she told the
Doc. ''He has *three hours* to worry about each unpleasant
surprise—and there's a strictly limited amount he can do
about it.''

The Doc opened his mouth and then shut it tight and let her
tell it. A good doctor hates forming opinions in ignorance.

''The first thing I asked him when he told me was why

hadn't he warned Phil and Mabel and the others. And then I caught myself and said, 'What a dumb question! How're you going to keep six people away from their desks *without telling them why*? Forget I asked that.'

" 'It's worse than that,' he told me. 'It's not that I'm trying to preserve some kind of secret identity—it's that it wouldn't do the slightest bit of good anyway, I can ameliorate—to some extent. But I *cannot* prevent. No matter what. I'm not . . . not permitted.'

" 'Permitted by who?' I asked.

" 'By whoever or whatever sends me these damned premonitions in the first place,' he said. 'I haven't the faintest idea who.'

" 'What exactly are the limitations?'

" 'If a pot of water is going to boil over and scald me, I can't just not make tea that night. Sooner or later I *will* make tea and scald myself. The longer I put off the inevitable, the worse I get burned. But if I accept it and let it happen in its natural time, I'm allowed to, say, have a pot of ice water handy to stick my hand in. When I saw that my neighbor's steering box was going to fail, I couldn't keep him from driving that day, but I could remind him to wear his seatbelt, and so his injuries were minimized. But if I'd seen him dying in that wreck, I couldn't have done *anything*—except arrange to be near the wife when she got the news. It's . . . it's especially bad to try to prevent a death. The results are . . .' I saw him start to say 'horrible' and reject it as not strong enough. He couldn't find anything strong enough.

" 'Okay, Cass,' I said real quick. 'So at least you can help some. That's more than some doctors can do. I think that was really terrific of you, to bring me that stuff like that, take a chance that I'd think you were—hey, how did you get hold of narcotics on three hours' notice?'

" 'I had three hours' warning for the last big blackout,' he told me. 'I took two suitcases of stuff out of Smithtown General while they were trying to get their emergency generator going. I . . . have uses for the stuff.' "

She looked down into her empty cup, then handed it to

Eddie, who had it refilled. While he was gone, she stared at her lap, breathing with her whole torso, lungs cycling slowly from absolutely full to empty.

"I was grateful to him. I felt sorry for him. I figured he needed somebody to help him. I figured after a manic-oppressive like Freddie, a quiet, phlegmatic kind of guy might suit me better. His favorite expression was, 'What's done is done.' I started dating him. One day Bobby fell . . . fell out of a tree and broke his leg, and Uncle Cass just happened to be walking by with a hypo and splints." She looked up and around at us, and her eyes fastened on me. "Maybe I wanted my kid to be safe." She looked away again. "Make a long story short, I married him."

I spilled a little Bushmill's down my beard. No one seemed to notice.

"It's . . . funny," she said slowly, and getting out that second word cost her a lot. "It's really damned funny. At first . . . at first, there, he was really good for my nerves. He never got angry. Nothing rattled him. He never got emotional the way men do, never got the blues. It's not that he doesn't *feel* things. I thought so at first, but I was wrong. It's just that . . . living with a thing like that, either he could be irritable enough to bite people's heads off all the time, or he could learn how to hold it all in. That's what he did, probably back when he was a little kid. 'What's done is done,' he'd say, and keep on going. He *does* need to be held and cared for, have his shoulders rubbed out after a bad one, have one person he can tell about it. I *know* I've been good for him, and I guess at first it made me feel kind of special. As if it took some kind of genius person to share pain." She closed her eyes and grimaced. *"Oh, and Bobby came to love him so!"*

There was silence.

"Then the weirdness of it started to get to me. He'd put a Band-Aid in his pocket, and a couple of hours later he'd cut his finger chopping lettuce. I'd get diarrhea and run to the john, and there'd be my favorite magazine on the floor. I'd come downstairs at bedtime for vitamins and find every pot in the house full of water, and go back up to bed wondering what the hell, and wake up a little while later to find that a socket short had set the living room on fire before it tripped the breaker and he had it under control. I'd catch him concealing some little preparation from me, and know that it was for me or Bobby, and I'd carry on and beg him to tell me—and the *best* of those times were when all I could make him tell me was, 'What's done is done.'

"I started losing sleep and losing weight.

"And then one day the principal called just before dinner to tell me that a school bus had been hit by a tractor-trailer and fourteen students were critically injured and Bobby and another boy were . . . I threw the telephone across the room at him, I jumped on him like a wild animal and punched him with my fists, I screamed and screamed. 'YOU DIDN'T EVEN TRY!' '' she screamed again now, and it rang and rang in the stillness of Callahan's Place. I wanted to leap up and take her in my arms, let her sob it out against my chest, but something held me back.

She pulled herself together and gulped cold coffee. You could hear the air conditioner sigh and the clock whir. You could not hear cloth rustle or a chair creak. When she spoke again, her voice was under rigid control. It made my heart sick to hear it.

"I left him for a week. He must have been hurting more than *I* was. So I left him and stayed in a crummy motel, curled up around my own pain. He made all the arrangements, and made them hold off burying Bobby until I came back, and when I did, all he said was . . . what I expected him to say, and we went on living.

"I started drinking. I mean, I started in that motel and kept it up when I went home. I never had before. I drank alone. I don't know if he ever found out. He must have. He never said anything. I . . . I started growing *away* from him. I knew it wasn't right or fair, but I just turned off to him completely. He never said anything. All this started happening about six months ago. I just got more and more self-destructive, more crazy, more . . . hungry for something."

She closed her eyes and straightened her shoulders.

"Tonight is Cass's bowling night. This afternoon I . . ." She opened her eyes. ". . . I made a date with a stockboy at the Pathmark supermarket. I told him to come by around ten, when my husband was gone. After supper he got his ball and shoes ready, like always, and left. I started to clean up in the kitchen so I'd have time to get juiced before Wally showed up. Out of the corner of my eye I saw Cass tiptoe back into the living room. He was carrying a big manila envelope and something else I couldn't see; the envelope was in the way. I pretended not to see him, and in a few seconds I heard the door close behind him.

"I dried my hands. I went into the living room. On the mantel, by the bedroom door, was the envelope, tucked behind the flowerpot. Tucked behind it was his service revolver. I left it there and walked out the door and came here and started drinking, and now I've had enough of this fucking coffee. I want a screwdriver."

Fast Eddie deserves his name. He was the first of us to snap out of the trance, and it probably didn't take him more than thirty seconds. He walked over to the bar on his banty little legs and slapped down a dollar and said, "Screwdriver, Mike."

Callahan shook his head slightly. He drew on his cigar and frowned at it for having gone out. He flung it into the fireplace and built a screwdriver, and he never said a mumblin' word. Eddie brought her the drink. She drained half at once.

Shorty Steinitz spoke up, and his voice sounded rusty. "I service air-conditioning systems. The big ones. I was over at Century Lanes today. Their unit has an intermittent that I can't seem to trace. It keeps cuttin' in and out."

She shut her eyes and did something similar to smiling and nodded her head. "That's it, all right. He'll be home early."

Then she looked me square in the eye.

"Well, Jake, do you understand now? I'm scared as hell! Because I'm here instead of there, and so he's not going to kill me after all. And he tells me that if you try to prevent a death, something worse happens, and I'm going out of my mind wondering what could be worse than getting killed!''

Total horror flooded through me; I thought my heart would stop.

I *knew* what was worse than getting killed.

Dear Jesus, no, I thought, and I couldn't help it. I wanted very badly to keep my face absolutely straight and my eyes holding hers, and I couldn't help it. There was just that tiny hope, and so I glanced for the merest instant at the Counterclock and then back to her. And in that moment of moments, scared silly and three-quarters bagged, she was seeing me clearly enough to pick up on it and know from my face that something was wrong.

It was 10:15.

My heart was a stone. I knew the answers to the next questions, and again I couldn't help myself: I had to ask them.

"Mrs.—"

"Kathy Anders. What's the *matter*?" Just what I had asked her, a few centuries ago.

"Kathy, you . . . you didn't lock the house behind you when you left?"

Callahan went pale behind the bar, and his new cigar fell out of his mouth.

"No," she said. "What the *hell* has that—"

"And you were too upset to think of—"

"Oh, *Christ*," she screamed. "Oh, no, I never thought! Oh, Christ, *Wally*, that dumb cocky kid. He'll show up at ten and find the door wide open and figure I went to the corner for beer and decide it's cute to wait for me in bed, and—" She whirled and found the clock, and puzzled out the time somehow, and wailed, "*No!*" And I tore in half right down the middle. She sprang from her chair and lurched toward the bar. I could not get to my feet to follow her. Callahan was already holding out the telephone, and when she couldn't dial it, he got the number out of her and dialed it for her. His face was carven from marble. I was just getting up on my hind legs by then. No one else moved. My feet made no sound at all on the sawdust. I could clearly hear the phone ringing on the other end. Once. Twice. Three times. "Come on, Cass, damn you, answer me!" Four times. *Oh dear God,* I thought, *she still doesn't get it.* Five times. *Maybe she does get it—and won't have it.* Six times.

It was picked up on the seventh ring, and at once she was shrieking, "You *killed* him, you *bastard*. He was just a jerk kid, and you had to—"

She stopped and held the phone at arm's length and stared at it. It chittered at her, an agitated chipmunk. Her eyes went round.

"Wally?" she asked it weakly. Then even more weakly she said to it, "That's his *will* in that manila envelope," and she fainted.

"*Mike!*" I cried, and leaped forward. The big barkeep understood me somehow and lunged across the bar on his belly and caught the phone in both hands. That left me my whole attention to deal with her, and I needed that and all my strength to get her to the floor gently.

"Wally," Callahan was saying to the chipmunk, "Wally, *listen to me*. This is a friend. I know what happened, and—*listen* to me, Wally, I'm trying to keep your ass out of the slam. Are you listening to me, son? Here's what you've got to do—"

Someone crowded me on my left, and I almost belted him before I realized it was Doc Webster with smelling salts.

"—No, *screw* fingerprints, this ain't TV. Just make up the goddamn bed and put yer cigarette butts in yer pocket and *don't touch anything else*—"

She coughed and came around.

"—sure nobody sees you leave, and then you get your ass over to Callahan's bar, off 25A. We got thirty folks here'll swear you been here all night, but it'd be nice if we knew what you looked like."

She stared up at us vacantly, and as I was helping her get up and into a chair, I was talking. I wanted her to be involved in listening to me when full awareness returned. It would be very hard to hold her, and I was absolutely certain I could do it.

"Kathy, you've got to listen carefully to me, because if you don't, in just another minute now you're going to try and swallow one giant egg of guilt, and it will, believe me, stick in your throat and choke you. You're choking on a couple already, and this one might kill you—and it's not fair, it's not right, it's not just. You're gonna award yourself a guilt that you don't deserve, and the moment you accept it and pin it on it'll stay with you for the rest of your life. Believe me, I *know*. Damn it, *it's okay to be glad you're still alive!*"

"What the hell do you know about it?" she cried out.

"I've been there," I said softly. "As recently as an hour ago."

Her eyes widened.

"I came in here tonight so egocentrically wrapped up in my own pain that I sat next to you for fifteen minutes and never noticed you, until some friends woke me up. This is a kind of anniversary for me, Kathy. Five years and one day ago I had a wife and a two-year-old daughter. And I had a *Big Book of Auto Repair*. I decided I could save thirty dollars easy by doing my own brake job. I tested it myself and drove maybe a whole block. Five years ago tonight all three of us went to the drive-in movie. I woke up without a scratch on me. Both dead. I smiled at the man who was trying to cut my door open, and I climbed out the window past him and tried to get my wrists on his chainsaw. He coldcocked me, and I woke up under restraint." I locked eyes with her. "I was glad to be alive, too. That's why I wanted to die so bad."

She blinked and spoke very softly. "How . . . how did you keep alive?"

"I got talking with a doctor the size of a hippo named Sam Webster, and he got me turned loose and brought me around here."

She waited for me to finish. "You—that's it? What is that?"

"Dis is Callahan's Place," Eddie said.

"This place is magic," I told her.

"Magic? *Bull*shit, magic, it's a *bar*. People come here to get blind."

"No. Not this one. People come to this bar to see. That's why I'm ashamed at how long it took me to see you. This is a place where people care. For as long as I sat here in my pain, my friends were in pain with me and did what they could to help. They told stories of past blunders to make it a little easier for me to make my annual toast to my family. You know what gives me the courage to keep on living? The courage to love myself a little? It's having a whole bunch of friends who really give a goddamn. When you share pain, there's less of it, and when you share joy, there's more of it. That's a basic fact of the universe, and I learned it here. I've seen it work honest-to-God miracles."

"Name me a miracle."

"Of all the gin joints in all the world, you come into this one. Tonight, of all the nights in the year. And you look like her, and your name is Kathy."

She gaped. "I—your wife?—I look—?"

"Oh, not a ringer—that only happens on *The Late Late Show*. But close enough to scare me silly. Don't you see, Kathy? For five years now I've been using that word, *fivesight*, not in conversation, just in my head, as a private label for precognition. I jumped when you said it. For five years now I've been wishing to God I'd been born with it. I was wishing it earlier tonight.

"Now I know better."

Her jaw worked, but she made no sound.

"We'll help you, Kathy," Callahan said.

"Damn straight," Eddie croaked.

"We'll help you find your own miracle," Long-Drink assured her. "They come by here regular."

There were murmurs of agreement, encouraging words. She stared around the place as though we had all turned into toads. "And what do you want from me?" she snapped.

"That you hold up your end," I said. "That you not leave us holding the bag. Suicide isn't just a cop-out; it's a rip-off."

She shook her head, as violently as she dared. "People don't *do* that; people don't act this way."

My voice softened, saddened. "Upright apes don't. People do."

She finished her drink. "But—"

"Listen, we just contradicted something you said earlier. It seems like it *does* take some kind of genius person to share pain. And I think you did a better job than I could have done. Two, three *years* you stayed with that poor bastard? Kathy, that strength and compassion you gave to Cass for so long, the imagination and empathy you have so much of, those are things we badly need here. We get a lot of incoming wounded. You could be of use here, while you're waiting for your own miracle."

She looked around at every face, looked long at Callahan and longest at me.

Then she shook her head and said, "Maybe I already got it," and she burst finally and explosively into tears, flinging herself into my arms. They were the right kind of tears. I smiled and smiled for some considerable time, and then I saw the clock and got very businesslike. Wally would be along soon, and there was much to be done. "Okay, Eddie, you get her address from her purse and ankle over there. Make sure that fool kid didn't screw up. Pyotr, you Litvak Samaritan, go on out and wake up your wheels. Here, Drink, you get her out to the parking lot; I can't hold her up much longer. Margie, you're the girl friend she went to spend the weekend with yesterday, okay? You're gonna put her up until she's ready to face the cops. Doc, you figure out what she's contracted that she doesn't want to bother her husband by calling. Shorty, if nobody discovers the body by, say, tomorrow noon, you make a service call to the wrong address and find him. Mike—"

Callahan was already holding out one finger of Irish.

"Say, Jake," Callahan said softly, "didn't I hear your wife's name was Diane? Kinda short and red-haired and jolly, gray eyes?"

We smiled at each other. "It was a plausible miracle that didn't take a whole lot of buildup and explanation. What if I'd told her we stopped an alien from blowing up the earth in here once?"

"You talk good on your feet, son."

I walked up to the chalk line. "Let me make the toast now," I said loudly. "The same one I've made annually for five years—with a little addition."

Folks hushed up and listened.

"To my family," I said formally, then drained the Irish and gently underhanded my glass onto the hearth.

And then I turned around and faced them all and added, "Each and every one of you."

Concerning "Fivesight":

There's been a wave of stuff about precognition in the popular media these days—people who dream disasters before they happen and so forth. Whether or not there's anything to it I couldn't say, but I'm willing to believe it can happen.

But when I will become seriously interested in precognition is the first time I hear of a disaster averted because of precognition. If some guy dreams a given flight is going to go down, and they cancel the flight and discover on inspection that it would have gone down, then I will join my local Support Your Prophets Club.

Unless and until that happens, I suspect the kindest thing to do for precognitors is to shoot them. Kindest for the future victims, too—if you know the date and manner of my death, kindly keep it to yourself.

Life's greatest virtue is its ability to surprise.

Postscript: both of the anecdotes told by Tommy Janssen and Long-Drink McGonnigle early in "Fivesight" actually occurred, exactly as described—but not to them. Each stole his story from me (that's all right—I've stolen them back). The first happened to my old college chum, Dirty Jack, and the second happened to my brother-in-law, John Moore.

Honest.

SOUL SEARCH

Rebecca Howell stood beside the plexiglass tank that contained the corpse of her husband Archer, trembling with anticipation.

A maelstrom of conflicting emotions raged within her: fondness, yearning, awe, lust, triumphant satisfaction, fierce joy and an underlayer of fear all trying to coexist in the same skull. Perhaps no one in all human history had experienced that precise mix of emotions, for her situation was close to unique. Because she was who and what she was, it would shortly lead her to develop the first genuinely new motive for murder in several thousand years.

"Go ahead," she said aloud, and eight people in white crowded around the transparent cryotank with her. In practiced silence, they began doing things.

John Dimsdale touched her shoulder. "Reb," he said softly, "come on. Let them work."

"No."

"Reb, the first part is *not* pretty. I think you should—"

"Dammit, I know that!"

"I think," he repeated insistently, "you should come with me."

She stiffened; and then she saw some of the things the technicians were doing. "All right. Doctor Bharadwaj!"

One of the white-suited figures looked up irritably.

"Call me before you fire the pineal. Without fail." She let Dimsdale lead her from the room, down white tile corridors to Bharadwaj's offices. His secretary looked up as they entered, and hastened to open the door leading into the doctor's inner sanctum for them. Dimsdale dismissed him, and Howell sat down heavily in the luxurious desk chair, putting her feet up on Bharadwaj's desk. They were both silent for perhaps ten minutes.

"Eight years," she said finally. "Will it really work, John?"

"No reason why it shouldn't," he said. "Every reason why it should."

"It's never been done before."

"On a human, no; not successfully. But the problems have been solved. It worked with those cats, didn't it? And that ape?"

"Yes, but—"

"Look, Bharadwaj knows perfectly well you'll have his skull for an ashtray if he fails. Do you think he'd try it at all if he weren't certain?"

After a pause she relaxed. "You're right, of course." She looked at him then, really seeing him for the first time that day, and her expression softened. "Thank you, John. I . . . thank you for everything. This must be even harder for you than it—"

"Put it out of your mind."

"I just feel so—"

"There is nothing for you to feel guilt over, Reb," he insisted. "I'm fine. When . . . when love cannot possess, it is content to serve."

She started. "Who said that?"

Dimsdale blushed. "Me," he admitted. "About fifteen years ago." *And frequently thereafter*, he added to himself. "So put it out of your mind, all right?"

She smiled. "As long as you know how grateful I am for you. I could never have maintained Archer's empire without you."

"Nonsense. What are your plans—after, I mean?"

"When he's released? As few as possible. I thought perhaps he might enjoy a cruise around the world, sort of a reorientation. But I'm quite content to hole up in Luna or up in Alaska instead—or whatever he wants. As long as I'm with him, I . . ."

Dimsdale knew precisely how she felt. After this week it might be weeks or years before he saw her again.

The phone rang, and he answered it. "Right. Let's go, Reb. They're ready."

The top of the cryotank had been removed now, allowing direct access to Archer Howell's defrosted body. At present it was only a body—no longer a corpse, not yet a man. It was "alive" in a certain technical sense, in that an array of machinery circulated its blood and pumped its lungs—but it was not yet Archer Howell. Dr. Bharadwaj awaited Rebecca Howell's command, as ordered, before firing the complex and precise charge through the pineal gland that he believed would restore independent life-function—and conscious-ness—to the preserved flesh.

"The new liver is in place and functioning correctly," he told her when she arrived. "Indications are good. Shall I—"

"At once."

"Disconnect life support," he snapped, and this was done. As soon as the body's integrity had been restored, he pressed a button. The body bucked in its plexiglass cradle, then sank back limply. A technician shook her head, and Bharadwaj, sweating prodigiously, pressed the button a sec-ond time. The body spasmed again—and the eyes opened. The nostrils flared, and drew in breath; the chest expanded; the fingers clenched spasmodically. Rebecca Howell cried out, Dimsdale stared with round eyes, Bharadwaj and his support team broke out in broad grins of relief and triumph . . .

And the first breath was expelled. In a long, high, unmis-takably infantile wail.

Rebecca Howell's mind was both tough and resilient. The moment her subconscious decided she was ready to handle consciousness again, it threw off heavy sedation like a flan-nel blanket. The physician monitoring her telemetry in the next room started violently, wondering if he could have cat-napped without realizing it.

"What's wrong?" Dimsdale demanded.

"Nothing. Uh, she—a second ago she was deep under, and—"

"—now she's wide awake," Dimsdale finished. "All right, stand by." He got up stiffly and went to her door. "Now comes the hard part," he said, too softly for the other to hear. Then he squared his shoulders and went in.

"Reb . . ."

"It's all right, John. Truly—I'm okay. I'm terribly disappointed, of course, but when you look at it in perspective this is really just a minor setback."

"No," he said very quietly. "It isn't."

"Of course it is. Look, it's perfectly obvious what's happened. Some kind of cryonic trauma wiped his mind. All his memories are gone, he'll have to start over again as an infant. But *he's got a mature brain*, John. He'll be an adult again in ten years, you wait and see if he isn't. I *know* him. Oh, he'll be different. He won't be the man I knew; he'll have no memories in common with that man, and the new 'upbringing' is bound to alter his personality some. I'll have to learn how to make him love me all over again. But *I've got my Archer back!*"

Dimsdale was struck dumb—as much by admiration for her indomitable spirit as by reluctance to tell her that she was dead wrong. He wished there were some honorable way he could die himself.

"What's ten years?" she chattered on, oblivious. "Hell, what's twenty years? We're both forty, now that I've caught up with him. With the medical *we* can afford, we're both good for a century and a quarter. At least sixty more *years* we can have together, that's four times as long as we've already had! I can be patient another decade or so for that." She smiled, then made herself become businesslike. "I want you to start making arrangements for his care at once. I want him to have the best rehabilitation this planet can provide, the ideal childhood. *I* don't know what kind of experts we need to hire, you'll have to—"

"*No!*" he cried.

She started, and looked at him closely. "John, what in

God's name is wrong with—'' She paled. ''Oh my God, they lost him, didn't they?''

''No,'' he managed to say. ''No, Reb, they haven't lost him. They never had him.''

''What the fuck are you talking about?'' she blazed. ''I heard him cry, saw him wave his arms and piss himself. He was *alive*.''

''He still is. Was when I came in here, probably still is. But he is not Archer Howell.''

''What are you saying?''

''Bharadwaj said a lot I didn't understand. Something about brain waves, something about radically different indices on the something-or-other profile, something about different reflexes and different—he was close to babbling. Archer was born after the development of brain-scan, so they have tapes on him from infancy. Eight experts and two computers agree: Archer Howell's body is alive down the hall, but that's not him in it. Not even the infant Archer. Someone completely different.'' He shuddered. ''A new person. A new, forty-year-old person.''

The doctor outside was on his toes, feeding tranquilizers and sedatives into her system in a frantic attempt to keep his telemetry readings within acceptable limits. But her will was a hot sun, burning the fog off her mind as fast as it formed. ''Impossible,'' she cried, and sprang from the bed before Dimsdale could react, ripping loose tubes and wires. ''You're wrong, all of you. That's my Archer!''

The doctor came in the door fast, trained and ready for anything, and she kicked him square in the stomach and leaped over him as he went down. She was out the door and into the hallway before Dimsdale could reach her.

When he reached the room assigned to Archer Howell, Dimsdale found her sitting beside the bed, crooning softly and rocking back and forth. An intern and a nurse were sprawled on the floor, the nurse bleeding slowly from the nose. Dimsdale looked briefly at the diapered man on the bed, and glanced away. He had once liked Archer Howell a great deal. ''Reb—''

She glanced up and smiled. The smile sideswiped him.

"He knows me. I'm sure he does. He smiled at me." As she spoke, a flailing hand caught one of hers, quite by accident. "See?" It clutched, babylike, but with adult strength; she winced, but kept the smile.

Dimsdale swallowed. "Reb, it's not him. I swear it's not. Bharadwaj and Nakamura are absolutely—"

The smile was gone now. "Go away, John. Go far away, and don't ever come back. You're fired."

He opened his mouth, and then spun on his heel and left. A few steps down the hall he encountered Bharadwaj, alarmed and awesomely drunk. "She knows?"

"If you value your career, Doctor, leave her be. She knows—and she doesn't believe it."

Three years later she summoned him. Responding instantly cost him much, but he ignored it. He was at her Alaskan retreat within an hour of the summons, slowed only by her odd request that he come alone, in disguise, and without telling anyone. He was conveyed to her den, where he found her alone, seated at her desk. Insofar as it was possible for one of her wealth and power, she looked like hell.

"You've changed, Reb."

"I've changed my mind."

"That surprises me more."

"He's the equivalent of a ten or twelve year old in a forty-three year old body. Even allowing for all that, he's not Archer."

"You believe in brain-scans now?"

"Not just them. I found people who knew him at that age. They helped me duplicate his upbringing as closely as possible." Dimsdale could not guess how much that had cost, even in money. "They agree with the scans. It's not Archer."

He kept silent.

"How do you explain it, John?"

"I don't."

"What do you think of Bharadwaj's idea?"

"Religious bullshit. Or is that redundant? Superstition."

" 'When you have eliminated the impossible . . .' " she began to quote.

"—there's nothing left," he finished.

"If you cannot think of a way to prove or disprove a proposition, does that make it false?"

"*Damn* it, Reb! Do you mean to tell me you're *agreeing* with that hysterical Hindu? Maybe he can't help his heritage, but *you*?"

"Bharadwaj is right."

"Jesus Christ, Rebecca," he thundered, "is this what love can do to a fine mind?"

She overmatched his volume. "*I'll thank you to respect that mind.*"

"Why should I?" he said bitterly.

"Because it's done something no one ever did in all history. I said *you* cannot think of a way to prove or disprove Bharadwaj's belief. No one ever has." Her eyes flashed. "*I* can. I did."

He gaped at her. Either she had completely lost her mind, or she was telling the truth. They seemed equally impossible.

At last he made his choice. "How?"

"Right here at this desk. Its brain was more than adequate, once mine told it what to do. I'm astonished it never occurred to anyone before."

"You proved the doctrine of reincarnation. With your desk."

"With the computers it has access to. That's right."

He found a chair and sat down. Her hand moved, and the chair's arm emitted a drink. He gulped it gratefully.

"It was so simple, John. I picked an arbitrary date twenty-five years ago, picked an arbitrary hour and minute. That's as close as I could refine it; death records are seldom kept to the second. But it was close enough. I got the desk to—"

"—collect all the people who died or were born at that minute," he cried, slopping his drink. "Oh my God, of course!"

"I told you. Oh, there were holes all over. Not all deaths are recorded, not by a damn sight, and not all of the recorded ones are nailed down to the minute, even today. The same with birth records, of course. And the worst of it was that picking a date that far back meant that a substantial number of the deaders were born before brain-scan, giving me incomplete data."

"But you *had* to go that far back," he said excitedly, "to get live ones with jelled personalities to compare."

"Right," she said, and smiled approvingly.

"But with all those holes in the data—"

"John, there are fifteen billion people in the solar system. That's one hell of a statistical universe. The desk gave me a tentative answer. Yes. I ran it fifteen more times, for fifteen more dates. I picked one two years ago, trading off the relative ambiguity of immature brain-scans for more complete records. I got fifteen tentative yeses. Then I correlated all fifteen and got a definite yes."

"But—but damn it all to hell, Reb, the fucking *birthrate* has been rising since forever! Where the hell do the *new ones* come from?"

She frowned. "I'm not certain. But I note that the animal birthrate *declines* as the human increases."

His mouth hung open.

"Do you see, John? *You're* a religious fanatic too. The only difference between you and Bharadwaj is, he's right. Reincarnation exists."

He finished his drink in a gulp. milked the chair for more.

"When we froze Archer, he *died*. His soul went away. He was recycled. When we forced life back into his body, his soul was elsewhere engaged. We got pot luck."

The whiskey was hitting him. "Any idea who?"

"I think so. Hard to be certain, of course, but I believe the man we revived was a grade three mechanic named Big Leon. He was killed on Luna by a defective lock-seal, at the right instant."

"Good Christ." He got up and began pacing around the room. "Is that why there are so many freak accidents? Every time you conceive a child you condemn some poor bastard? Of all the grotesque—'' He stopped in his tracks, stood utterly motionless for a long moment, and whirled on her. *''Where is Archer now?''*

Her face might have been sculpted in ice. ''I've narrowed it down to three possibilities. I can't pin it down any better than that. They're all eleven years old, of course. All male, oddly enough. Apparently we don't change sex often. Thank God.''

Dimsdale was breathing heavily. ''Rebecca,'' he began dangerously.

She looked him square in the eyes. ''I've had a fully equipped cryotheater built into this house. His body's already refrozen. There are five people in my employ who are competent to set this up so it cannot possibly be traced back to me. There is not one of them I can trust to have that much power over me. You are the only person living I trust that much, John. And you are not in my employ, which is another plus.''

''God damn it—''

''This is the only room in the system that I am certain is not bugged, John. I want three *perfectly* timed, untraced murders.''

''But the bloody cryotechs are *witnesses*—''

''To what? We freeze and thaw him again, hoping it will bring him out of it somehow. From the standpoint of conventional medicine it's as good an idea as any. No one listened to Bharadwaj, there *is* no accepted explanation for Archer's change. And no one but you and I know the real one for certain—even the desk doesn't remember.'' She snorted. ''Nine more attempted defrostings since Archer, none of 'em worked, and *still* nobody's guessed. There's a moratorium on defrosting, but it's unofficial. *We can do it, John.*'' She stopped, and sat back in her chair, became totally expressionless. ''If you'll help me.''

He left the room, left the house, and kept going on foot. Four days later he re-emerged from the forest, bristling with beard, his cheeks gaunt, his clothes torn and filthy. Most of his original disguise was gone, but he was quite unrecognizable as John Dimsdale. The security people who had monitored him from a distance conveyed him to her, as they had been ordered, and reluctantly left him alone with her.

"I'm your man," he said as soon as they had gone.

She winced, and was silent for a long time.

"You'll have to kill Bharadwaj too," she said at last.

"I know."

Rebecca Howell gazed again at the defrosted thing that had once been Archer Howell, but the torrent of emotions was tamed this time, held in rigid control. *It may not work on this shot,* she reminded herself. *I'm only guessing that his soul will have an affinity for his old body. He may end up in a crib in Bombay—this time.* She smiled. *But sooner or later I'll get him.*

"*Señora,* it would be well to do it now."

The smile vanished and she turned to the chief surgeon. "Doctor Ruiz-Sanchez, I said 1200 hours. To the second. You have made me repeat myself."

Her voice was quite gentle, and a normal man would have gone very pale and shut up, but good doctors are not normal men. "*Señora,* the longer he is on machine life-support—"

"HUMOR ME!" she bellowed, and he sprang back three steps and tripped over a power cable, landing heavily on his back. Technicians jumped, then went expressionless and looked away. Ruiz-Sanchez got slowly to his feet, flexing his fingers. He was trembling. "*Si, señora.*"

She turned away from him at once, returned to contemplation of her beloved. There was dead silence in the cryotheater, save for the murmur and chuckle of life-support machinery and the thrum of powerful generators. Cryotechnology was astonishingly power-thirsty, she reflected. The "restarter" device alone drank more energy than her desk, though it delivered only a tiny fraction of that to the pineal gland. She disliked the noisy, smelly generators on principle, but a drain this large *had* to be unmetered. Especially if it had to be repeated several times. *Mass murder is easy,* she thought.

All you need is a good mind and unlimited resources. And one trusted friend.

She checked the wall-clock. It lacked five minutes of noon. The tile floor felt pleasantly cool to her bare feet; the characteristic cryotheater smell was subliminally invigorating. "Maybe this time, love," she murmured to the half-living body. "Maybe not. But soon."

The door banged open and a guard hurled backward into the room, landing asprawl. Dimsdale stepped over him, breathing hard. He was wild-eyed and seemed drunk.

Only for the barest instant did shock paralyze her, and even for that instant only the tightening of the corners of her mouth betrayed her fury at his imprudence.

"*Señor*," Ruiz-Sanchez cried in horror, "you are not sterile!"

"No, thank God," Dimsdale said, looking only at her.

"What are you doing here, John?" she asked carefully.

"Don't you see, Reb?" He gestured like a beggar seeking alms. "Don't you see—it's all got to *mean* something. If it *is* true, there's got to be a point to it, some kind of purpose. Maybe we get just a hair smarter each time round the track. A bit more mature. Maybe we *grow*. Maybe what you're trying to do is get him demoted. I've studied all three of them, and so help me God every one of them is making more of his childhood than Archer did. They may not grow up to be as successful as he was. But they'll be happier."

Her voice cracked like a whip now. "John! *This room is not secure.*"

He started, and awareness came into his eyes. He glanced around at terrified doctors and technicians.

"Rebecca, I studied them all first hand. I made it my business. I had to. Three eleven year old boys, Rebecca. They have parents. Grandparents. Brothers and sisters, playmates, hopes and dreams. They have *futures*," he cried, and stopped. He straightened to his full height and met her eyes squarely. "I will not murder them, even for you. I can't."

"*Madre de dios,* no!" Ruiz-Sanchez moaned in terror.

The anesthesiologist began singing his death-song, softly and to himself. A technician bolted hopelessly for the door.

Rebecca Howell screamed with rage, a hideous sound, and slammed her hands down on the nearest console. One hand shattered an irrigator, which began fountaining water. "You *bastard,*" she raged. "You filthy bastard!"

He did not flinch. "I'm sorry. I thought I could."

She took two steps backward, located a throwable object and let fly. It was a tray of surgical instruments.

Dimsdale stood his ground. The tray itself smashed into his mouth, and a needle-probe *stuck* horribly in his shoulder. Technicians began fleeing.

"Reb," he said, blood starting down his chin, "whoever orders this incredible circus, you and your fucking desk can't outwit Him! Archer *died,* eleven years ago. You cannot have him back. If you'll only *listen* to me, I can—"

She screamed again and leaped for him. Her intention was plainly to kill him with her hands, and he knew she was more than capable of it, and again he stood his ground.

And saw her foot slip in the puddle on the floor, watched one flailing arm snarl in the cables that trailed from the casing of the pineal restarter and yank two of them loose, saw her land face first in water at the same instant as the furiously sparking cables, watched her buck and thrash and begin to die.

Frantically he located the generator that fed the device and sprang for it. Ruiz-Sanchez blocked his way, holding a surgical laser like a dueling knife. Dimsdale froze, and the doctor locked eyes with him. Long after his ears and nose told him it was too late, Dimsdale stood motionless.

At last he slumped. "Quite right," he murmured softly.

Ruiz-Sanchez continued to aim the laser at his heart. They were alone in the room.

"I have no reason to think this room has been bugged by anyone but Rebecca," Dimsdale said wearily. "And the only thing you *know* about me is that I won't kill innocent people. Don't try to understand what has happened here. You and your people can go in peace; I'll clean up here. I won't even bother threatening you."

Ruiz-Sanchez nodded and lowered the laser.

"Go collect your team, Doctor, before they get themselves into trouble. You can certify her accidental death for
me."

The doctor nodded again and began to leave.

"Wait."

He turned.

Dimsdale gestured toward the open cryotank. "How do I
pull the plug on this?"

Ruiz-Sanchez did not hestiate. "The big switch. There, by
the coils at this end." He left.

An hour and a half later, Dimsdale had achieved a meeting
of minds with her chief security officer and her personal
secretary, and had been left alone in the den. He sat at her
desk and let his gaze rest on the terminal keyboard. At this
moment thousands of people were scurrying and thinking
furiously; her whole mammoth empire was in chaos.
Dimsdale sat at its effective center, utterly at peace. He was
in no hurry; he had all the time in the world, and everything
he had ever wanted.

We do *get smarter every time*, he thought. *I'm sure of it.*

He made the desk yield up the tape of what had transpired
in the cryotheater, checked one detail of the tape very carefully, satisfied himself that it was the only copy, and wiped
it. Then, because he was in no hurry, he ordered scotch.

When she's twenty, I'll only be fifty-seven, he thought
happily. *Not even middle-aged. It's going to work. This time
it's going to work for both of us.* He set down the scotch and
told the desk to locate him a girl who had been born at one
minute and forty-three seconds before noon. After a moment, it displayed data.

"Orphan, by God!" he said aloud. "That's a break."

He took a long drink of scotch on the strength of it, and
then he told the desk to begin arranging for the adoption. But
it was the courtship he was thinking about.

Concerning "Soul Search":

I have always felt faintly guilty about the Campbell Award.

Every year the members of the World Science Fiction Society* vote on the Hugo Awards for professional and fannish achievement in sf. Since 1973 they have also voted the John W. Campbell Award for Best New Writer. It is technically a non-Hugo, and has been privately sponsored by Conde-Nast Publications, former publishers of Analog *(formerly* Astounding*), the magazine which the late John Campbell used to invent modern science fiction. Davis Publications, Analog's new owner, will continue the tradition. The award was originally suggested by Ben Bova, who was named editor of* Analog *when John died. Anyone whose first professional sf publication took place within the previous years is eligible.***

In 1974 Lisa Tuttle and I tied for the second Campbell Award.

It was the first award of any kind that I ever won (barring a scholarship), and I tied for it fair and square, and I'm quite proud of it. And yet there is a certain sense in which I feel a little funny about it.

You see, I suspect in my heart of hearts that if he had lived, John W. Campbell would have hated my stuff.

Or at least failed to buy it with any regularity. I don't write watchacall your average Astounding *story. I've never written a story with an engineer as the protagonist. I'm massively ignorant of science, and rarely write stories about physical problems. I don't know how to design a planet, and I don't much want to learn; I tend to keep my stories in and around known ones. The second Callahan story ever published, "The Time Traveler," caused one* Analog *reader to cancel*

---

* - *i.e., anybody in the world who chooses to bother. You, if you like.*
**- *each year George Martin publishes an anthology of original stories by all the Campbell Award nominees, called* New Voices. *(Pocket) Highly recommended.*

his subscription because they'd "stopped printing science fiction."

Don't get me wrong. I think that if we had ever met, John and I would have found many many things to agree about. It's hard to be certain what those things would have been; I understand that his thought was, like a UFO, capable of sudden 180° course changes without structural damage. But I'd guess that we would have agreed on a number of important things: the value of reason and technology and liberty and hope and conscience and competence for a start. I have enjoyed a lot of the stories that John Campbell paid money for.

I just don't think he would have bought much of my particular brand of sf for Analog.

Until now. When I sent the manuscript of "Soul Search" to Ben Bova (at Omni, where he has lately gone after seven years as editor of Analog), I said in the cover letter, "This is the first story I've written that I really think John Campbell would have bought."

It's such a Campbellian notion, precisely the kind of idea he used to toss at writers over those famous lunches. "Okay, assume reincarnation. Now: what happens to cryogenics?" Whether he would have actually bought the story you have just read or not can never be known, but I think it's the kind of story idea that would have made John's eyes light up.

Incidentally, while I know many people who emphatically believe in reincarnation, I have never met or read one who could satisfactorily explain population growth. As far as I know the hypothesis I offer in "Soul Search"—that human population is inversely proportional to that of other species—is original with me. The beauty of it is that since I haven't specified which species (Cats, dogs and dolphins, certainly. But do goats have souls? Owls? Salmon? Oats? Cockroaches? Viruses? Computers?)* the hypothesis cannot be disproved unless and until we have a complete and accurate census of all life on Earth.

---

* - When I lived on the Fundy Shore, there was a stand of rock maples back up the Mountain that I got to know pretty well. Some of 'em even became volunteer blood-donors for my pancakes. I'm sure they had souls.

(Come to think, why limit souls to earth? What about that old sf notion that the Martian race has been dying off as ours expands? Could our population explosion have been triggered by a supernova halfway across the universe? Could our cycles of warfare correspond to the breeding cycle of some distant race of methane breathers? Excuse me while I go write a couple more stories.)

In short, the Steady State Theory of the Continuum of Souls is still tenable—at least cannot be disproved—while the Big Bang Theory raises more questions than it answers. (By the way, if you do limit the continuum of souls to Terra, neither theory addresses planetary disaster, either past [glaciation] or projected [the ecodeath scenario so beloved by Luddities].)

The point, the purely Campbellian point is that reincarnation cannot be disproved today, and may conceivably become provable in the near future, with tools a-buildin' today. Therefore it's past time to begin speculating about it.

Concerning "Spider vs. The Hax Of Sol III":

I know a simple, four-letter word whose meaning can, by the transposition of the last two letters, be precisely reversed—without altering its pronunciation.

To substantiate this claim, I have to go back just over five years.

Five years ago Jim Baen was the editor of Galaxy magazine, in the process of making it the second-best-selling magazine in the business. I was a novice sf writer, with no novels and fewer than half a dozen short stories published. Jim had bought exactly one of these for Galaxy (well, it was the only one I showed him), and a couple of times when I'd passed through New York he had thrown me a double sawbuck for a day's worth of reading slushpile. "Slush" is the technical term for unsolicited manuscripts, and for about 99.6% of them, it is a very charitable description indeed. The remaining four tenths of a percent are what keeps sf alive and growing, and in particular they were what was keeping Galaxy alive and growing five years ago, as the publisher gave Jim a monthly budget of two cheese sandwiches, a firkin of salt and a buffalo nickel with which to produce the magazine. Furthermore each month's budget tended to actually leave the accounting department in the following fiscal year, or worse. Jim needed his slush combed pretty thoroughly.

(I wish to note here that to my knowledge Jim always warned his writers at point-of-sale to expect late payment. I have known editors less forthright.)

Anyway, I was on the phone with him one day, I forget who called who or why, I remember I was in North Dartmouth, Massachusetts, working on a story called "Stardance" with my wife Jeanne, and didn't want to be distracted.

"Here's a good question," he said. "What's the difference between a critic and a book reviewer?"

I thought about it. "I guess I'd say a critic is someone who evaluates books in terms of the objective standards of serious literature. A reviewer is someone who believes those standards to be either imaginary or irrelevant, and evaluates books in terms of his own prejudices."

"Say it simpler."

I was itching to get back to my little basement writing-nook. "Uh . . . a critic tells you whether or not it's Art; a reviewer tells you whether or not it's any damn good to read."

"Done," he said.

"Huh?"

"The pay is half a cheese sandwich."

"What?"

"All right, all right, you can have the buffalo nickel; Pournelle and Geis are splitting the salt."

"What the hell are you talking about?"

"You're my new book reviewer. Deadline is next week; we'll call it a guest column and then phase you in permanently in a couple of months."

"You've got a book reviewer. One of the biggest names in the business."

"I had a book reviewer. Sturgeon has this bad habit."

"Eh?"

"Eating. We owe him a great many cheese sandwiches."

"Ah. I take it the cheese sandwiches you are offering me are similarly promissory in nature?"

"You've got it. Same as buying stories: I promise to pay you before you die—but you have to promise not to die." *

You can't let editors push you around in this business or you're finished. "Let me see if I've got this straight. You want me to stop work on a novella which is no question going to win the Hugo, Nebula and Locus next year, ** *just put that on hold for awhile, read about a dozen books and think of something coherent to say about them, type the whole thing up and send it in by next week, stick my neck out by telling people what I think is good and bad on the basis of my three*

---

*—*Actually, Jim got me every penny I was owed. Eventually.*
**—*no, I haven't got fivesight. I say that about every story; it just happened to be true this time.*

whole years in the business—and furthermore you want me to do this month after month—and furthermost, the pay for all this is cheese sandwiches that arrive so late I can't even Edam; is that, in essence, your offer?''

''Well summarized.''

''It's a deal.''

Which might make me sound like a bit of a chump. After all, each month's column took three weeks to prepare, leaving one week in which to earn a living. But consider: for the next several years (until I resigned over a disagreement with the publisher as to which of us was writing the column) my name was featured prominently on the cover of every issue of Galaxy, *in plain view of a great many citizens. At least seventy-five thousand people took a copy into their homes and exposed their families and friends to it each month. Untold thousands of people who left the magazine-stand without a copy yet carried away the subconscious impression that this Robinson must be some kind of prominent or prolific guy, to be featured on every cover. Now this was no inducement at all to Ted Sturgeon, whose reputation simply could not be any bigger or better. He didn't need exposure, he needed cheese sandwiches.* But me? Since the age of thirteen I have stood six-one and weighed one hundred and fifteen pounds: such a metabolism can survive on the promise of cheese sandwiches.*

And so was born ''Spider vs. The Hax Of Sol III.''

And things began happening.

At the end of my first year as a reviewer, I was named Best Critic of the Year by the readers of Locus, *the excellent newspaper of sf. (The word ''critic'' itched me a bit—but* Locus, *apparently agreeing that to call me a critic is some kind of travesty, and unwilling to court semantic dispute by establishing a ''reviewer'' category, solved the problem by dropping ''critic'' altogether from its poll.) Incoming correspondence peaked at about twenty letters a week, and has remained constant. My only major overhead—buying sf— disappeared, and in fact my problem now is disposing of the*

**Ted raises rabbits.*

surplus. (Most of the books I receive for review are surplus.)
I acquired a number of new friends in the business (a small
number, as most writers seem to believe a good review is only
what they deserve), and a number of new enemies (a rather
larger number, as most writers seem to believe that a bad
review can only come from an admixture of envy, stupidity
and innate evil).

And, as a side effect, readership of my own stories increased. People who liked my columns decided that if I was
that entertaining talking about books, imagine how entertaining I'd be telling stories. People who hated my columns
wanted to prove that I had no business criticizing anyone
else's work.

The net result is that as I write this, five years almost to the
day since Jim Baen decided to take a chance on an unknown
(a decision for which he says he received a huge amount of
static from some quarters), I'm making a (tenuous) living at
my trade.

So it seems to me that if you take the word "bane"
("Nemesis; cause of destruction or ruin.") and reverse the
last two letters, you totally reverse the meaning. It is at Jim
Baen's insistence that the following, my first-ever "guest"
review column, is reprinted here, despite its amateurishness,
and I understand how he feels. He has reason to be proud.

And I have reason to be grateful.

(Lest, however, you put this book down with the erroneous
impression that any editor is a totally nice guy, I direct your
attention to the logo at the head of the following column. It is
the original logo for "Spider vs. The Hax," commissioned
by Baen and drawn by Freff. I first saw it when it was
printed, and I sent what I considered a mild letter [no
specific death threats] to Jim, suggesting that perhaps the
logo "lacked dignity" a trifle. Freff happened to be in the
office when my letter arrived, and their mutual response
follows the column.)

SPIDER VERSUS THE HAX OF SOL III

I'm sorry. I can't help it. I just have that kind of mind, and there's nothing I can do about it. When Jim Baen asks me for a guest review, all I can visualize is a psychopathic butler, ex-Army no doubt, who instead of announcing the guests as they arrive, lines them up and begins inspecting them for flaws. "Suck in that gut, sister. You there, call that a shave?" I'm sorry, honest.

So here's a guest review, Jim.

Laurels first, then brickbats, with the white elephant saved for last. I'm sorry to say that there are no perfect books waiting for you at your bookstore this month, genties and ladlemen. But some come closer than others.

Closest is *Deathbird Stories* by Harlan Ellison (Harper & Row, price unknown). This, friends, is one king hell collection of gutpunching, groin-kicking, arm-breaking short stories, subtitled "A Pantheon of Modern Gods" and dedicated to the proposition that if gods die when their followers stop believing, then gods are born when beliefs crystallize.

47

Harlan takes a look at some of the gods we're raising up these days, and makes it quite clear that we'd better start learning how to placate them, like pronto. Written over a period of ten years, the stories are superbly crafted and chillingly effective, the kind of which Heinlein once said that you should serve a whisk-broom with every shot, so that the customer can brush the sawdust off him when he gets back up. But in the three or four times I've met Harlan, I've noticed a severe strain on our relationship in that he has nothing to bitch at me about, and so I ought to add some beefs.

First, most of these stories will probably already be familiar to you (a margarine dildo to the first reader who can name an anthology of anything by anyone in the past year that *hasn't* contained *Deathbird*), reminding one of those ten Billie Holiday albums with three albums worth of songs endlessly shuffled and re-dealt. "Maggie Moneyeyes," "Along the Scenic Route," "Paingod" and "Shattered Like A Glass Goblin" aren't exactly obscure, for instance.

But thass alright—somehow all these stories do belong thematically in one book. My main beef is that *all* of Harlan's new gods are scary. Pessimism is okay—but unrelieved pessimism seems a little unrealistic. Maybe all that's on the other side is the sixteen-year-old perfect goombah and his divine Maserati, but why don't we take a look?

But how can you complain about a book that has "Whimper of Whipped Dogs" in it?

Next in line is *The Shockwave Rider* (Harper & Row, price unknown—while this latter phrase reoccurs frequently because I'm working from galleys, for obvious reasons I can't abbreviate it) by John Brunner, a Spring '75 selection for the SF Book Club. This one had seeds of greatness, but maybe it needed more vermiculite. It's not a bad book—but somehow it just misses. Close though.

The protagonist is Nickie Haflinger, who was drafted as a child into the government's behaviorist-oriented genius factory, Tarnover. Not content with encouraging natural geniuses to mature, the directors of this institution are attempting to grow genetically-modified geniuses from ova in the laboratory. As a young man Nickie stumbles across a deformed and imbecile Mark I, becomes disillusioned with behaviorism and splits, removing himself from the national data-net and establishing a succession of aliases with a stolen computer-code, dedicating himself to the overthrow of Tarnover and all it stands for. A dandy plot, and one that in Brunner's hands should have been Hugo material. I dunno; maybe he was in a hurry. Both his villains and the community of Precipice (Tarnover's underground antithesis) are cut from cardboard, and there are a series of debate-lectures between Nickie and the government interrogator who's wringing out his memory that just don't ring true.

But the book reads well all the same. Individual sections are often brilliant, in the way that John seems to have copyrighted, and the message is incisive and timely. But as a story it limps. So call it the worst book he's written in five years, and you've still put it two notches above average. It kept me turning the page, and its closing question has yet to be answered.

Onward to a pleasant surprise. Somehow or other I got on Doubleday's SF review list a couple of years back, and as a result my stove here in Nova Scotia has never lacked for fire-starter. Honest to God, you never saw such stuff in your life. Comic-books without the pictures. But I hear they've got a new SF editor lately, and here on my desk, by Jesus, is an actual first-rate science-fiction novel from Doubleday, *Newton and the Quasi-Apple*, by Stanley Schmidt. I'd never have read it if I hadn't recognized Stanley's name from some fine stories in *Analog*, but I'm glad I gave it a chance. The planet of Ymrek, see, is at a crisis point in its cultural development. The civilized types in the city of Yngmer are threatened by the barbarian Ketaxil, and have for defense only crude cannon which they don't know how to aim very well. A pair of human xenologists reluctantly decide to interfere by giving the Yngmerians technological aid in the form of "quasi-matter," a wondrous stuff they hope to pass off as "nothing more than simple magic." Unfortunately, at the same time a native genius named Terek has singlehandedly duplicated the work of Copernicus, Galileo and Newton, deducing laws of motion with which *he* hopes to save the day by inventing ballistics, to aim the cannon better. The local shaman reacts little better than did Galileo's inquisitors, and just as Terek has begun to convince him that perhaps *il se muovo* after all, in come the xenologists—with quasimatter trinkets that don't obey Newton's Laws! Poor Terek is ceremonially proclaimed a Dunce, and the rest of the book deals with the attempts of the meddling but well-intentioned xenologists to set things right. It's a dandy, and I'm proud of Stanley for his refusal to yield to temptation and pull rabbits out of a hat for an ending.

My only complaint is his failure to explain quasimatter rather than simply describe it—but as a man with a trunkfull of letters saying, "your last story was okay—but it's not science fiction," possibly I should shut up. Tasty stuff, Stan.

Cliff Simak's new book, *Enchanted Pilgrimage* (Putnam-Berkley) is another one of those that gave me mixed feelings. If there's a sequel planned, I withdraw most of my objections, but as it stands it raises more questions than it answers.

To say that it's well told would be more unnecessarily redundant than is absolutely called for—it is, after all, a Simak. The characters are well-drawn, the menaces chilling, the succession of events compelling. But the book frustrates me, dammit. The first half reads like alternate-universe sword-and-sorcery—a little strange for Cliff, but what the hell. In this alternate universe men have never really left the Middle Ages, and gobblins, trolls, elves and unicorns festoon the countryside. A quest is undertaken (incidentally, quests involving a chalice or grail are a separate subgenre called cup-and-sorcery) by a band of good joes. Fine.

Then halfway through the book, a modern-day human appears from our time-stream, complete with firestick and a Honda dragon, and one not unnaturally assumes that some of the strange goings-on are going to get mundane explanations. Only some do, and some don't, and one of the most impressive menaces turns out for no apparent reason to be an alien, which dies in giving birth to a robot (!) that seems to do nothing to advance the plot. We learn that there are *three* alternate universes (why only three?) and that the third of these is a "humanist" world in which all the problems of man have been solved—but all we ever get to see of it is two characters who appear only by rumor. Nor do we ever learn how travel between the universes is managed, nor why only one not-especially-bright inhabitant of our own time-stream (named Jones, forsooth) pulled it off. Worst, the quest turns out to have been a wild-goose chase for all but one of its members.

Oh hell—Cliff is just too good a craftsman to leave such gaping holes in the foundations: there *has* to be a sequel. But I wish there'd been words to that effect somewhere in the galleys.

The missing man in Katherine MacLean's book of the same name (Putnam-Berkley) seems to be the protagonist—the one we are given just doesn't seem real to me. No, amend that: he seems real for the first chapter (which, if my memory serves, appeared somewhere or other as a novelette—and a damned good one* and then vanishes, leaving behind a cardboard simulacrum. There's just no consistency to his character: he's an ex-teengang member, big and strong when the plot requires it, but most of the time he acts like a timid chump; he is a professional empath, and yet he gets suckered into buying the metaphysics of a sociopath gang leader with nary a quiver. And the final group of villains to be dragged onstage, comic-opera Com-Yew-Nists Who Want To Make

*-1980 update; to give you an idea how well my memory serves me, the shortest version, a novella, won the Nebula in 1971.

The World A Conformist Utopia So They Can Power Trip Us (but get this: they're telepathic, see . . .) went down like two tablespoons of peanut butter.

Which leaves me astounded. For years I have watched Kate MacLean write circles around a large lot of folks, and upon receiving the first novel I've seen by her I rejoiced, expecting something above average. But this is barely adequate. The first chapter, in which we meet George, the high-sensitivity empath who works as a locater for the Rescue Squad, is really excellent—but the book as a whole lacks an internal consistency somehow, and suspending that disbelief starts to give you cramps. I'm disappointed. I don't object to a simple series-of-episodes—but the cast should be continuous.

Getting near the bottom, now. Funny SF novels, when they work, are among the funniest things ever written: e.g., Niven & Gerrold's *The Flying Sorcerer,* a sizable chunk of Keith Laumer's work, and the new Bester novel. Some are a trifle strained, but still make you giggle consistently: e.g. Bob Toomey's *World of Trouble.* And some are as strained as the stuff that goes in I.V. bottles: e.g., *The Wilk Are Among Us,* by Isidore Haiblum (Doubleday, $5.95).

Since Stan Schmidt's book had turned out so well, I decided to try the one that came with it; but when I got to the part where the ferocious and homidical *nill* says to the alien protagonist, "If I wasn't a bit under the weather, and you didn't have that crude mind-block on—really, under ordinary conditions it wouldn't do at all, you know—I'd give you such a hit!" I began to suspect that the stack of handkerchiefs I'd laid in against tears of laughter might be superfluous. Everybody in the book is named Leonard or Ernest or Marvin, extraterrestrials who've never heard of Earth call each other *boychik,* and at odd intervals Haiblum succumbs to Zelazny's Syndrome: the habit of stringing together sentence fragments.

As paragraphs.

In groups of six of seven.

For no discernible reason.
Like a freshman art student.
Making a collage.
Or some.
Thing.

Followed by two skipped lines and a block of more or less standard copy. There's a lot of action, a cast of thousands, and a plot that would confound a panel consisting of Ketih Laumer, P.G. Wodehouse and Avram Davidson, and if you use an Ashley wood-burning stove and don't subscribe to a newspaper you'll be interested to know that the hardcover edition fits snugly into the firebox and will support a good base of kindling and mixed hardwood. I recommend maple if you can get it.

And so at last we come to Sprague de Camp's Antique Shoppe.

I know there are a horde of you Lovecraft freaks out there, and maybe some of you *are* Trekkie-type groupies, and I really truly do believe that a reviewer has a duty to finish a book before publishing his views on it, but honest to Christ, fellas. *The Life of H.P. Lovecraft* by L. Sprague de Camp (Doubleday, $12.95) is simply above and beyond the call of whatever Baen is underpaying me. [*"Sold!" he shrieked.—Ed.*] It is no bigger than a Smith-Corona portable, clearly the result of a literally incredible amount of time and energy, and I tried, cross my heart. But do any of you really want to know that at the age of two, Lovecraft's golden curls led his landlady to call him "Little Sunshine"?

I have in my possession a volume of comparable size, which was commissioned by state legislature, printed at taxpayers' expense in 1947, and bought by the same taxpayers for the State University Library system, from which I ultimately stole it, leaving behind five identical copies none of which has ever been checked out. It is an 800-page study of the ruffed grouse, a bird so stupid you can blow out the brains of one without disturbing the one next to it. It took six men to write, and one of the men later produced a 400-page sequel. I take it down from the shelf whenever I'm feeling especially useless and futile, and pore over the maps and graphs and close-ups of grouse droppings, and I feel better.

At long last I've found a companion volume.

If you're an English major who believes you must know the man to properly read and evaluate his works (don't laugh—I was one once) then by all means pick this book up—if you can (little joke there). If you're an Ashley user, I should advise you that the binding is damnably difficult to destroy, and it's too big to use all at once. If you're H.P. Lovecraft, let me know what you think of it.

And so opens 1975 in the SF publishing world. Me, I think I'm going to get back in the time-capsule and get some sleep. Wake me up when Heinlein's next book comes out, will you? Thanks.

Also concerning "Spider vs. The Hax Of Sol III":

God, that hurt to proofread.

One final word on this column. Since its publication I have had an opportunity to apologize privately to L. Sprague de Camp, an apology he most graciously accepted; I would like to do so now publicly. When I first met that worthy gentleman, he suggested with exquisitely gentle politeness that perhaps I had been a trifle harsh in reviewing his Lovecraft biography. I suggest that what I was was a horse's ass. To heap scorn and abuse on a book one doesn't happen to be excited about, on the grounds of its thoroughness, is the mark of an amateur playing to the bloodthirsty. One of the major agonies of reviewing is that you cannot recall an opinion which later reflection reveals to be fatheaded. There isn't enough time for anything but snap judgements, and often you end up regretting them, and there's no practical way to retract them. Writing a book gives you time for reflection: a year after you mail off the manuscript, they mail it back copy-edited and you re-read it carefully, changing what now strikes you as imprudent or ill-advised. Six months later you get galley proofs—again you can make sure that's what you meant to say. A few months after that, people are reading it—and there's still time to make changes for the paperback edition.

A book review column is always due last week. You hammer it out on horseback, race to the post office, nap on the doorstep for a few hours until they open up, mail the manuscript—and then the next time you see it is the same time everybody else does, in print. It generally has not been copy-edited; all your mistakes and syntactical horrors are intact and the typesetter has suggested some of his own. It contains opinions you cannot imagine yourself having entertained, let alone expressed, and if you sit down right now and dash off a letter to recant or clarify it will see print five or six months from now; half the readers won't know what the hell you're talking about. It's too late.

This is the only time I've ever had an opportunity to retract something I said in a column, and it feels good.

No one interested in the life of H.P. Lovecraft should be without Sprague de Camp's definitive biography.

Ironic update: Stan Schmidt, whom I praised in this first column, is now my employer. "Doc" Schmidt recently became editor of Analog, *for which magazine I do quarterly book-reviews. Funny how things work out.*

DOG DAY EVENING

It absolutely *had* to happen. I mean, it was so cosmically preordained-destined-fated flat out *inevitable* that I can't imagine how we failed to be expecting it. Where else on God's earth could Ralph and Joe possibly have ended up but at Callahan's Place?

It was Tall Tales Night at Callahan's, the night on which the teller of the most outrageous shaggy-dog story gets his night's tab refunded. "Animals" had been selected as the night's generic topic, and we had suffered through *hours* of stinkers about pet rocks and talking dogs and The Horse That Was Painted Green and the Fastest Dog in the World and the Gay Rooster and a dozen others you probably know already. In fact, most of the Tale-Tellers had been disqualified when someone shouted the punchline before they got to it—often after only a sentence or two. The fireplace was filled to overflowing with broken glasses, and it was down to a tight contest between Doc Webster and me. I thought I had him on the run, too.

A relative newcomer named B.D. Wyatt had just literally crapped out, by trying to fob off that old dumb gag about the South Sea island where "there lives a bird whose digestive system is so incredibly rank that, if its excrement should contact your skin, re-exposure of the contaminated skin to air is invariably fatal." Named for its characteristic squawk, it is of course the famous Foo Bird, and the punchline—as I'm certain you know already—is, "If the Foo shits, wear it." Unfortunately for B.D. ("Bird Doo"?), we already knew it too. But it gave me an idea.

"You know," I drawled, signalling Callahan for a fresh

Bushmill's, "like all of us, I've heard that story before. So many times, in fact, that I decided there might be a grain of truth in it—hidden, of course, by a large grain of salt. So my friend Thor Lowerdahl and I decided to check it out. We investigated hundreds of south sea islands without success, until one day our raft, the *Liki Tiki*, foundered on an uncharted atoll. No sooner did we stagger ashore than we heard a distant raucous cry: 'Foo! Foo!'

"Instantly, of course, we dove back into the surf, and didn't stick our heads up until we were far offshore. We treaded water for awhile, hoping for a glimpse of the fabulous bird, to no avail. Suddenly a seal passed us underwater, trailing a cloud of sticky brown substance. Some of it got on Thor's leg, and with a snort of disgust, he wiped it off. He expired at once. Realizing the truth in an instant, I became so terrified that I *swam* back to the States."

I paused expectantly, and Fast Eddie (sensing his cue) obliged me with a straight line.

"What truth, Jake?"

"That atoll," I replied blithely, "was far more dangerous than anyone suspected—as any seal can plainly foo."

A general howl arose. Long-Drink chanced (by statistical inevitability) to have his glass to his mouth at the time; he bit a piece off clean and spat it into the fireplace. I kept my face straight, of course, but inwardly I exulted. *This* time I had Doc Webster beat for sure, and with an *impromptu* pun at that. I ordered another.

But when the tumult died down, the Doc met my eyes with a look of such mild, placid innocence that my confidence faltered.

"Fortunate indeed, Jacob," he rumbled, patting his ample belly, "that you should have rendered so un*bear*able a pun. It reminds me of a book about a bear I read the other day by Richard Adams—*Shardik,* it's called. Any of you read it?"

There were a few nods. The Doc smiled and sipped scotch.

"For those of you who missed it," he went on, "it's about a primitive empire that forms around an enormous, semi-mythical bear. Well, it happens I know something about that empire that Adams forgot to mention, and now's as good a time as any to pass it along. You see, the only way to become a knight in Shardik's empire was to apply for a personal interview with the bear. This had its drawbacks. If he liked your audition, you were knighted on the spot—but if you failed, Lord Shardik was quite likely to club your head off your shoulders with one mighty paw. Even so, there were many applicants—for the peasantry were poor farmers, and if a candidate failed for knighthood his family received, by way of booby-prize, a valuable sheepdog from the Royal Kennels. This consoled them greatly, for truly it is written . . .''

And here he actually paused to sip his scotch again, daring us to guess the punchline:

''.   .   . 'For the mourning after a terrible knight, nothing beats the dog of the bear that hit you.''

A howl again began to arise—and then suddenly a howl arose.

I mean a *real* howl.

So of course we all swiveled around in our chairs, and damned if there wasn't a guy with a German shepherd sitting near the door. I hadn't seen them come in, and it took me a second to notice that the dog had a glass of gin on the floor in front of him, half-empty.

As we gaped, open-mouthed, the dog picked up the half-full glass in his teeth (without spilling a drop), carried it to the hearth, and with a flick of his powerful head, flung it into the fireplace hard enough to bust it. He turned and looked at us then, wagging his tail as if to make sure we understood that he was commenting on the *Doc's* tale. Then, to underline the point, he turned back to the fireplace, lifted his leg and put out a third of the fire.

We roared with laughter, a great simultaneous outburst of total glee, and the dog trotted proudly back to his master. I looked the guy over: medium height, a little thin, nose like an avalanche about to happen and a great sprawling fungus of a mustache clinging to its underside. He wore Salvation Army rejects like Mr. Emmett Kelly used to wear, clothes that looked like what starts fires in old warehouses. But his eyes were alert and aware, and he was obviously quite proud of his dog.

Then he caught Callahan's eye, and winced. "You got a house-rule on dogs, Mister?" he asked. You could hardly see his lips move under that ridiculous mustache.

Callahan considered the matter. "We try not to be human-chauvinists around here," he allowed at last. "Only house-rule on dogs, Mister?" he asked. You could hardly see his lips move under that ridiculous mustache.

"Are you kiddin'?" the guy mumbled. "*This* dog mess on the floor? Why, this is the Smartest Dog In The World." He said it just like that, with capital letters.

"Uh-huh," said Long-Drink. "He talks, right?"

A strange gleam came into the shabby man's eyes.

"Yep."

"Oh for God's sake," Doc Webster groaned. "Don't tell me. A talking dog has walked into Callahan's Place on Tall Tales Night. If that hound tops my story, I'm going on the wagon—for the whole night."

That broke everyone up, and Long-Drink McGonnigle was particularly tickled (say that three times fast with whiskey in your mouth). "Patron saint of undershorts," he whooped, "it makes so much sense I almost believe it."

"You think I'm kidding?" the stranger asked.

"That or crazy," the Doc asserted. "A dog hasn't got the larynx to talk—let alone the mouth structure—even if he *is* as smart as you say."

"I've got two hundred dollars says you're wrong," the stranger announced. He displayed a fistfull of bills. "Any takers?"

Well, now. We're a charitable bunch at Callahan's, not normally inclined to cheat the mentally disturbed. And yet there was a clarity to his speech that belied his derelict's clothes, a twinkle in his eye that looked entirely sane, and a challenging out-thrust to his chin that reminded us of a kid daring you to hit him. And there was that wildly improbable handful of cash in his hand. "I'll take ten of that," I said, digging for my wallet, and a dozen other guys chimed in. "Me too." "I'll take ten." "I'm in for five." Doc Webster took a double sawbuck's worth, and even Fast Eddie produced a tattered single. The guy collected the dough in a hat that looked like its former owner had been machine-gunned in the head, and the whole time that damn dog just sat there next to the table, watching the action.

When the guy had it all counted, there was a hundred and seventy bucks in the hat. "There's thrity unfaded," he said, and looked around expectantly.

Callahan came around the bar, a red-headed glacier descending on the shabby man. The barkeep picked him up by the one existing lapel and the opposite collar, held him at arm's length for a while, and sighed.

"I like a good gag as well as the next guy," he said conversationally. "But that's serious money in that hat. Now if you was to ask that dog his name, and he said 'Ralph! Ralph!' and then you was to ask him what's on top of a house and he said 'Roof! Roof!' and then you was to ask him who was the greatest baseball player of all time and he said 'Ruth! Ruth!', why, I'd just naturally have to sharpen your feet and drive you into the floor. You would become like a Gable roof: Gone With The Wind. What I mean, there are *very* few gags I've never heard, and if yours is of that calibre you are in dire peril. Do we have a meeting of the minds?" He was still holding the guy at arm's length, the muscles of his arms looking like hairy manila, absolutely serene.

"I'm telling you the truth," the guy yelped. "The dog can talk."

Callahan slowly lowered him to the floor. "In that case," he decided, "I will fade your thirty." He went back behind the bar and produced an apple. "Would you mind putting this in your mouth?"

The guy blinked at him.

"I believe you implicitly," Callahan explained, "but someone without my trusting nature might suspect you was a ventriloquist tryin' to pull a fast one."

"Okay," said the guy at once, and he stuffed the apple in his face. He beckoned to the dog, who came at once to the center of the room and sat on his haunches. He gazed up inquisitively at the shabby man, who nodded.

"I hope you will forgive me," said the dog with the faintest trace of a German accent, "but I'm afraid my name actually *is* Ralph."

There was silence, as profound as that which must exist on the Moon now that the tourist season is past. Then, slowly at first, glasses began to hit the fireplace. Soon there was a shower of glasses shattering on the hearth, and not a drop of liquid in any of 'em. Callahan passed fresh beers around the room, bucket-brigade fasion, his face impassive. Not a word was spoken.

At last every had been lubed, and the big Irishman wiped off his hands and came around the bar. He pulled up a chair in front of the dog, dropped heavily into it, and put a fresh light to his cigar.

"Sure is a relief," he sighed, "to take the weight offa my d . . . to sit down."

You must understand—we were all still so stunned that not one of us thought to ask him if he was bitching.

"So tell me, Ralph," he went on, "how do you like my bar?"

"Nice place," the dog said pleasantly. "You guys always tell shaggy- . . . uh, -person stories?"

"Only on Wednesday nights," Callahan told him, and explained the game and current topic.

"That sounds very interesting," Ralph said, parodying Artie Johnson. His voice was slightly hoarse but quite intelligible. "Mind if I take a shot at it?"

"You just heard the Doc's stinker," Callahan said. "If you can beat that, you're top . . ."

"Please," Ralph interrupted with a pained look. "As you told me a moment ago, I've heard them all before. All right, then: I have an animal story. Did any of you know that until very recently, a tribe of killer monkeys lived undetected in Greenwich Village?"

The Doc had nearly found his own voice, but now he lost it

again. Me, I'd already crapped out—but it was fun to see the champ sweat. I resolved to buy the dog a beer.

"To some extent," the German shepherd went on, "it was not surprising that they escaped notice for so long. They had extremely odd sleeping habits, hibernating for 364 days out of every year (365 in Leap Years) and emerging from the caverns of the Village sewers only on Christmas Day. Even so, one might have thought they could hardly help but cause talk, since they tended when awake to be enormous, ferocious, carnivorous, and *extremely* hungry. Yet in Greenwich Village of all places on earth they went unnoticed until last year, when they were finally destroyed."

The dog paused and looked expectant. Sighing, Callahan reached over the bar and got him a glass of gin. Ralph lapped it up in a twinkling, looked up at us, and delivered.

"Everyone *knows*," he said patiently, "that Yule gibbons ate only nuts and fruits."

Not, I am certain, since the days when Rin-Tin-Tin ran in neighborhood theaters has a German shepherd received such thunderous applause. We gave him a standing ovation, and I want to say Doc Webster was the first one to rise (despite the fact that, by virtue of his earlier rash promise, he was now on the wagon for the evening). Callahan nearly fell off his chair, and Fast Eddie tried to strike up "At The Zoo," but he was laughing so hard his left hand was in G and his right in Eb. As the applause trickled off we toasted the dog and blitzed the fireplace as one.

And the man in shabby clothes, whose existence we had nearly forgotten, stepped up to the bar (minus his apple now) and claimed the hatful of money.

Callahan blinked, then his grin widened and he returned behind the bar. "Mister," he said, drawing another gin for Ralph, "that was worth every penny it cost us. Your friend is terrific, and I'm honored to have you both in my joint. Here's another gin for him, and what're you drinking?"

"Scotch," the shabby man said, and Callahan nodded and reached for the scotch—but I used to work in a boiler factory once, and so I choked on my drink.

Callahan looked around, puzzled. "What is it, Jake?"

"His lips, Mike," I croaked, wiping fine whiskey from my beard. "His *lips*."

Callahan turned back to the guy, gently lifted the scrofulous mustache and examined the guy's lips. There were two. "So?" he said, peering at them.

"I read lips," I managed at last. "You know that. That guy's voice said 'scotch,' *but his lips said 'bourbon.'* "

"How the hell could you tell?" Callahan asked reasonably.

"I swear, Mike—he said 'bourbon.' Here: look." I wear a mustache myself, middlin' sanitary, but I covered most of it and all of my mouth with my hand. Then I said, " 'Scotch' . . . 'Bourbon' . . . See what I mean? It *ain't* the lips, entirely—the mustache, the cheek muscles—I'm telling you, Mike, the guy said 'bourbon'."

Callahan looked at the guy, then at me . . . and then at the dog.

"I'm sorry, Joe," the dog said miserably. "I thought sure you'd want to stick with scotch."

The shabby man shrugged eloquently.

"Well, I'll be a son of a . . .." Long-Drink began, then caught himself. "*You're* the ventriloquist!"

Doc Webster roared with laughter, and Callahan's eyes widened the barest trifle. "I surely will be go to hell," he breathed. "I shoulda guessed."

But I was watching the look exchanged by Joe and Ralph, the way both of them ever so casually got ready to bolt for the door, and I spoke up quickly.

"It's okay, fellas. Don't go away—*tell* us about it."

They froze, undecided, and the rest of the boys jumped in. "Hell, yeah." "Give us the yarn, Ralph." "Let's hear it." "Get that dog another drink."

Ralph looked around at us, poised to flee, and then he met Callahan's eyes for a long moment. He looked *exactly* like a dog that's been kicked too often, and I thought he'd go. But he must have heard the sincerity in our voices, or else he read something on Callahan's face, because all at once he relaxed and curled up on the floor.

"It's all right, Joe," he said to the shabby man, who still stood undecided. "These people will not make trouble for us." The shabby man nodded philosophically and accepted a bourbon from Callahan.

"How come you can talk?" Fast Eddie asked Ralph. "I mean, if it ain't no poisonal question or nuttin'."

"Not at all," Ralph answered. "I was . . . created, I suppose you'd say, by a demented genius of a psychology major named Malion, who was desperate for a doctoral thesis. He had a defrocked veterinary surgeon modify my larnyx and mouth in my infancy, apparently in the mad hope that he could condition me to parrot human speech. But I'm afraid his experiment blew up in his face. You see," he said rather proudly, "I seem to be a mutant.

"This, naturally, was the one thing Malion had never planned for. How could he? Who could guess that a dog could actually have human intelligence? For all I know I am unique—in fact I fervently and desperately hope so. If there are other dogs of my intelligence, but without the capacity for speech, *who would ever know?*" Ralph shuddered. "At any rate, I destroyed all of Malion's hopes the first time I got tired of his damned yammering and told him what I thought of him *and* Pavlov *and* Skinner in no uncertain terms. At first, naturally, he was tremendously excited. But within a few hours, as I reminded him of highlights of our past life together, I could see dawning in him the fear that any lab-researcher—let alone a behaviorist—might feel upon realizing that one of his experimental animals is an aware attack-dog.

And eventually, of course, he realized the same thing that had kept my own mouth shut for so many months: that if he attempted to write *me* up for his doctorate, they'd laugh him off the campus. He abandoned me, simply kicked me out in the streets and locked my doggy-door. The next day he left town, and hasn't been heard from since."

"Cripes," said Eddie, "dat's awful. Abandoned by yer creator."

"Like Frankenstein," Doc Webster said.

"Damn right," Ralph agreed. "I'd like to get my paws on that pig, Malion."

Then he realized what he'd just said and barked with laughter. The Doc drained his own glass with a gulp and tossed it over his shoulder, squarely into the fire.

"I beg your pardon," the shepherd continued. "Anyhow, I got by for quite a while. It's not too hard for a big dog to survive in Suffolk County, especially when the summer people go. But what drove me crazy was *having nobody to talk to*. After all those years of keeping my mouth shut, so as not to spoil my meal ticket with Malion, I was like a pent-up river ready to burst its dam. But every time I tried to strike up a conversation, the other party ran away rather abruptly. A few children would talk to me, but I soon stopped that, too—their parents gave them endless grief for telling lies, and one day I found myself obliged to bite one. He took a shot at me—with a silver bullet.

"So I tried to sublimate. I found a serviceable typewriter in a junk-yard, swiped paper and stamps and became a writer—of speculative fiction, of course. Since I lived mostly in the remaining farmland east of here, I selected pastoral pen names like Trout and Bird and Farmer— although occasionally I wrote under an old family name, Von Wau Wau."

"Holy smoke," Wyatt breathed. "So that's what that hoax was all about . . ."

"Eventually I acquired something of a following . . . but answering fan mail is not the same as *talking* with someone. Besides, I couldn't cash the checks.

"Then one day, outside a bar in Rocky Point, I happened to overhear some fools making fun of Joe here, because he was a mute. 'Dummy,' they called him, and his face was red and he was desperate for a voice with which to curse them. So *I* did. They fled the bar, screaming like chickens, and ten minutes later Joe and I left the empty bar with the beginnings of a partnership."

"I get it," I said, striking my forehead with my hand. "You teamed up."

"Precisely," Ralph agreed. "I could have the pleasure of conversing with people, at least by proxy—and so could Joe, simply by letting me put words in his mouth. He grew that mustache to help, and we worked out a fairly simple 'script' and 'cues.' To support ourselves, we hit upon the old talking-dog routine, which we have been working in taverns from Ronkonkoma to Montauk over the last six months. The beauty of it is that while people virtually always pay up, they *never* believe I can truly speak. Always they speak only to Joe, congratulating *him* on his fine trick even if they can't figure out how he does it. I suppose I should be annoyed by this, but truthfully, I find it hilarious. And at any rate, it's a living."

Doc Webster shook his head like . . . well, like a dog shaking off water is the only simile I can think of. "And to think it took you guys all this time to come to Callahan's Place," he said dizzily.

"I feel the same," Ralph said seriously. "You are the first men who have ever accepted Joe and me as we are, who knew the truth about us and did not run away. Or worse, laugh at us.

"I thank you."

And Joe pointed at his own chest and nodded vigorously. *Me too!*

Callahan's face split in a broad grin. "Sure and hell welcome, fellas," he boomed, "sure and hell welcome— *any* time. I can't think of any two guys I'd rather have in my joint."

And another cheer went up. "To Ralph and Joe," Long-Drink hollered, and two dozen voices chorused, *"To Ralph'n'Joe."* The toast was drunk, the glasses disposed of in unison, and the place started to get real merry. But an idea struck me.

"Hey Ralph," I called out. "You want a job? A real job?"

Ralph paused in mid-lap and looked up. "Are you crazy? Who'd hire a talking dog?"

"I know the only place around that might," I told him

confidently. "Jim Friend over at WGAB has been talking about taking a year off, and he's a good friend of mine. How'd you like to run a radio talk-show at 4 A.M. every morning?"

Ralph looked stunned.

"Yeah," Callahan agreed judiciously, "WGAB would hire a talking dog. Hell, maybe they got one already. Whaddya say, Ralph?"

I could see Ralph was tempted—but German shepherds are notoriously loyal. "What about Joe?"

"Hmmm." I thought hard, but I was stumped.

Joe was gesticulating furiously, but Ralph ignored him. "No," he decided. "I could not leave my friend."

"I'll think of something," Callahan promised, but Ralph shook his head.

"Thank you," he said, "but there's no use in raising false hopes. I'm resigned to this life."

"Mister," Callahan said firmly, "that's what this Place is all about. We raise hopes, here—until they're old enough to fend for themselves. Wait—I *got* it! Joe!"

The shabby man looked up from his drink, shamefaced.

"Get that frown off yer phiz," Callahan demanded. "You can type, can't ya?"

Joe nodded, puzzled. "I taught him," Ralph said.

"Then I can help ya," the big Irishman told Joe. "How would you like a job over at Brookhaven National Lab?"

Joe looked dubious, and Ralph spoke up again. "I told you, Mr. Callahan—writing just isn't the same as talking to people."

"Hold on and listen," Callahan insisted. "Over at Brookhaven, they got a new computer they're real proud of—they claim it's almost alive. So they're reviving the old gag about having experts try to tell the computer from a guy on a teletype. They're lookin' for a guy right now, who don't mind carryin' on conversations through one-way glass on a teletype all day long. I bet we could get you the job. How 'bout it?" And he hauled out the blackboard he uses to keep score for dart games, and gave it and some chalk to Joe.

The shabby man took the chalk and carefully printed, "THANK YOU. I'LL GIVE IT A TRY," in large letters.

"Well Ralph," Callahan said to the dog, "it looks like you're a DJ."

And Ralph yelped happily, nuzzling Joe with his head, while we all started cheering once again.

And, hours later, as we all got ready to bottle it up and go, Ralph turned to Joe and said, almost sadly, "So, Joe my friend. After tomorrow, perhaps we go our separate ways. No longer will I dog your heels."

Joe winced and wrote, "NO LONGER WILL I HEEL MY DOG, EITHER."

Doc Webster made a face at the plain Coca Cola that sat before him on the bar. "I might have to heal the both of you if you keep it up," he growled, and I could see he was still a little miffed over his defeat by Ralph.

"Oh no," Ralph protested. "I want to get my new job right away. The only other work for a dog of my intelligence is as a seeing eye dog, *ja?* And radio-work is better than replacing a cane, *nein?*"

"*Cane-nein?*" the Doc exploded. "*Canine?* Why you . . ."

But over what the portly sawbones said then, let us draw a censoring veil of silence. His bark always was worse than his bite.

Say—if Ralph really makes it on radio, and becomes a dog star: is that Sirius?

Concerning "Dog Day Evening":

For some reason, as I mentioned in this book's foreword, funny stories don't seem to get nominated for Hugos. In the last ten years, fewer than five percent of the Hugo nominees have been funny stories, and very few of those have won.

"Dog Day Evening" was nominated in 1978, and didn't win. There are four very good reasons why it didn't win: the other four stories nominated, all of which were superb (the winner was Harlan Ellison's "When Jeffty Was Five"). But I can think of only one reason why it was even nominated in the first place, while other, and I think better, Callahan stories failed of this honor.

Every year at the World Science Fiction Convention there is an event organized and produced by Gale Burnick called the Authors Forum, at which sf writers read their newest works aloud. It is always well attended and well received, and the only small problem with it is that a great many stories which are terrific on the printed page just lay there when read aloud. As Samuel R. Delany has noted, writing and marketplace storytelling are different trades, related but different.

But the stories that do seem to read aloud the best are funny stories.

Lines that would, in one's living room, cause one corner of the mouth to twitch upward will, when read aloud in a roomful of sweaty strangers, elicit howls of laughter. Lines that would make a solitary reader chuckle will leave an audience gasping for breath. Puns that would provoke a private wince bring a public outcry of terrifying proportions.

Let me run a little experiment here. The last time I was at Callahan's, Fast Eddie brought in a jug of his moonshine to pass around. He said he called it Mother's Milk. As he was setting it down on the bar, the jug slipped from his fingers and headed for the floor. Fast Eddie is fast, but it was Doc Webster who caught the jug—and in the stop-frame stillness *that usually follows such events, he sang clearly, "Catch that paps-y spirit . . ."**

See now? Sitting there in your arm-chair (or whatever), you may have smiled slightly, or at most groaned softly—most likely you displayed no outward reaction at all. But if you'd been there at Callahan's when it happened, likely you'd still have sawdust in your hair from rolling on the floor, like the rest of us.

We like to have company when we laugh. Sharing a joke seems to make it better. (From this we derive the fundamental principle of Callahan's: that shared pain is lessened, and shared joy is increased.)

So I read "Dog Day Evening" aloud at the 1977 Worldcon, and it made the '78 Hugo list.

At the '78 Worldcon I read a serious story, of which I was exceeding proud; it proceeded to vanish without a ripple.

At this year's Worldcon I will do my damndest to have a funny story to read.

"Dog Day Evening," by the way, is told with the gracious permission of Philip José Farmer, author of the famous Riverworld Series, literary agent for Ralph Von Wau Wau (not to mention Kilgore Trout, Leo Queequeg Tincrowdor and the Earl of Greystoke), and Friend of Cordwainer Bird.

Oh, and this story spawned what is so far the only Callahan's Place Christmas card I have seen. A woman reprinted the "Yule gibbons" gag on cards and sent it to all those who up until then had been her friends. She asked my permission. Life is strange.

**Actually there are nine puns that could have been made here—but the Doc lactate. Just as well—one shouldn't milk a joke, if he wishes to put his breast-feed forward.*

GOD IS AN IRON

I smelled her before I saw her. Even so, the first sight of her was shocking.

She was sitting in a tan plastic-surfaced armchair, the kind where the front comes up as the back goes down. It was back as far as it would go. It was placed beside the large living-room window, whose curtains were drawn. A plastic block table next to it held a digital clock, a dozen unopened packages of Peter Jackson cigarettes, an empty ashtray, a full vial of cocaine, and a lamp with a bulb of at least 150 watts. It illuminated her with brutal clarity.

She was naked. Her skin was the color of vanilla pudding. Her hair was in rats, her nails unpainted and untended, some overlong and some broken. There was dust on her. She sat in a ghastly sludge of feces and urine. Dried vomit was caked on her chin and between her breasts and down her ribs to the chair.

These were only part of what I had smelled. The predominant odor was of fresh-baked bread. It is the smell of a person who is starving to death. The combined effluvia had prepared me to find a senior citizen, paralyzed by a stroke or some such crisis.

I judged her to be about twenty-five years old.

I moved to where she could see me, and she did not see me. That was probably just as well, because I had just seen the two most horrible things. The first was the smile. They say that when the bomb went off at Hiroshima, some people's shadows were baked onto walls by it. I think that smile got baked on the surface of my brain in much the same way. I don't want to talk about that smile.

The second horrible thing was the one that explained all the rest. From where I now stood I could see a triple socket in the wall beneath the window. Into it were plugged the lamp, the clock, and her.

I knew about wireheading, of course—I had lost a couple of acquaintances and one friend to the juice. But I had never *seen* a wirehead. It is by definition a solitary vice, and all the public usually gets to see is a sheeted figure being carried out to the wagon.

The transformer lay on the floor beside the chair where it had been dropped. The switch was on, and the timer had been jiggered so that instead of providing one five- or ten- or fifteen-second jolt per hour, it allowed continuous flow. That timer is required by law on all juice rigs sold, and you need special tools to defeat it. Say, a nail file. The input cord was long, fell in crazy coils from the wall socket. The output cord disappeared beneath the chair, but I knew where it ended. It ended in the tangled snarl of her hair, at the crown of her head, ended in a miniplug. The plug was snapped into a jack surgically implanted in her skull, and from the jack tiny wires snaked their way through the wet jelly to the hypothalamus, to the specific place in the medial forebrain bundle where the major pleasure center of her brain was located. She had sat there in total transcendent ecstasy for at least five days.

I moved finally. I moved closer, which surprised me. She saw me now, and impossibly the smile became a bit wider. I was marvelous. I was captivating. I was her perfect lover. I could not look at the smile; a small plastic tube ran from one corner of the smile and my eyes followed it gratefully. It was held in place by small bits of surgical tape at her jaw, neck and shoulder, and from there it ran in a lazy curve to the big fifty-litre water-cooler bottle on the floor. She had plainly meant her suicide to last: she had arranged to die of hunger rather than thirst, which would have been quicker. She could take a drink when she happened to think of it; and if she forgot, well, what the hell.

My intention must have shown on my face, and I think she even understood it—the smile began to fade. That decided me. I moved before she could force her neglected body to react, whipped the plug out of the wall and stepped back warily.

Her body did not go rigid as if galvanized. It had already been so for many days. What it did was the exact opposite, and the effect was just as striking. She seemed to shrink. Her eyes slammed shut. She slumped. Well, I thought, it'll be a long day and a night before *she* can move a voluntary muscle again, and then she hit me before I knew she had left the chair, breaking my nose with the heel of one fist and bouncing the other off the side of my head. We cannoned off each other and I managed to keep my feet; she whirled and grabbed the lamp. Its cord was stapled to the floor and would not yield, so she set her feet and yanked and it snapped off clean at the base. In near-total darkness she raised the lamp on high and came at me and I lunged inside the arc of her swing and punched her in the solar plexus. She said *guff!* and went down.

I staggered to a couch and sat down and felt my nose and fainted.

I don't think I was out very long. The blood tasted fresh. I woke with a sense of terrible urgency. It took me a while to work out why. When someone has been simultaneously starved and unceasingly stimulated for days on end, it is not the best idea in the world to depress their respiratory center. I lurched to my feet.

It was not completely dark, there was a moon somewhere out there. She lay on her back, arms at her sides, perfectly relaxed. Her ribs rose and fell in great slow swells. A pulse showed strongly at her throat. As I knelt beside her she began to snore, deeply and rhythmically.

I had time for second thoughts now. It seemed incredible that my impulsive action had not killed her. Perhaps that had been my subconscious intent. Five days of wireheading alone should have killed her, let alone sudden cold turkey.

I probed in the tangle of hair, found the empty jack. The hair around it was dry. If she hadn't torn the skin in yanking herself loose, it was unlikely that she had sustained any more serious damage within. I continued probing, found no soft places on the skull. Her forehead felt cool and sticky to my hand. The fecal smell was overpowering the baking bread now, sourly fresh.

There was no pain in my nose yet, but it felt immense and pulsing. I did not want to touch it, or to think about it. My shirt was soaked with blood; I wiped my face with it and tossed it into a corner. It took everything I had to lift her. She was unreasonably heavy, and I have carried drunks and corpses. There was a hall off the livingroom, and all halls lead to a bathroom. I headed that way in a clumsy staggering trot, and just as I reached the deeper darkness, with my pulse at its maximum, my nose woke up and began screaming. I nearly dropped her then and clapped my hands to my face; the temptation was overwhelming. Instead I whimpered like a dog and kept going. Childhood feeling: runny nose you can't wipe. At each door I came to I teetered on one leg and kicked it open, and the third one gave the right small-room, acoustic-tile echo. The light switch was where they almost always are; I rubbed it on with my shoulder and the room flooded with light.

Large aquamarine tub, styrofoam recliner pillow at the head end, nonslip bottom. Aquamarine sink with ornate handles, cluttered with toiletries and cigarette butts and broken shards of mirror from the medicine cabinet above. Aquamarine commode, lid up and seat down. Brown throw rug, expensive. Scale shoved back into a corner, covered with dust in which two footprints showed. I made a massive effort and managed to set her reasonably gently in the tub. I rinsed my face and hands of blood at the sink, ignoring the broken glass, and stuffed the bleeding nostril with toilet paper. I adjusted her head, fixed the chin strap. I held both feet away from the faucet until I had the water adjusted, and then left with one hand on my nose and the other beating against my hip, in search of her liquor.

There was plenty to choose from. I found some Metaxa in the kitchen. I took great care not to bring it near my nose, sneaking it up on my mouth from below. It tasted like

burning lighter fluid, and made a sweat spring out on my
forehead. I found a roll of paper towels, and on my way back
to the bathroom I used a great wad of them to swab most of
the sludge off the chair and rug. There was a growing pool of
water siphoning from the plastic tube and I stopped that.
When I got back to the bathroom the water was lapping over
her bloated belly, and horrible tendrils were weaving up from
beneath her. It took three rinses before I was satisfied with
the body. I found a hose-and-spray under the sink that mated
with the tub's faucet, and that made the hair easy.

I had to dry her there in the tub. There was only one towel
left, none too clean. I found a first aid spray that incorporated
a good topical anesthetic, and put it on the sores on her back
and butt. I had located her bedroom on the way to the
Metaxa. Wet hair slapped my arm as I carried her there. She
seemed even heavier, as though she had become water
logged. I eased the door shut behind me and tried the light-
switch trick again, and it wasn't there. I moved forward into a
footlocker and lost her and went down amid multiple crashes,
putting all my attention into guarding my nose. She made no
sound at all, not even a grunt.

The light switch turned out to be a pull chain over the bed.
She was on her side, still breathing slow and deep. I wanted
to punt her up onto the bed. My nose was a blossom of pain. I
nearly couldn't lift her the third time. I was moaning with
frustration by the time I had her on her left side on the
king-size mattress. It was a big brass four-poster bed, with
satin sheets and pillowcases, all dirty. The blankets were
shoved to the bottom. I checked her skull and pulse again,
peeled up each eyelid and found uniform pupils. Her
forehead and cheek still felt cool, so I covered her. Then I
kicked the footlocker clear into the corner, turned out the
light and left her snoring like a chainsaw.

Her vital papers and documents were in her study, locked
in a strongbox on the closet shelf. It was an expensive box,
quite sturdy and proof against anything short of nuclear
explosion. It had a combination lock with all of twenty-seven
possible combinations. It was stuffed with papers. I laid her

life out on her desk like a losing hand of solitaire, and studied it with a growing frustration.

Her name was Karen Scholz, and she used the name Karyn Shaw, which I thought phony. She was twenty-two. Divorced her parents at fourteen, uncontested no-fault. Since then she had been, at various times, waitress, secretary to a lamp salesman, painter, freelance typist, motorcycle mechanic and unlicensed masseuse. The most recent paycheck stub was from The Hard Corps, a massage parlor with a cutrate reputation. It was dated almost a year ago. Her bank balance combined with paraphernalia I had found in the closet to tell me that she was currently self-employed as a tootlegger, a cocaine dealer. The richness of the apartment and furnishings told me that she was a foolish one. Even if the narcs missed her, very shortly the IRS was going to come down on her like a ton of bricks. Perhaps subconsciously she had not expected to be around.

Nothing there; I kept digging. She had attended community college for one semester as an art major, and dropped out failing. She had defaulted on a lease three years ago. She had wrecked a car once, and been shafted by her insurance company. Trivia. Only one major trauma in recent years: a year and a half ago she had contracted out as host-mother to a couple named Lombard/Smyth. It was a pretty good fee— she had good hips and the right rare blood type—but six months into the pregnancy they had caught her using tobacco and canceled the contract. She fought, but they had photographs. And better lawyers, naturally. She had to repay the advance, and pay for the abortion, of course, and got socked for court costs besides.

It didn't make sense. To show clean lungs at the physical, she had to have been off cigarettes for at least three to six months. Why backslide, with so much at stake? Like the minor traumas, it felt more like an effect than a cause. Self-destructive behavior. I kept looking.

Near the bottom I found something that looked promising. Both her parents had been killed in a car smash when she was eighteen. Their obituary was paperclipped to her father's will. That will was one of the most extraordinary documents I have ever read. I could understand an angry father cutting off his only child without a dime. But what he had done was worse. Much worse.

Damn it, it didn't work either. So-there suicides don't wait four years. And they don't use such a garish method either: it devalues the tragedy. I decided it had to be either a very big and dangerous coke deal gone bad, or a very reptilian lover. No, not a coke deal. They'd never have left her in her own apartment to die the way she wanted to. It could not be murder: even the most unscrupulous wire surgeon needs an awake, consenting subject to place the wire correctly.

A lover, then. I was relieved, pleased with my sagacity, and irritated as hell. I didn't know why. I chalked it up to my nose. It felt as though a large shark with rubber teeth was rhythmically biting it as hard as he could. I shoveled the papers back into the box, locked and replaced it, and went to the bathroom.

Her medicine cabinet would have impressed a pharmacist. She had lots of allergies. It took me five minutes to find aspirin. I took four. I picked the largest shard of mirror out of the sink, propped it on the septic tank and sat down backward on the toilet. My nose was visibly displaced to the right, and the swelling was just hitting its stride. I removed the toilet tissue plug from my nostril, and it resumed bleeding. There was a box of Kleenex on the floor. I ripped it apart, took out all the tissues and stuffed them into my mouth. Then I grabbed my nose with my right hand and tugged out and to the left, simultaneously flushing the toilet with my left hand. The flushing coincided with the scream, and my front teeth met through the kleenex. When I could see again the nose looked straight and my breathing was unimpaired. When the bleeding stopped again I gingerly washed my face and hands and left. A moment later I returned; something had caught my eye. It was the glass and toothbrush holder. There was only one toothbrush in it. I looked through the medicine chest again, and noticed this time that there was no shaving cream, no razor manual or electric, no masculine toiletries of any kind. All the prescriptions were in her name.

I went thoughtfully to the kitchen, mixed myself a

Preacher's Downfall by moonlight and took it to her bedroom. The bedside clock said five. I lit a match, moved the
footlocker in front of an armchair, sat down and put my feet
up. I sipped my drink and listened to her snore and watched
her breathe in the feeble light of the clock. I decided to run
through all the possibilities, and as I was formulating the first
one daylight smacked me hard in the nose.

My hands went up reflexively and I poured my drink on
my head and hurt my nose more. I wake up hard in the best of
times. She was still snoring. I nearly threw the empty glass at
her.

It was just past noon, now; light came strongly through the
heavy curtains, illuminating so much mess and disorder that I
could not decide whether she had trashed her bedroom herself or it had been tossed by a pro. I finally settled on the
former: the armchair I'd slept on was intact. Or had the pro
found what he wanted before he got that far?

I gave it up and went to make myself breakfast. The milk
was bad, of course, but I found a tolerable egg and the
makings of an omelet. I don't care for black coffee, but
Javanese brewed from frozen beans needs no augmentation. I
drank three cups.

It took me an hour or two to clean up and air out the livingroom. The cord and transformer went down the oubliette,
along with most of the perished items from the fridge. The
dishes took three full cycles for each load, a couple of hours
all told. I passed the time vacuuming and dusting and snoop-
ing, learning nothing more of significance. The phone rang.
She had no answering program in circuit, of course. I ener-
gized the screen. It was a young man in a business tunic,
wearing the doggedly amiable look of the stranger who wants
you to accept the call anyway. After some thought I did
accept, audio-only, and let him speak first. He wanted to sell
us a marvelous building lot in Forest Acres, South Dakota. I
was making up a shopping list about fifteen minutes later
when I heard her moan. I reached her bedroom door in
seconds, waited in the doorway with both hands in sight and
said slowly and clearly, "My name is Joseph Templeton,

Karen. I am a friend. You are all right now.''

Her eyes were those of a small, tormented animal.

''Please don't try to get up. Your muscles won't work properly and you may hurt yourself.''

No answer.

''Karen, are you hungry?''

''Your voice is ugly,'' she said despairingly, and her own voice was so hoarse I winced. ''*My* voice is ugly.'' She sobbed gently. ''It's *all* ugly.'' She screwed her eyes shut.

She was clearly incapable of movement. I told her I would be right back and went to the kitchen. I made up a tray of clear strong broth, unbuttered toast, tea with maltose and saltine crackers. She was staring at the ceiling when I got back, and apparently it was vile. It put the tray down, lifted her and made a backrest of pillows.

''I want a drink.''

''After you eat,'' I said agreeably.

''Who're you?''

''Mother Templeton. Eat.''

''The soup, maybe. Not the toast.'' She got about half of it down, did nibble at the toast, accepted some tea. I didn't want to overfill her. ''My drink.''

''Sure thing.'' I took the tray back to the kitchen, finished my shopping list, put away the last of the dishes and put a frozen steak into the oven for my lunch. When I got back she was fast asleep.

Emaciation was near total; except for breasts and bloated belly she was all bone and taut skin. Her pulse was steady. At her best she would not have been very attractive by conventional standards. Passable. Too much waist, not enough neck, upper legs a bit too thick for the rest of her. It's hard to evaluate a starved and unconscious face, but her jaw was a bit too square, her nose a trifle hooked, her blue eyes just the least little bit too far apart. Animated, the face might have been beautiful—any set of features can support beauty—but even a superb makeup job could not have made her pretty. There was an old bruise on her chin, another on her left hip. Her hair was sandy blonde, long and thin; it had dried in snarls that would take an hour to comb out. Her breasts were magnificent, and that saddened me. In this world, a woman whose breasts are her best feature is in for a rough time.

I was putting together a picture of a life that would have depressed anyone with the sensitivity of a rhino. Back when I had first seen her, when her features were alive, she had looked sensitive. Or had that been a trick of the juice? Impossible to say now.

But damn it all to hell, I could find nothing to really explain the socket in her skull. You can hear worse life stories in any bar, on any street corner. I was prepared to match her scar for scar myself. Wireheads are usually addictive personalities, who decide at last to skip the small shit. There were no tracks on her anywhere, no nasal damage, no sign that she used any of the coke she sold. Her work history, pitiful and fragmented as it was, was too steady for any kind of serious jones; she had undeniably been hitting the sauce hard lately, but only lately. Tobacco seemed to be her only serious addiction.

That left the hypothetical bastard lover. I worried at that for a while to see if I could make it fit. Assume a really creatively sadistic son of a bitch has gutted her like a trout, for the pure fun of it. You can't do that to someone as a visitor or even a guest, you have to live with them. So he does a worldclass job of crippling a lady who by her history is a tough little cookie, and when he has broken her he vanishes. Leaving not even so much as empty space in drawers, closets or medicine chest. Unlikely. So perhaps after he is gone *she* scrubs all traces of him out of the apartment—and then discovers that there is only one really good way to scrub memories. No, I couldn't picture such a sloppy housekeeper being so efficient.

Then I thought of my earlier feeling that the bedroom might have been tossed by a pro, and my blood turned to ice water. Suppose she wasn't a sloppy housekeeper? The jolly sadist returns unexpectedly for one last nibble. And finds her in the livingroom, just like I did. And leaves her there. Carefully removes his spoor and leaves her there.

After five minutes' thought I relaxed. That didn't parse either. True, this luxury co-op did inexplicably lack security cameras in the halls, relying on door-cameras—but for that very reason its rich tenants would be sure to take notice of comings and goings. If he had lived here for any time at all, his spoor was too diffuse to erase—so he would not have tried. Besides, a monster of that unique and rare kind thrives on the corruption of innocence. Tough little Karen was simply not toothsome enough.

At that point I went to the bathroom, and that settled it. When I lifted the seat to urinate I found written on the underside with magic marker: "It's so nice to have a man around the house!" The handwriting was hers. She had lived alone.

I was relieved, because I hadn't relished thinking about my hypothetical monster or the necessity of tracking and killing him. But I was irritated as hell again.

I wanted to *understand*.

For something to do I took my steak and a mug of coffee to the study and heated up her terminal. I tried all the typical access codes, her birthdate and her name in numbers and such, but none of them would unlock it. Then on a hunch I tried the date of her parents' death and that did it. I ordered the groceries she needed, instructed the lobby door to accept delivery, and tried everything I could think of to get a diary or a journal out of the damned thing, without success. So I punched up the public library and asked the catalog for *Britanica* on wireheading. It referred me to brain-reward, autostimulus of. I skipped over the history, from discovery by Olds and others in 1956 to emergence as a social problem in the late '80s when surgery got simple; declined the offered diagrams, graphs and technical specs; finally found a brief section on motivations.

There was indeed one type of typical user I had overlooked. The terminally ill.

Could that really be it? At her age? I went to the bathroom and checked the prescriptions. Nothing for heavy pain, nothing indicating anything more serious than allergies. Back before telephones had cameras I might have conned something out of her personal physician, but it would have been a chancy thing even then. There was no way to test the hypothesis.

It was possible, even plausible—but it just wasn't *likely* enough to satisfy the thing inside me that demanded an explanation. I dialed a game of four-wall squash, and made sure the computer would let me win. I was almost enjoying myself when she screamed.

It wasn't much of a scream; her throat was shot. But it fetched me at once. I saw the problem as I cleared the door. The topical anesthetic had worn off the large ''bedsores'' on her back and buttocks, and the pain had woken her. Now that I thought about it, it should have happened earlier; that spray was only supposed to be good for a few hours. I decided that her pleasure-pain system was weakened by overload.

The sores were bad; she would have scars. I resprayed them, and her moans stopped nearly at once. I could devise no means of securing her on her belly that would not be nightmare-inducing, and decided it was unnecessary. I thought she was out again, and started to leave. Her voice, muffled by pillows, stopped me in my tracks.

''I don't know you. Maybe you're not even real. I can tell you.''

''Save your energy, Karen. You—''

''Shut up. You wanted the karma, you got it.''

I shut up.

Her voice was flat, dead. ''All my friends were dating at twelve. *He* made me wait until fourteen. Said I couldn't be trusted. Tommy came to take me to the dance, and he gave Tommy a hard time. I was so embarassed. The dance was nice for a couple of hours. Then Tommy started chasing after Jo Tompkins. He just left me and went off with her. I went into the ladies' room and cried for a long time. A couple of girls got the story out of me, and one of them had a bottle of vodka in her purse. I never drank before. When I started tearing up cars in the parking lot, one of the girls got ahold of Tommy. She gave him shit and made him take me home. I don't remember it, I found out later.''

Her throat gave out and I got water. She accepted it without meeting my eyes, turned her face away and continued.

"Tommy got me in the door somehow. I was out cold by then. He'd been fooling around with me a little in the car I think. He must have been too scared to try and get me upstairs. He left me on the couch and my underpants on the rug and went home. The next thing I knew I was on the floor and my face hurt. *He* was standing over me. *Whore* he said. I got up and tried to explain and he hit me a couple of times. I ran for the door but he hit me hard in the back. I went into the stairs and banged my head real hard."

Feeling began to come into her voice for the first time. The feeling was fear. I dared not move.

"When I woke up it was day. Mama must have bandaged my head and put me to bed. My head hurt a lot. When I came out of the bathroom I heard him call me. Him and Mama were in bed. He started in on me. He wouldn't let me talk, and he kept getting madder and madder. Finally I hollered back at him. He got up off the bed and started in hitting me again. My robe came off. He kept hitting me in the belly and tits, and his fists were like hammers. *Slut,* he kept saying. *Whore.* I thought he was going to kill me so I grabbed one arm and bit. He roared like a dragon and threw me across the room. Onto the bed; Mama jumped up. Then he pulled down his underpants and it was big and purple. I screamed and screamed and tore at his back and Mama just stood there. Her eyes were big and round, just like in cartoons. His breath stank and I screamed and screamed and—"

She broke off short and her shoulders knotted. When she continued her voice was stone dead again. "I woke up in my own bed again. I took a real long shower and went downstairs. Mama was making pancakes. I sat down and she gave me one and I ate it, and then I threw it up right there on the table and ran out the door. She never said a word, never called me back. After school that day I found a Sanctuary and started the divorce proceedings. I never saw either of them again. I never told this to anybody before."

The pause was so long I thought she had fallen asleep.

"Since that time I've tried it with men and women and boys and girls, in the dark and in the desert sun, with people I cared for and people I didn't give a damn about, and I have never understood the pleasure in it. The best it's ever been for me is not uncomfortable. God, how I've wondered . . . . . . now I know." She was starting to drift. "Only thing my whole life turned out *better* 'n cracked up to be." She snorted sleepily. "Even alone."

I sat there for a long time without moving. My legs trembled when I got up, and my hands trembled while I made supper.

That was the last time she was lucid for nearly forty-eight hours. I plied her with successively stronger soups every time she woke up, and once I got a couple of pieces of tea-soggy toast into her. Sometimes she called me by others' names, and sometimes she didn't know I was there, and everything she said was disjointed. I listened to her tapes, watched some of her video, charged some books and games to her computer account. I took a lot of her aspirin. And drank surprisingly little of her booze.

It was a time of frustration for me. I still couldn't make it all fit together, still could not quite understand. There was a large piece missing. The animal who sired and raised her had planted the charge, of course, and I perceived that it was big enough to blow her apart. But why had it taken eight years to go off? If his death four years ago had not triggered it, what had? I could not leave until I knew. I prowled her apartment like a caged bear, looking everywhere for something else to think about.

Midway through the second day her plumbing started working again; I had to change the sheets. The next morning a noise woke me and I found her on the bathroom floor on her knees in a pool of urine. I got her clean and back to bed and just as I thought she was going to drift off she started yelling at me. "Lousy son of a bitch, it could have been over! I'll never have the guts again now! How could you *do* that, you *bastard*, it was so *nice!*" She turned violently away from me and curled up. I had to make a hard choice then, and I gambled on what I knew of loneliness and sat on the edge of the bed and stroked her hair as gently and impersonally as I knew how. It was a good guess. She began to cry, in great racking heaves first, then the steady wail of total heartbreak. I had been praying for this, and did not begrudge the strength it cost her.

She cried for so long that every muscle in my body ached from sitting still by the time she fell off the edge into sleep. She never felt me get up, stiff and clumsy as I was. There was something different about her sleeping face now. It was not slack but relaxed. I limped out in the closest thing to peace I had felt since I arrived, and as I was passing the livingroom on the way to the liquor I heard the phone.

As I had before, I looked over the caller. The picture was undercontrasted and snowy; it was a pay phone. He looked like an immigrant construction worker, massive and florid and neckless, almost brutish. And, at the moment, under great stress. He was crushing a hat in his hands, mortally embarassed. I mentally shrugged and accepted.

"Sharon, don't hang up," he was saying. "I *gotta* find out what this is all about."

Nothing could have made me hang up.

"Sharon? Sharon, I know you're there. Terry says you ain't there, she says she called you every day for almost a week and banged on your door a few times. But I know you're there, now anyway. I walked past your place an hour ago and I seen the bathroom light go on and off. Sharon, will you please tell me what the hell is going on? Are you listening to me? I know you're listening to me. Look, you gotta understand, I thought it was all set, see? I mean I thought it was *set*. Arranged. I put it to Terry, cause she's my regular, and she says not *me*, lover, but I know a gal. Look, was she lying to me or what? She told me for another bill you play them kind of games, sometimes."

Regular two hundred dollar bank deposits plus a cardboard box full of scales, vials, bags, razor and milk powder makes her a coke dealer, right, Travis McGee? Don't be misled by the fact that the box was shoved in a corner, sealed with tape and covered with dust. After all, the only other illicit profession that pays regular sums at regular intervals is hooker, and *two* bills is too much for square-jawed, hook-nosed, wide-eyed little Karen, breasts or no breasts.

For a garden variety hooker . . .

"Dammit, she told me she *called* you and set it up, she gave me your *apartment* number." He shook his head violently. "I can't make no sense out of this. Dammit, she *couldn't* be lying to me. It don't figure. You let me in, didn't even look first, it was all arranged. Then you screamed and I . . . done like we arranged, and I thought you was maybe overdoing it a bit but Terry *said* you was a terrific little actress. I was real careful not to really hurt you, I know I was. Then I put on my pants and I'm putting the envelope on the dresser and you bust that chair on me and come at me with that knife and I hadda bust you one. It just don't make no sense, will you *goddammit say something to me?* I'm twisted up inside going on two weeks now. I can't even eat."

I tried to shut off the phone, and my hand was shaking so bad I missed, spinning the volume knob to minimum. "Sharon you gotta believe me," he hollered from far far away, "I'm into rape fantasy, I'm not into rape!" and then I had found the right switch and he was gone.

I got up very slowly and toddled off to the liquor cabinet, and I stood in front of it taking pulls from different bottles at random until I could no longer see his face, his earnest, baffled, half ashamed face hanging before me.

Because his hair was thin sandy blond, and his jaw was a bit too square, and his nose was a trifle hooked, and his blue eyes were just the least little bit too far apart. They say everyone has a double somewhere. And Fate is such a witty little motherfucker, isn't he?

I don't remember how I got to bed.

I woke later that night with the feeling that I would have to bang my head on the floor a couple of times to get my heart started again. I was on my makeshift doss of pillows and blankets beside her bed, and when I finally peeled my eyes open she was sitting up in bed staring at me. She had fixed her hair somehow, and her nails were trimmed. We looked at each other for a long time. Her color was returning somewhat, and the edge was off her bones. She sighed.

"What did Jo Ann say when you told her?"

I said nothing.

"Come on, Jo Ann's got the only other key to this place, and she wouldn't give it to you if you weren't a friend. So what did she say?"

I got painfully up out of the tangle and walked to the window. A phallic church steeple rose above the lowrises a couple of blocks away.

"God is an iron," I said. "Did you know that?"

I turned to look at her and she was staring. She laughed experimentally, stopped when I failed to join in. "And I'm a pair of pants with a hole scorched through the ass?"

"If a person who indulges in gluttony is a glutton, and a person who commits a felony is a felon, then God is an iron. Or else He's the dumbest designer that ever lived."

Of a thousand possible snap reactions she picked the most flattering and hence most irritating. She kept silent, kept looking at me, and thought about what I had said. At last she said, "I agree. What particular design screwup did you have in mind?"

"The one that nearly left you dead in a pile of your own shit,'" I said harshly. "Everybody talks about the new menace, wireheading, fifth most common cause of death in less than a decade. Wireheading's not new—it's just a technical refinement."

"I don't follow."

"Are you familiar with the old cliche, 'Everything in the world I like is either illegal, immoral or fattening'?"

"Sure."

"Didn't that ever strike you as damned odd? What's the most nutritionally useless and physiologically dangerous 'food' substance in the world? White sugar. Glucose. And it seems to be beyond the power of the human nervous system to resist it. They put it in virtually all the processed food there is, which is next to all the food there is, because *nobody can resist it*. And so we poison ourselves and whipsaw our dispositions and rot our teeth. Maltose is just as sweet, but it's less popular, precisely because it doesn't kick your blood-sugar in the ass and then depress it again. Isn't that odd? There is a primitive programming in our skulls that rewards us, literally overwhelmingly, every time we do something damned silly. Like smoke a poison, or eat or drink or snort or shoot a poison. Or *over*eat *good* foods. Or engage in complicated sexual behavior without procreative intent, which if it were not for the pleasure would be pointless and insane. And which, if pursued for the pleasure alone, quickly becomes pointless and insane anyway. A suicidal brain-reward system is built into us.''

"But the reward system is for survival."

"So how the hell did ours get wired up so that survival threatening behavior gets rewarded best of all? Even the pro-survival pleasure stimuli are wired so that a dangerous *overload* produces the maximum pleasure. On a purely biological level man is programmed to strive hugely for more than he needs, more than he can profitably use.

"The error doesn't show up as glaringly in other animals. Even surrounded by plenty, a stupid animal has to work hard simply to meet his needs. But add in intelligence and everything goes to hell. Man is capable of outgrowing any ecological niche you put him in—he survives at all because he is The Animal That Moves. Given half a chance he kills himself of surfeit.''

My knees were trembling so badly I had to sit down. I felt feverish and somehow larger than myself, and I knew I was talking much too fast. She had nothing whatever to say, with voice, face or body.

"It is illuminating,'' I went on, fingering my aching nose, ''to note that the two ultimate refinements of hedonism, the search for 'pure' pleasure, are the pleasure of cruelty and the pleasure of the despoliation of innocence. We will overlook the tempting example of your father because he was not a normal human being. Consider instead the obvious fact that no sane person in search of sheerly physical sexual pleasure would select an inexperienced partner. Everyone knows that mature, experienced lovers are more competent, confident and skilled. Yet there is not a skin mag in the world that prints pictures of men or women over twenty-five if they can possibly help it, and in the last ten years or so teenagers and pre-teens have been much preferred. Don't tell me about recapturing lost youth: the root is that a fantasy object over twenty cannot plausibly possess innocence, can no longer be corrupted.

"Man has historically devoted *much* more subtle and ingenious thought to inflicting cruelty than to giving others pleasure, which given his gregarious nature would seem a much more survival-oriented behavior. Poll any hundred people at random and you'll find at *least* twenty or thirty who know all there is to know about psychological torture and psychic castration—and maybe two that know how to give a terrific backrub. That business of your father leaving all his money to the Church and leaving you 'a hundred dollars, the going rate'—that was *artistry*. I can't imagine a way to make you feel as good as that made you feel rotten. That's why sadism and masochism are the last refuge of the jaded, the most enduring of the perversions; their piquancy is—"

"Maybe the Puritans were right," she said. "Maybe pleasure is the root of all evil. Oh God! but life is bleak without it."

"One of my most precious possessions," I went on blindly, "is a button that my friend Slinky John used to hand-paint and sell below cost. He was the only practicing anarchist I ever met. The button reads: 'GO, LEMMINGS, GO!' A lemming surely feels intense pleasure as he gallops to the sea. His self-destruction is programmed by nature, a part of the very same life force that insisted on being conceived and born in the first place. If it feels good, do it." I laughed, and she flinched. "So it seems to me that God is either an iron, or a colossal jackass. I don't know whether to be admiring or contemptuous."

All at once I was out of words, and out of strength. I yanked my gaze away from hers and stared at my knees for a long time. I felt vaguely ashamed, as befits one who has thrown a tantrum in a sickroom.

After a time she said, "You talk good on your feet."

I kept looking at my knees. "I think I used to be an actor once."

"Will you tell me something?"

"If I can."

"What was the pleasure in putting me back together again?"

I jumped.

"Look at me. There. I've got a half-ass idea of what shape I was in when you met me, and I can guess what it's been like since. I don't know if I'd have done as much for Jo Ann, and she's my best friend. You don't look like a guy whose favorite kick is sick fems, and you sure as *hell* don't look like you're so rich you got time on your hands. So what's been your pleasure, these last few days?"

"Trying to understand," I snapped. "I'm nosy."

"And do you understand?"

"Yeah. I put it together."

"So you'll be going now?"

"Not yet," I said automatically. "You're not—"

And caught myself.

"There's something else besides pleasure," she said. "Another system of reward, only I don't think it has much to do with the one I got wired up to my scalp here. Not brain-reward. Call it mind-reward. Call it . . . joy—the thing like pleasure that you feel when you've done a good thing or passed up a real tempting chance to do a bad thing. Or when the unfolding of the Universe just seems especially apt. It's nowhere near as flashy and intense as pleasure can be. *Believe* me! But it's got *some*thing going for it. Something that can make you do without pleasure, or even accept a lot of pain, to get it.

"That stuff you're talking about, that's there, that's true. What's messing us up is the animal nervous system and instincts we inherited. But you said yourself, Man is the animal that outgrows and moves. Ever since the first brain grew a mind we've been trying to outgrow our instincts, grow new ones. Maybe we will yet." She pushed hair back from her face. "Evolution works slow, is all. It took a couple of hundred million years to develop a thinking ape, and you want a smart one in a lousy few thou? That lemming drive you're talking about is there—but there's another kind of drive, another kind of force that's working against it. Or else there wouldn't still be any people and there wouldn't be the words to have this conversation and—'' She paused, looked down at herself. ''And I wouldn't be here to say them.''

''That was just random chance.''

She snorted. ''What isn't?''

''Well that's *fine*,'' I shouted. ''That's *fine*. Since the world is saved and you've got everything under control I'll just be going along.''

I've got a lot of voice when I yell. She ignored it utterly, continued speaking as if nothing had happened. ''Now I can say that I have sampled the spectrum of the pleasure system at both ends—none and all there is—and I think the rest of my life I will dedicate myself to the middle of the road and see how that works out. Starting with the very weak tea and toast I'm going to ask you to bring me in another ten minutes or so. With maltose. But as for this other stuff, this joy thing, that I would like to begin learning about, as much as I can. I don't really know a God damned thing about it, but I understand it has something to do with sharing and caring and what did you say your name was?''

''It doesn't matter,'' I yelled.

''All right. What can *I* do for *you*?''

''Nothing!''

''What did you come here for?''

I was angry enough to be honest. ''To burgle your fucking apartment!''

Her eyes opened wide, and then she slumped back against the pillows and laughed until the tears came, and I tried and could not help myself and laughed too, and we shared laughter for a long time, as long as we had shared her tears the night before.

And then straightfaced she said, ''You'll have to wait a week or so; you're gonna need help with those stereo speakers. Butter on the toast.''

Concerning "God Is An Iron":

Only two things need to be said about this story, and the first is that it forms Chapter Two of my next novel, Mindkiller.

The second is that, while the character of Karen Scholz is not *drawn from life and is wholly imaginary, the business involving her father is* not *fiction. It is a transcript, as near verbatim as my memory will produce, of a story a woman told me in 1967. (And if she's still alive out there, I'd love to hear from her.) Animals like her father are not made up by writers for shock value; they exist.*

God is an iron . . . and that's a hot one.

Concerning "Rah Rah R.A.H.":

When Jim Baen left Galaxy, *shortly before I did, it was to become sf editor of Ace Books. Ace promptly became the largest publisher of sf in the world, printing more titles in 1977 than any other house.*

Suddenly Jim found himself in custody of a great many cheese sandwiches.

So he built the magazine he had always wanted Galaxy *to be and couldn't afford to make it, and he named it* Destinies. *It was a quarterly paperback bookazine from Ace, a book filled with fiction and speculative fact and artwork and all the little extras that make up a magazine, and it was the most consistently satisfying and thought-provoking periodical that came into my house, not excluding* Omni *and the* Scientific American. *I did review columns for the first five issues, dropping out for reasons that in retrospect seem dumb.*

So one day shortly after I quit writing reviews for Destinies, *Jim called and offered me a proposition: he would send me a xerox of the newest Robert Heinlein manuscript, months in advance of publication, if I would use the book as a springboard for a full-length essay on the lifework of Heinlein, for* Destinies. *The new book was* Expanded Universe, *which by now you will almost certainly have seen and therefore own; let me tell you, it blew me away.*

The following is what came spilling out of me when I was done reading Expanded Universe—*and when I used it as my Guest of Honor speech at Bosklone, the 1980 Boston sf convention, it was received with loud and vociferous applause. Perhaps I overestimated the amount of attention people pay to critics. Perhaps the essay was unnecessary.*

But oooh *it was fun!*

RAH RAH R.A.H.!

A swarm of petulant blind men are gathered around an elephant, searching him inch by inch for something at which to sneer. What they resent is not so much that he towers over them, and can see farther than they can imagine. Nor is it that he has been trying for nearly half a century to warn them of the tigers approaching through the distant grasses downwind. They do resent these things, but what they really, bitterly resent is his damnable contention that they are not blind, *his insistent claim that they can open up their eyes any time they acquire the courage to do so.*

Unforgivable.

How shall we repay our debt to Robert Anson Heinlein?

I am tempted to say that it can't be done. The sheer size of the debt is staggering. He virtually invented modern science fiction, and did not attempt to patent it. He opened up a great many of sf's frontiers, produced the first reliable maps of most of its principal territories, and did not complain when each of those frontiers filled up with hordes of johnny-come-latelies, who the moment they got off the boat began to complain about the climate, the scenery and the employment opportunities. I don't believe there can be more than a handful of science fiction stories published in the last forty years that do not show his influence one way or another. He has written the definitive time-travel stories ("All You Zombies—" and "By His Bootstraps"), the definitive longevity books (*Methuselah's Children* and *Time Enough For Love*), the definitive theocracy novel (*Revolt In 2100*),

95

heroic fantasy/sf novel (*Glory Road*), revolution novel (*The Moon Is A Harsh Mistress*), transplant novel (*I Will Fear No Evil*), alien invasion novel (*The Puppet Masters*), technocracy story ("The Roads Must Roll"), arms race story ("Solution Unsatisfactory"), technodisaster story ("Blowups Happen"), and about a dozen of the finest science fiction juveniles ever published. These last alone have done more for the field than any other dozen books. And perhaps as important, he broke sf out of the pulps, opened up "respectable" and lucrative markets, broached the wall of the ghetto. He continues to work for the good of the entire genre: his most recent book sale was a precedent-setting event, representing the first-ever SFWA Model Contract signing. (The Science Fiction Writers of America has drawn up a hypothetical ideal contract, from the sf writer's point of view—but until *"The Number of the Beast–"* no such contract had ever been signed.) Note that Heinlein did not do this for his own benefit: the moment the contract was signed it was renegotiated *upward*.

You *can't* copyright ideas; you can only copyright specific arrangements of words. If you could copyright ideas, every living sf writer would be paying a substantial royalty to Robert Heinlein.

So would a lot of other people. In his spare time Heinlein invented the waldo and the waterbed (and God knows what else), and he didn't patent them either. (The first waldos were built by Nathan Woodruff at Brookhaven National Laboratories in 1945, three years after Heinlein described them for a few cents a word. As to the waterbed, see *Expanded Universe*.) In addition he helped design the spacesuit as we now know it.

Above all Heinlein is better educated, more widely read and traveled than anyone I have ever heard of, and has consistently shared the Good Parts with us. He has learned prodigiously, and passed on the most interesting things he's learned to us, and in the process passed on some of his love of learning to us. Surely that is a mighty gift. When I was five years old he began to teach me to love learning, and to be skeptical about what I was taught, and he did the same for a great many of us, directly or indirectly.

How then shall we repay him?

Certainly not with dollars. Signet claims 11.5 million Heinlein books in print. Berkley claims 12 million. Del Rey figures are not available, but they have at least a dozen titles. His latest novel fetched a record price. Extend those figures worldwide, and it starts to look as though Heinlein is very well repaid with dollars. But consider: at today's prices you could own all 42 of his books for about a hundred dollars plus sales tax. Robert Heinlein has given me more than a C-note's worth of entertainment, knowledge and challenging skullsweat, more by several orders of magnitude. His books do *not* cost five times the price of Philip Roth's latest drool; hence they are drastically underpriced.

We can't repay him with awards, nor with honors, nor with prestige. He has a shelf-full of Hugos (voted by his readers), the first-ever GrandMaster Nebula for Lifetime Contribution To Science Fiction (voted by his fellow writers), he is an Encyclopedia Britanica authority, he is the only man ever to be a World Science Fiction Convention Guest of Honor three times—it's not as though he needs any more flattery.

We can't even thank him by writing to say thanks—we'd only make more work for his remarkable wife Virginia, who handles his correspondence these days. There are, as noted, *millions* of us (possibly hundreds of millions)—a quick thank-you apiece would cause the U.S. Snail to finally and forever collapse—and if they were actually delivered they would make it difficult for Heinlein to get any work done.

I can think of only two things we could do to thank Robert Heinlein.

First, give blood, now and as often as you can spare a half hour and a half pint. It pleases him; blood donors have saved his life on several occasions. (Do you know the *I Will Fear No Evil* story? The plot of that book hinged on a character having a rare blood type; routine [for him] research led Heinlein to discover the National Rare Blood Club; he went out of his way to put a commercial for them in the forematter of the novel. After it was published he suffered a medical emergency, requiring transfusion. Surprise: Heinlein has a rare blood type. His life was saved by Rare Blood Club members. There is a persistent rumor, which I am unable to either verify or disprove, that at least one of those donors had joined because they read the blurb in *I Will Fear No Evil*.)

The second suggestion also has to do with helping to ensure Heinlein's personal survival—surely the sincerest form of flattery. Simply put, we can all do the best we personally can to assure that the country Robert Heinlein lives in is not ruined. I think he would take it kindly if we were all to refrain from abandoning civilization as a failed experiment that requires too much hard work. (I think he'll make out okay even if we don't—but he'd be a lot less comfortable.) I think he would be pleased if we abandoned the silly delusion that there are any passengers on Starship Earth, and took up our responsibilities as crewmen—as he has.

Which occasionally involves giving the Admiral your respectful attention. Even when the old fart's informed opinions conflict with your own ignorant prejudices.

The very size of the debt we all owe Heinlein has a lot to do with the savagery of the recent critical assaults on him. As Jubal Harshaw once noted, gratitude often translates as resentment. Sf critics, parasitic on a field which would not exist in anything like its present form or size without Heinlein, feel compelled to bite the hand that feeds them. Constitutionally unable to respect anything except insofar as it resembles themselves, some critics are compelled to publicly display disrespect for a talent of which not one of them can claim the tenth part.

And some of us pay them money to do this.

Look, Robert Heinlein is not a god, not even an angel. He is "merely" a good and great man, and a good and great writer, no small achievements. But there seems to be a dark human compulsion to take the best man around, declare him a god, and then scrutinize him like a hawk for the sign of human weakness that will allow us to slay him. Something in us likes to watch the mighty topple, and most especially the good mighty. If someone wrote a book alleging that Mother Theresa once committed a venial sin, it would sell a million copies.

And some of the cracks made about Robert Heinlein have been pretty personal. Though the critics swear that their concern is with criticizing literature, few of them can resist the urge to criticize Heinlein the man.

Alexei Panshin, for instance, in *Heinlein In Dimension*, asserts as a biographical fact, without disclaimer of hearsay, that Heinlein "cannot stand to be disagreed with, even to the point of discarding friendships." I have heard this allegation quoted several times in the twelve years since Panshin committed it to print. Last week I received a review copy of Philip K. Dick's new short story collection, *The Golden Man* (Berkley); I quote from its introduction:

> I consider Heinlein to be my spiritual father, even though our political ideologies are totally at variance. Several years ago, when I was ill, Heinlein offered his help, anything he could do, and we had never met; he would phone me up and see how I was doing. He wanted to buy me an electric typewriter, God bless him—one of the few true gentlemen in this world. *I don't agree with any ideas he puts forth in his writing, but that is neither here nor there.* One time when I owed the IRS a lot of money and couldn't raise it, Heinlein loaned the money to me. . . . he knows I'm a flipped-out freak and still he helped me and my wife when we were in trouble. That is the best in humanity, there; that is who and what I love.
>
> (italics mine—SR)

Full disclosure here: Robert Heinlein has given me, personally, an autograph, a few gracious words, and a couple of hours of conversation. Directly. But when I was five he taught me, with the first and weakest of his juveniles, three essential things: to make up my own mind, always; to think it through *before* doing so; to get the facts *before* thinking. Perhaps someone else would have taught me those things sooner or later; that's irrelevant: it was Heinlein who did it. That is who and what *I* love.

Free speech gives people the right to knock who and what I love; it also give me the right to rebut.

Not to "defend". As to the work, there it stands, invulnerable to noise made about it. As to the man, he once said that "It is impossible to insult a man who is not unsure of himself." Fleas can't bite him. Nor is there any need to defend his literary reputation; people who read what critics tell them to deserve what they get.

No, I accepted this commission because I'm personally annoyed. I grow weary of hearing someone I love slandered; I have wasted too many hours at convention parties arguing with loud nits, seen one too many alleged "reference books" take time out to criticize Heinlein's alleged political views and literary sins, heard one too many talentless writers make speeches that take potshots at the man who made it possible for them to avoid honest work. At the next convention party I want to be able to simply hand that loud nit a copy of *Destinies* and go back to having fun.

So let us consider the most common charges made against Heinlein. I arrange these in order of intelligence, with the most brainless first.

I. PERSONAL LAPSES

(Note: all these are most-brainless, as not one of the critics is in any position to know anything about Heinlein the man. The man they attack is the one they infer from his fiction: a mug's game.)

(1) *"Heinlein is a fascist."* This is the most popular Heinlein shibboleth in fandom, particularly among the young—and, of course, exclusively among the ignorant. I seldom bother to reply, but in this instance I am being paid. Dear sir or madam: kindly go to the library, look up the dictionary definition of fascism. For good measure, read the history of fascism, asking the librarian to help you with any big words. Then read the works of Robert Heinlein, as you have plainly not done yet. If out of 42 books you can produce

one shred of evidence that Heinlein—or any of his protagonists—is a fascist, I'll eat my copy of *Heinlein In Dimension*.

(2) *"Heinlein is a male chauvinist."* This is the second most common charge these days. That's right, Heinlein populates his books with dumb, weak, incompetent women. Like Sister Maggie in "If This Goes On—"; Dr. Mary Lou Martin in "Let There Be Light"; Mary Sperling in *Methuselah's Children*; Grace Cormet in "—We Also Walk Dogs"; Longcourt Phyllis in *Behond This Horizon*; Cynthia Craig in "The Unpleasant Profession of Jonathan Hoag"; Karen in "Gulf"; Gloria McNye in "Delilah And The Space-Rigger"; Allucquere in *The Puppet Masters*; Hazel and Edith Stone in *The Rolling Stones*; Betty in *The Star Beast*; all the women in *Tunnel In The Sky*; Penny in *Double Star*; Pee Wee and the Mother Thing in *Have Spacesuit— Will Travel;* Jill Boardman, Becky Vesant, Patty Paiwonski, Anne, Miriam and Dorcas in *Stranger In A Strange Land*; Star, the Empress of Twenty Universes, in *Glory Road*; Wyoh, Mimi, Sidris and Gospazha Michelle Holmes in *The Moon Is A Harsh Mistress*; Eunice and Joan Eunice in *I Will Fear No Evil*; Ishtar, Tamara, Minerva, Hamadryad, Dora, Helen Mayberry, Llita, Laz, Lor and Maureen Smith in *Time Enough For Love*; and Dejah Thoris, Hilda Corners, Gay Deceiver and Elizabeth Long in *"The Number of the Beast—"*.*

Brainless cupcakes all, eh? (Virtually every one of them is a world-class expert in at least one demanding and competitive field; the exceptions plainly will be as soon as they grow up. Madame Curie would have enjoyed chatting with any one of them.) Helpless housewives! (Any one of them could take Wonder Woman three falls out of three, and polish off Jirel of Joiry for dessert.)

I think one could perhaps make an excellent case for Heinlein as a *female* chauvinist. He has repeatedly insisted that women average smarter, more practical and more courageous than men. He consistently underscores their

*An incomplete list, off the top of my head.

biological and emotional superiority. He married a woman he proudly described to me as "smarter, better educated and more sensible than I am." In his latest book, *Expanded Universe*—the immediate occasion for this article—he suggests without the slightest visible trace of irony that the franchise be taken away from men and given exclusively to women. He consistently created strong, intelligent, capable, independent, sexually aggressive women characters for a quarter of a century *before* it was made a requirement, right down to his supporting casts.

Clearly we are still in the area of delusions which can be cured simply by reading Heinlein while awake.

(3) *"Heinlein is a closet fag."* Now, this one I have only run into twice, but I include it here because of its truly awesome silliness, and because one of its proponents is Thomas Disch. In a speech aptly titled, "The Embarassments of Science Fiction," reprinted in Peter Nicholls' *Explorations of the Marvelous*, Disch asserts, with the most specious arguments imaginable, that there is an unconscious homosexual theme in *Starship Troopers*. He apparently feels (a) that everyone in the book is an obvious fag (because they all act so macho, and we all know that all macho men are really fags, right? Besides, some of them wear jewelry, as *real* men have never done in all history.); (b) that Heinlein is clearly unaware of this (because he never overtly raises the issue of the sex habits of infantry in a book intended for children and published in 1962), and (c) that (a) and (b), stipulated and taken together, would constitute some kind of successful slap at Heinlein or his book or soldiers . . . or something. Disch's sneers at "swaggering leather boys" (I can find no instance in the book of anyone wearing leather) simply mystify me.

The second proponent of this theory was a young woman at an sf convention party, ill-smelling and as ugly as she could make herself, who insisted that *Time Enough For Love* proved that Heinlein wanted to fuck himself. I urged her to give it a try, and went to another party.

(4) *"Heinlein is right wing."* This is not *always* a semantic confusion similar to the "fascist" babble cited above;

occasionally the loud nit in question actually has some idea of what "right-wing" means, and is able to stretch the definition to fit a man who bitterly opposes military conscription, supports consensual sexual freedom and women's ownership of their bellies, delights in unconventional marriage customs, champions massive expenditures for scientific research, suggests radical experiments in government; and has written with apparent approval of anarchists, communists, socialists, technocrats, limited-franchise-republicans, emperors and empresses, capitalists, dictators, thieves, whores, charlatans and even career civil servants (Mr. Kiku in *The Star Beast*). If this indeed be conservatism, then Teddy Kennedy is a liberal, and I am Marie of Roumania.

And if there *were* anything to the allegation, when exactly was it that the conservative viewpoint was proven unfit for literary consumption? I missed it.

(5) "*Heinlein is an authoritarian.*" To be sure, respect for law and order is one of Lazarus Long's most noticeable characteristics. Likewise Jubal Harshaw, Deety Burroughs, Fader McGee, Noisy Rhysling, John Lyle, Jim Marlowe, Wyoming Knott, Manuel Garcia O'Kelly-Davis, Prof de la Paz and Dak Broadbent. In his latest novel, "*The Number of the Beast*—", Heinlein seems to reveal himself authoritarian to the extent that he suggests a lifeboat can have only one captain at a time. He also suggests that the captain be elected, by unanimous vote.

(6) "*Heinlein is a libertarian.*" Horrors, no! How dreadful. Myself, I'm a serf.*

(7) "*Heinlein is an elitist.*" Well, now. If by that you mean that he believes some people are of more value to their species than others, I'm inclined to agree—with you and with him. If you mean he believes a learned man's opinion is likely to be worth more than that of an ignoramus, again I'll go along. If by "elitist" you mean that Heinlein believes the strong should rule the weak, I strongly *dis*agree. (Remember

---

*I know it sounds crazy, but I've heard "libertarian" used as a pejorative a few times lately.

frail old Professor de la Paz, and Waldo, and recall that
Heinlein himself was declared "permanently and totally
disabled" in 1934.) If you mean he believes the wealthy
should exploit the poor, I refer you to *The Moon Is A Harsh
Mistress* and *I Will Fear No Evil*. If you mean he believes
the wise should rule the foolish and the competent rule the
incompetent, again I plead guilty to the same offense. *Somebody's* got to drive—should it not be the best driver?

How do you *pick* the best driver? Well, Heinlein has given
us a multiplicity of interesting and mutually exclusive
suggestions; why not examine them?

(8) *"Heinlein is a militarist."* Bearing in mind that he
abhors the draft, this is indeed one of his proudest boasts.
Can there really be people so naive as to think that their way
of life would survive the magic disappearance of their armed
forces by as much as a month? Evidently; I meet 'em all over.

(9) *"Heinlein is a patriot."* (Actually, they always say
"superpatriot." To them there is no other kind of patriot.)
Anyone who sneers at patriotism—and continues to *live* in
the society whose supporters he scorns—is a parasite, a
fraud, or a fool. Often all three.

Patriotism does not mean that you think your country is
perfect, or blameless, or even particularly likeable on balance; nor does it mean that you serve it blindly, go where it
tells you to go and kill whom it tells you to kill. It means that
you are committed to keeping it alive and making it better,
that you will do whatever seems necessary (up to and including dying) to protect it whenever you, personally, perceive a
mortal threat to it, military or otherwise. This is something to
be ashamed of? I think Heinlein has made it abundantly clear
that in any hypothetical showdown between species patriotism and national patriotism the former, for him, would
win hands down.

(10) *"Heinlein is an atheist,"* or *"agnostic,"* or *"solip-
sist,"* or *"closet fundamentalist,"* or *"hedonistic Cal-
vinist,"* or . . . Robert Heinlein has consistently refused to
discuss his personal religious beliefs; in one of his stories a
character convincingly argues that it is *impossible* to do so
meaningfully. Yet everyone is sure they know where he

stands. *I* sure don't. The one thing I've *never* heard him called (yet) is a closet Catholic (nor am I suggesting it for a moment), but in my new anthology, *The Best of All Possible Worlds* (Ace Books), you will find a story Heinlein selected as one of his personal all-time favorites, a deeply religious tale by Anatole France (himself generally labeled an agnostic) called "Our Lady's Juggler," which I first heard in Our Lady of Refuge grammar school in the Bronx, so long ago that I'd forgotten it until Heinlein jogged my memory.

In any event his theology is none of anybody's damned business. God knows it's not a valid reason to criticize his fiction.

(11) *"Heinlein is opinionated."* Of course, I can't speak for him, but I suspect he would be willing to accept this compliment. The people who offer it as an insult are always, of course, as free of opinions themselves as a newborn chicken.

Enough of personal lapses. What are the indictments that have been handed down against Heinlein's *work*, his failures as a science fiction writer? Again, we shall consider the most bone-headed charges first.

II. LITERARY LAPSES

(1) *"Heinlein uses slang."* Sorry. Flat wrong. It is *very* seldom that one of his *characters* uses slang or argot; he in authorial voice never does. What he uses that is *miscalled* "slang" are idiom and colloquialism. I won't argue the (to me self-evident) point that a writer is *supposed* to preserve them—not at this time, anyway. I'll simply note that you can't very well criticize a man's use of a language whose terminology you don't know yourself.

(2) *"Heinlein can't create believable women characters."* There's an easy way to support this claim: simply disbelieve in all Heinlein's female characters, and maintain that all those who believe them are gullible. You'll have a problem, though: several of Heinlein's women bear a striking resemblance to his wife Virginia, you'll have to disbelieve in her, too—which could get you killed if your paths

cross. Also, there's a lady I once lived with for a long time, who used to haunt the magazine stores when *I Will Fear No Evil* was being serialized in *Galaxy*, because she could not wait to read the further adventures of the "unbelievable" character with whom she identified so strongly—you'll have to disbelieve in her, too.

Oddly, this complaint comes most often from radical feminists. Examination shows that Heinlein's female characters are almost invariably highly intelligent, educated, competent, practical, resourceful, courageous, independent, sexually aggressive and sufficiently personally secure to be able to stroke their men's egos as often as their own get stroked. I will—reluctantly—concede that this does *not* sound like the average woman as I have known her, but I am bemused to find myself in the position of trying to convince *feminists* that such women can in fact exist.

I think I know what enrages the radicals: two universal characteristics of Heinlein heroines that I left out of the above list. They are always beautiful and proud of it (regardless of whether they happen to be pretty), and they are often strongly interested in having babies. *None* of them bitterly regrets and resents having been born female—which of course makes them not only traitors to their exploited sex, but unbelievable.

(3) *"Heinlein's male characters are all him."* I understand this notion was first put forward by James Blish in an essay titled, "Heinlein, Son of Heinlein," which I have not seen. But the notion was developed in detail by Panshin. As he sees it, there are three basic male personae Heinlein uses over and over again, the so-called Three-Stage Heinlein Individual. The first and youngest stage is the bright but naive youth; the second is the middle-aged man who knows how the world works; the third is the old man who knows how it works and why it works, knows how it got that way. All three, Panshin asserts, are really Heinlein in the thinnest of disguises. (Sounds like the average intelligent man to me.)

No one ever does explain what, if anything, is *wrong* with this, but the implication seems to be that Heinlein is unable to get into the head of anyone who does not think like him. An interesting theory—if you overlook Dr. Ftaeml, Dr. Mahmoud, Memtok, David McKinnon, Andy Libby, all the characters in "Magic, Inc." and "And He Built a Crooked House," Noisy Rhysling, the couple in "It's Great To Be Back," Lorenzo Smythe, The Man Who Traveled in Elephants, Bill Lermer, Hugh Farnham, Jake Salomon, *all* the extremely aged characters in *Time Enough For Love*, all the extremely young characters in *Tunnel In The Sky* except Rod Walker, and all four protagonists of *"The Number of the Beast—"* (among many others). Major characters all, and none of them fits on the three-stage age/wisdom chart. (Neither, by the way, does *Heinlein*—who was displaying third-stage wisdom and insight in his early thirties.)

If all the male Heinlein characters that *can* be forced into those three pigeonholes are Heinlein in thin disguise, why is it that I have no slightest difficulty in distinguishing (say) Juan Rico from Thorby, or Rufo from Dak Broadbent, or Waldo from Andy Libby, or Jubal Harshaw from Johann Smith? If Heinlein writes in characterizational monotone, why don't I confuse Colonel Dubois, Colonel Baslim and Colonel Manning? Which of the four protagonists of *"The Number of the Beast—"* is the *real* Heinlein, and how do you know?

To be sure, some generalizations can be made of the majority of Heinlein's heros—he seems fascinated by competence, for example, whereas writers like Pohl and Sheckley seem fascinated by incompetence. Is this a flaw in *any* of these three writers? If habitual use of a certain type of character *is* a literary sin, should we not apply the same standard to Alfred Bester, Kurt Vonnegut, Phil Dick, Larry Niven, Philip Roth, Raymond Chandler, P.G. Wodehouse, J.P. Donleavy and a thousand others?

(4) *"Heinlein doesn't describe his protagonists physically."* After I have rattled off from memory extensive physical descriptions of Lazarus and Dora and Minerva Long, Scar Gordon, Jubal Harshaw and Eunice Branca,

complainers of this type usually add, "unless the mechanics of the story require it." Thus amended, I'll chop it—as evidence of the subtlety of Heinlein's genius. A maximum number of his readers can identify with his characters.

What these types are usually complaining about is the absence of any *poetry* about physical appearance, stuff like, "Questing eyes like dwarf hazelnuts brooded above a strong yet amiable nose, from which depended twin parentheses framing a mouth like a pink Eskimo Pie. Magenta was his weskit, and his hair was the color of mild abstraction on a winter's morning in Antigonish." In Heinlein's brand of fiction, a picture is seldom worth a thousand words—least of all a portrait.

But I have to admit that Alexei Panshin put his finger on the fly in the ointment on p. 128 of *Heinlein In Dimension:* ". . . while the reader doesn't notice the lack of description while he reads, afterwards individual characters aren't likely to stand out in the mind." In other words, if you leave anything to the reader's imagination, you've lost better than half the critics right there. Which may be the best thing to do with them.

(5) "*Heinlein can't plot.*" One of my favorite parts of *Heinlein In Dimension* is the section on plot. On p. 153 Panshin argues that Heinlein's earliest works are flawed because "they aren't told crisply. They begin with an end in mind and eventually get there, but the route they take is a wandering one." On the *very next page* Panshin criticizes Heinlein's later work for *not* wandering, for telling him only those details necessary to the story.

> In "Gulf," for instance, Heinlein spends one day in time and 36 pages in enrolling an agent. He then spends six months, skimmed over in another 30-odd pages, in training the agent. Then, just to end the story, he kills his agent off in a job that takes him one day, buzzed over in a mere 4 pages. The gradual loss of control is obvious.

Presumably the significant and interesting parts of Panshin's life come at steady, average speed. Or else he wanted the boring and irrelevant parts of Joe's life thrown in to balance some imaginary set of scales. (Oh, and just to set the record straight, it is clearly stated in "Gulf" that Joe's final mission takes him many days.)

All written criticism I have seen of Heinlein's plotting comes down to this same outraged plaint: that if you sit down and make an outline of the sequence of events in a Heinlein story, it will most likely not come out symmetrical and balanced. Right you are: it won't. It will just *seem* to sort of ramble along, just like life does, and at the end, when you have reached the place where the author wanted you to go, you will look back at your tracks and fail to discern in them any mathematical pattern or regular geometric shape. If you keep looking, though, you'll notice that they got you there in the shortest possible distance, as straightforwardly as the terrain allowed. And that you hurried.

That they cannot be described by any simple equation is a sign of Heinlein's excellence, not his weakness.

(6) *"Heinlein can't write sex scenes."* This one usually kicks off an entertaining hour defining a "good sex scene." Everybody disagrees with everybody on this, but most people I talk to can live with the following four requirements: a "good" sex scene should be believable, consensual (all parties consenting), a natural development of the story rather than a pasted-on attention-getter, and, hopefully, sexually arousing.

In order: Heinlein has never described *any* sexual activity that would cause either Masters or Johnson even mild surprise. In forty-two books I can recall only one scene of even attempted rape (unsuccessful, fatally so) and two depictions of extremely mild spanking. I have found *no* instances of gratuitous sex, tacked on to make a dull story interesting, and I defy anyone to name one.

As to the last point, if you have spent any time at all in a pornshop (and if you haven't, why not? Aren't you at all curious about people?) you'll have noticed that *none* of the clientele is aroused by more than 5-10% of the available material. Yet it all sells or it wouldn't be there. One man's meat is another man's person. Heinlein's characters may not behave in bed the way you do—so what?

It has been argued by some that "Heinlein suddenly started writing about sex after ignoring it for years . . ." They complain that all of Heinlein's early heros, at least, are Boy Scouts. Please examine any reasonably complete bibliography of early Heinlein—the one in the back of *Heinlein In Dimension* will do fine. Now: if you exclude from consideration (a) juvenile novels, in which Heinlein *could not* have written a sex scene, any more than any juveniles-novelist could have in the forties and fifties; (b) stories sold to John Campbell, from which Kay Tarrant cut all sex no matter who the author; (c) stories aimed at and sold to "respectable," slick, non-sf markets which were already breaking enough taboos by buying science fiction at all; (d) tales in which no sex subplot was appropriate to the story; and (e) stories for *Boy's Life* whose protagonists were *supposed* to be Boy Scouts; what you are left with as of 1961 is two novels and two short stories, all rife with sex. Don't take *my* word, go look it up. In 1961, with the publication of *Stranger In A Strange Land*, Heinlein became one of the first sf writers to openly discuss sex at any length, and he has continued to do so since. (Note to historians: I know Farmer's "The Lovers" came nine years earlier—but note that that story did not appear in book form until 1961, the same year as *Stranger* and a year after Sturgeon's *Venus Plus X*.) I know vanishingly few septuagenarians whose view of sex is half so liberal and enlightened as Heinlein's—damn few people of *any* age, more's the pity.

(7) *"Heinlein is preachy."* "preachy: inclined to preach." "preach: to expound upon in writing or speech; especially, to urge acceptance of or compliance with (specified religious or moral principles)."

Look: the classic task of fiction is to create a character or characters, give he-she-or-them a problem or problems, and then show his-her-their struggle to find a solution or solutions. If it doesn't do that, compraatively few people will pay cash for the privilege of reading it. (Rail if you will about "archaic rules stifling creative freedom": that's the way readers are wired up, and *we* exist for *their* benefit.) Now: if the solution proposed does not involve a moral principle (extremely difficult to pull off), you have a cook-book, a how-to manual, Spaceship Repair for the Compleat Idiot. If no optimal solution is suggested, if the problem is left unsolved, there are three possibilities: either the writer is propounding the *moral principle* that some problems have no optimal solutions (e.g. "Solution Unsatisfactory" by R.A.H.), or the writer is suggesting that *some*body should find a solution to this dilemma because it beats the hell out of him, or the writer has simply been telling you series of pointless and depressing anecdotes, speaking at great length without saying anything (e.g. most of modern mainstream litracha). Perhaps this is an enviable skill, for a politician, say, but is it really a requirement of good fiction?

Exclude the above cases and what you have left is a majority of all the fiction ever written, and the overwhelming majority of the good fiction.

But one of the oddities of humans is that while we all want our fiction to propose solutions to moral dilemmas, we do not want to admit it. Our writers are *supposed* to answer the question, "What is moral behavior?"—but they'd better not let us catch them palming that card. (Actually, Orson and I are just good friends.) The pill must be heavily sugar-coated if we are to swallow it. (I am not putting down people. *I'm* a people. That bald apes can be cajoled into moral specualtion by any means at all is a miracle, God's blessing on us all. Literature is the antithesis of authoritarianism and of most organized religions—which seek to replace moral speculation with laws—and in that cause we should all be happy to plunge our arms up to the shoulders in sugar.)

And so, when I've finished explaining that "preachy" is a *complimentary* thing to call a writer, the people who made the charge usually backpedal and say that what they *meant* was

(8) *"Heinlein lectures at the expense of his fiction."* Here,

at last, we come to something a little more than noise. This, if proved, would seem a genuine and serious literary indictment.

Robert Heinlein himself said in 1950:

> A science fiction writer may have, and often does have, other motivations *in addition to* pursuit of profit. He may wish to create "art for art's sake," he may want to warn the world against a course he feels disastrous (Orwell's *1984,* Huxley's *Brave New World*—but please note that each is intensely entertaining, and that each made stacks of money), he may wish to urge the human race toward a course which he considers desirable (Bellamy's *Looking Backwards,* Wells' *Men Like Gods*), he may wish to instruct, to uplift, or even to dazzle. But the science fiction writer—any fiction writer—must keep entertainment consciously in mind as his prime purpose . . . or he may find himself back dragging that old cotton sack.
>
> (from "Pandora's Box," reprinted in *Expanded Universe*)

The change is that in his most recent works, Robert Heinlein has subordinated entertainment to preaching, that he has, as Theodore Sturgeon once said of H.G. Wells' later work, "sold his birthright for a pot of message." In evidence the prosecution adduces *I Will Fear No Evil, Time Enough For Love*, the second and third most recent Heinlein novels, and when *"The Number of the Beast*—" becomes generally available, they'll probably add that one too.

Look: nobody wants to be lectured to, right? That is, no one wants to be lectured to by some jerk who doesn't know any more than they do. But do not good people, responsible people, enlightened citizens, *want* to be lectured to by someone who knows more than they do? Have we really been following Heinlein for forty years because he does great card tricks? Only?

Defense is willing to stipulate that, proportionately speaking, all three of People's Exhibits tend to be—*by comparison with early Heinlein*—rather long on talk and short on action (*Time Enough For Love* perhaps least so of the three).

Defense wishes to know, however, what if anything is wrong with that, and offers for consideration *Venus Plus X, Triton, Camp Concentration* and *The Thurb Revolution*.

I Will Fear No Evil concerns a man whose brain is transplanted into the body of a healthy and horny woman; to his shock, he learns that the body's original personality, its soul, is still present in his new skull (or perhaps, as Heinlein is careful not to rule out, he has a sustained and complex hallucination to that effect.). She teaches him about how to be female, and in the process learns something of what it's like to be male. Is there any conceivable way to handle this theme *without* lots of internal dialogue, lots of sharing of opinions and experiences, and a minimum of fast-paced action? Or is the theme itself somehow illegitimate for sf?

Time Enough For Love concerns the oldest man in the Galaxy (by a wide margin), who has lived *so* long that he no longer longs to live. But his descendants (and by inescapable mathematical logic most of the humans living by that point *are* his descendants) will not let him die, and seek to restore his zest for living by three perfectly reasonable means: they encourage him to talk about the Old Days, they find him something *new* to do, and they smother him with love and respect. Do not all of these involve a lot of conversation? As I mentioned above, this book *has* action aplenty, when Lazarus gets around to reminiscing (and lying); that attempted-rape scene, for instance, is a small masterpiece, almost a textbook course in how to handle a fight scene.

But who says that ideas are not as entertaining as fast-paced action?

"The Number of the Beast—" (I know, on the cover of the book it says *The Number of the Beast*, without quotes or dash; that is the publishers' title. I prefer Heinlein's.) I hesitate to discuss this book as it is unlikely you can have read it by now and I don't want to spoil any surprises (of which there are many). But I will note that there is more action here than in the last two books put together, and—since all four protagonists are extraordinarily educated people, who love to argue—a whole lot of lively and spirited dialogue. I also note

that its basic premise is utterly, delightfully preposterous—
and that I do not believe it can be disproved. (Maybe Heinlein
and Phil Dick aren't *that* far apart after all.) It held my
attention most firmly right up to the last page, and indeed
holds it yet.

Let me offer some more bits of evidence.

One: According to a press release which chanced to land
on my desk last week, three of Berkley Publishing Company's top ten all-time best-selling sf titles are *Stranger In A
Strange Land, Time Enough For Love,* and *I Will Fear No
Evil.*

Two: In the six years since it appeared in paperback, *Time
Enough For Love* has gone through thirteen printings—a feat
it took both *Stranger In A Strange Land* and *The Moon Is A
Harsh Mistress* ten years apiece to achieve.

Three: Gregg Press, a highly selective publishing house
which brings out quality hardcover editions of what it con-
siders to be the finest in sf, has already printed an edition of *I
Will Fear No Evil,* designed to survive a thousand readings.
It is one of the youngest books on the Gregg List.

Four: *The Notebooks Of Lazarus Long,* a 62-page excerpt
from *Time Enough For Love* comprising absolutely *nothing
but opinions,* without a shred of action, narrative or drama, is
selling quite briskly in a five-dollar paperback edition, par-
tially hand-lettered by D.F. Vassallo. I know of no parallel to
this in all sf (unless you consider Tolkien "sf").

Five: Heinlein's latest novel, *"The Number of the
Beast—"*, purchased by editors who, you can assume, knew
quite well the dollars-and-cents track record of Heinlein's
last few books, fetched an all-time genre-record-breaking
half a million dollars.

Plainly the old man has lost his touch, eh? Mobs of
customers, outraged at his failure to entertain them, are
attempting to drown him in dollars.

What's that? You there in the back row, speak up. You say
you aren't entertained, and that proves Heinlein isn't entertaining? Say, aren't you the same person I saw trying to
convince that guy from the *New York Times* that sf is not
juvenile brainless adventure but the literature of ideas? Social

relevance and all that?

What that fellow in the back row means is not that ideas and opinions do not belong in a science fiction novel. He means he disagrees with some of Heinlein's opinions. (Even that isn't strictly accurate. From the noise and heat he generates in venting his disagreement, it's obvious that he hates and bitterly resents Heinlein's opinions.)

I know of many cases in which critics have disagreed with, or vilified, or forcefully attacked Robert Heinlein's opinions. A few were even able to accurately identify those opinions.* I know of none who has succeeded in *disproving*, demonstrating to be false, a single one of them. I'm sure it could happen, but I'm still waiting to see it.

Defense's arms are weary from hauling exhibits up to the bench; perhaps this is the point at which Defense should rest.

Instead I will reverse myself, plead guilty with an explanation, and throw myself on the mercy of the court. I declare that I *do* think the sugar-coating on Heinlein's last few books is (comparatively) thin, and not by accident or by failure of craft. I believe there is a good reason *why* the plots of the last three books allow and require their protagonists to preach at length. Moral, spiritual, political and historical lessons which he once would have spent at least a novelette developing are lately fired off at the approximate rate of a half dozen per conversation. That his books do *not* therefore fall apart the way Wells' last books did is only because Heinlein is incapable of writing dull. Over four decades it has become increasingly evident that he is not the "pure entertainment" song and dance man he has always claimed to be, that he has sermons to preach—and the customers keep coming by the carload. Furthermore, with the passing of those four decades, the urgency of his message has grown.

And so now, with his very latest publication, *Expanded Universe*, Heinlein has finally blown his cover altogether. I think that makes *Expanded Universe*, despite a significant number of flaws, the single most important and valuable Heinlein book ever published.

*—As distinct from the opinions of his protagonists.

Let me tell you a little about the book. It is built around a previously available but long out of print Heinlein collection, *The Worlds of Robert A. Heinlein*, but it has been expanded by about 160%, with approximately 125,000 words of new material, for a total of about 202,500 words. Some of the new stuff is fiction, although little of it is science fiction (about 17,500 words). But the bulk of the new material, about 84,000 words, is non-fiction. Taken together it's as close as Heinlein is ever going to get to writing his memoirs, and it forms his ultimate personal statement to date. In ten essays, a polemic, one and a half speeches and extensive forewords and afterwords for most of thirteen stories, Heinlein lets us further inside his head than he ever has before. And hey, you know what? He doesn't resemble Lazarus Long much at all.

For instance, although he is plainly capable of imagining and appreciating it, Heinlein is not himself able to sustain Lazarus's magnificent ingrained indifference to the fate of any society. Unlike Lazarus, Heinlein loves the United States of America. He'll tell you why, quite specifically, in this book. Logical, pragmatic reasons why. He will tell you, for instance, of his travels in the Soviet Union, and what he saw and heard there. If, after you've heard him out, you still don't think that for all its warts (hell, running sores), the United States is the planet's best hope for an enlightened future, there's no sense in us talking further; you'll be wanting to pack. (Hey, have you heard? The current government of the People's Republic of China [half-life unknown] has allowed as how limited freedom of thought will be permitted this year. Provisionally.)* You know, the redneck clowns who chanted "America—love it or leave it!" while they stomped me back in the sixties didn't have a *bad* slogan. The only problem was that they got to define "love of America," and they limited its meaning to "blind worship of America." In addition they limited the definition of America to "the man in the White House."

These mistakes Heinlein certainly does not make. (Relevant quote from *Expanded Universe*: "Brethren and Sistren, have you ever stopped to think that *there has not been one*

*At press time, they have given every sign of having changed their minds.—SR

rational decision out of the Oval Office for fifty years?''—[italics his—SR]) In this book he identifies clearly, vividly and concisely the specific brands of rot that are eating out America's heart. He outlines each of the deadly perils that face the nation, and predicts their consequences. As credentials, he offers a series of fairly specific predictions he made in 1950 for the year 2000, updated in 1965, and adds 1980 updates supporting a claim of a 66% success rate—enormously higher than that of, say Jeanne Dixon. He pronounces himself dismayed not only by political events of the last few decades, but by the terrifying decay of education and growth of irrationalism in America. (Aside: in my own opinion, one of the best exemplars of this latter trend is Stephen King's current runaway bestseller *The Stand*, a brilliantly entertaining parable in praise of ignorance, superstition, reliance on dreams, and the sociological insights of feeble-minded old Ned Lud.)

It is worth noting in this connection that while Heinlein has many scathing things to say about the U.S. in *Expanded Universe*, he has prohibited publication of the book in any other country.* We don't wash family linen with strangers present. I don't know of any other case in which an sf writer deliberately (and drastically) limited his royalties out of patriotism, or for that matter any moral or ethical principle. I applaud.

Friends, one of the best educated and widely-traveled men in America has looked into the future, and he is not especially optimistic.

It cannot be said that he despairs. He makes *many* positive, practical suggestions—for real cures rather than bandaids. He outlines specifically how to achieve the necessary perspective and insight to form intelligent extrapolations of world events, explains in detail how to get a decent education (by the delightful device of explaining how *not* to get one), baldly names the three pillars of wisdom, and reminds us that ''Last to come out of Pandora's Box was a gleaming, beautiful thing—eternal Hope.''

But the last section of the book is a matched pair of

*—at presstime I learn that the book can be obtained in Canada. I follow the logic; the two countries are Siamese Twins.

mutually exclusive prophecies, together called "The Happy Days Ahead." The first is a gloomy scenario of doom, the second an optimistic scenario. He says, "I can risk great gloom in the first because I'll play you out with music at the end."

But I have to admit that the happy scenario, *Over The Rainbow*, strikes me as preposterously unlikely.

In fact, the only thing I can imagine that would increase its probability would be the massive widespread reading of *Expanded Universe*.

Which brings me to what I said at the beginning of this essay: if you want to thank Robert A. Heinlein, do what you can to see to it that the country he loves, the culture he loves, the magnificent ideal he loves, is not destroyed. If you have the wit to see that this old man has a genuine handle on the way the world wags, kindly stop complaining that his literary virtues are not classical and go back to doing what you used to do when sf was a ghetto-literature scorned by all the world: force copies of Heinlein on all your friends. Unlike most teachers, Heinlein has been successfully competing with television for forty years now. Anyone that *he* cannot convert to rationalism is purely unreachable, and you know, there are a hell of a lot of people on the fence these days.

I do not worship Robert Heinlein. I do not agree with everything he says. There are a number of his opinions concerning which I have serious reservations, and perhaps two with which I flat-out disagree (none of which I have the slightest intention of washing with strangers present). But all of these tend to keep me awake nights, because the only arguments I can assemble to refute him are based on "my thirty years of experience," of a very limited number of Americans and Canadians—and I'm painfully aware of just how poorly that stacks up against his seventy-three years of intensive study of the entire population and the entire history of the planet.

And I repeat: if there is anything that can divert the land of my birth from its current stampede into the Stone Age, it is the widespread dissemination of the thoughts and perceptions that Robert Heinlein has been selling as entertainment since 1939. You can thank him, not by buying his book, but by *loaning out* the copy you buy to as many people as will sit still for it, until it falls apart from overreading. (Be sure and loan *Expanded Universe* only to fellow citizens.) Time is short: it is no accident that his latest novel devotes a good deal of attention to the subject of lifeboat rules. Not that *Expanded Universe* contains a quick but thorough course in how to survive the aftermath of a nuclear attack. (When Heinlein said in his Guest of Honor speech at MidAmeriCon that "there will be nuclear war on Earth in your lifetime," some people booed, and some were unconvinced. But it chanced that there was a thunderstorm over the hotel next morning—and I woke up three feet in the air, covered with sweat.) Emergencies require emergency measures, so drastic that it will be hard to persuade people of their utter necessity.

If you want to thank Robert Heinlein, open your eyes and look around you—and begin loudly demanding that your neighbors do likewise.

Or—at the very least—please stop loudly insisting that the elephant is merely a kind of inferior snake, or tree, or large barrel of leather, or oversized harpoon, or flexible trombone, or . . .

(When I read the above as my Guest of Honor speech at the New England Science Fiction Association's annual regional convention, Bosklone, I took Heinlein's advice about playing them out with music literally, and closed with a song. I append it here as well. It is the second filksong* I've ever written, and it is set to the tune of Old Man River, *as arranged by Marty Paich on Ray Charles's* Ingredients In a Recipe For Soul. *[If you're not familiar with that arrangement, the scansion will appear to limp at the end.] Guitar chords are provided for would-be filksingers, but copyright is reserved for recording or publishing royalties, etc.)*

---

*A filksong is not a typo, but a generic term for any song or song-parody sung by or for sf fans.

Ol' Man Heinlein
(lyrics by Spider Robinson)

```
D       G7        D          G7
Ol' man Heinlein     That ol' man Heinlein
    D           A7           Bm          E7
He must know somethin'     His heart keeps pumpin'
    A      Asus        A     A+     D
He just keep writin'    And lately writin' 'em long
```

```
    D              G7          D            G7
He don't write for critics   Cause that stuff's rotten
       D           A7        Bm         E7
And them that writes it    Is soon forgotten
    A         Asus         A    A+     D
But ol' man Heinlein    keeps speculatin' along
```

```
F#m    C#7    F#m    C#7    F#m     C#7 \ F#m     C#7
You and me    Sit and think   Heads all empty except for drink
F#m    C#7    F#m    C#7     F#m      F#m  Em      A7
Tote that pen   Jog that brain   Get a little check in the mail from Baen . .
```

```
D   G7        D      G7
I get bleary      And feel like shirkin'
    D         A7         Bm          E7
I'm tired of writin'    But scared of workin'
    A         Asus       A      A+    D
But ol' man Heinlein    He keeps on rollin' along
```

```
Abm    Eb7    Abm    Eb7    Abm     Eb7   Abm  Eb7
You and me    Read his stuff   Never can seem to get enough
Abm    Eb7    Abm    Eb7     Abm    Eb7  Abm  F#m     B7
Turn that page   Dig them chops   Hope the old gentleman never stops . . .
```

```
    E          A7          E    A7
So raise your glasses      It's only fittin'
    E    B        C#m   F#7
The best sf that was ever written
    E    E+    E6     Am        E   C#m     F#7  B7  E
Is Old Man Heinlein     May he live as long as Lazarus Long!
```

HAVE YOU HEARD
THE ONE . . . ?

There is clearly a kind of delirious logic to the way things happen at Callahan's Place, a kind of artistic symmetry—if by "artistic" you mean, like, Salvador Dali or Maurits Escher.

It just happened, for instance, that in 1979 the Fourth of July fell on a rainy Wednesday night—and Wednesday night is customarily Tall Tales Night at Callahan's. So naturally it was that night that the Traveling Salesman arrived.

And even with that much hint, the punchline surprised me.

Oh, would you like to hear about it?

The house custom on Wednesday nights is that the teller of the tallest tale gets his or her bar-bill refunded, and I haven't missed a Wednesday in years. I have won a few times; I have lost quite a few times: there are some fearful liars at Callahan's bar. (Sometime customers include a paperback editor, a literary agent and a former realtor.) Lately, however, the stakes had increased. A lady named Josie Bauer had begun coming regular to Callahan's the month previous, and she was pleasant and bright and buxom and remarkably easy to talk to. And she was something I'd never encountered before: a humor groupie. It was her charming and unvarying custom to go home with whoever won the Tall Tales contest on Wednesday nights and the Punday Night competition on Tuesdays. This caused the competition, as Doc Webster observed, to stiffen considerably.

But I had hopes that night, and I was sorry to see Gentleman John Kilian approach the chalk line with a gin and gin in his hand. John is a short dapper Englishman with a quick mind and a wicked talent for summatory puns. He's not on this side of the lake much, and a lot of folks dropped what they were doing to listen.

"I commanded a submarine in Her Majesty's Navy during the last World War," he began, tugging at his goatee, "and I propose to tell you of a secret mission I was ordered to undertake. The famous spy Harry Lime, the celebrated Third Man, had developed a sudden and severe case of astigmatism—and many of his espionage activities forbade dependence on spectacles. At that time only one visionary in all the world was working on the development of a practical contact lens: a specialist at Walter Reed Hospital. I was ordered to convey Lime there in utmost secrecy and despatch, then wait round and fetch him home again."

"Is this gonna be a Limey story?" Long-Drink McGonnigle asked, and Callahan took a seltzer bottle to him.

John ignored it magnificently. "He was an excellent actor, of course, but before long I began to suspect that there was nothing atall wrong with his vision. I searched his quarters, and found correspondence indicating that he had a girlfriend who lived some twenty miles from the hospital. So I called him into my cabin. 'I can't prove a thing against you,' I said, 'but I'm ordering you—' " For effect, he paused and elegantly sipped gin.

I hated to do it. I'm a liar: I loved doing it. In any case I had seen the punchline coming long since, and so I delivered it before he could. " '—to go directly from the sub, Lime, to the Reed oculist.' "

"Oh, *damn*," he cried, and everyone broke up, Josie loudest of all. John glared at his gin, finished it in one gulp and pegged his glass into the fireplace.

"Sorry, John."

"Bullshit," he said, making an extra syllable out of the t. He grinned satanically and his eyes flashed. "Let's hear yours now, Jake."

"Aw, I haven't got any worth telling."

"None of that," he said sharply.

"And besides, you're so good at puns, John. You always smell 'em coming."

"Come out and fight like a man."

"Well . . ." I got up from the bar, took my Tullamore Dew to the chalk line before the fireplace. "I haven't got a tall tale, exactly." I wet my whistle. "What I've got is a true story that happened to me, that I've never been able to get anybody to believe."

"Better," said Gentleman John, mollified.

"No, *really*. I swear, this is true. Most of you know, I've been making a living with a guitar around the Island for some time now, and I've played a lot of *strange* places. I played the Village Pizza Restaurant Lounge, I played the Deer Park High School Senior Assembly, my old partner Dave and me played a joint once where the topless dancer had one arm, you had to show a razor and puke blood to get in. But the weirdest of all was a solo gig. I got a call from this big chain department store, Lincoln & Waltz; their PR lady heard me somewhere and wanted to know if I would come and sing in the Junior Miss Department. I thought she was drunk. Essentially they wanted something sufficiently odd to awaken the shoppers and attract a crowd, for which they would then have the local Girl Scouts model the new spring line. She figured I was hungry enough, and she figured right.

"Now, I'm not a superstitious man, but this is a pretty weird gig, even for me. So as I'm driving to the store I'm wondering if I've made a terrible mistake, and I kind of— there was a witness present—I look upward-like and I say out loud, 'Oh Lord, give me a sign. Will my paycheck get cosigned, or is that going off on a tangent?' " Sustained groans. "All right, I'm embellishing. What I really said was, 'Should I go through with this? Lord, give me a sign.' At that moment I stop for a stop sign, and overhead a bird electrocutes itself on the high-tension lines and drops dead on the front hood of my car—"

Whoops of laughter.

"I swear to God, feet sticking up, I have a *witness*."

Doc Webster popped a vest button, and Josie was smiling dreamily.

"So I sit there at the stop sign a while . . . shivering . . . tilt my head back and real soft I say, 'You didn't have to shout . . .' "

Roars. "Marvelous," Gentleman John cried. "You went home straightaway, of course?"

"Hell no, like a chump I showed up at the Junior Miss Department. To tell you the truth, I was curious. Nothing I played or sang or said attracted the attention of a single customer, and when they gave the Girl Scouts the go-ahead anyway, one of them stepped into my guitar-case and broke a hinge, and I set fire to a $50 dress with my cigar, and I didn't get paid. Worst single disaster of my career."

John was shaking his head. "Don't believe a word of it, old boy."

"Of *course* not. Neither did I; that's why I was stupid enough to go through with it after a warning like that. I didn't believe. In retrospect it's obvious, but I just thought the damn bird was a sparrow or magpie or some such . . ." I trailed off carefully.

"What was it then?" John bit. "Raven, I suppose?"

"I'm surprised at you, John," I said triumphantly. "Obviously it was an Omen Pigeon."

People grade a pun by their reaction to it. The very best, of course, as Bernard Shaw said, is when one's audience holds its collective nose and flees screaming from one's vicinity. Immediate laughter or groan is a *lesser* approbation. And in between these two is the *pause*, followed only after five or ten stunned seconds by cheers and jeers. It was this intermediate rating that I was accorded, and I savored the pause, and Josie's broad grin, and lifted my Irish whiskey to my lips to savor that too.

And sprayed a fine mist of Irish into the air.

Because before the pause could turn to applause, in that second or two of silence, we all heard—with a dreadful clarity—the unmistakable sound of hoofbeats on the roof.

Pretty near everyone had just drawn in a breath to cheer or groan; there was a vast *huff* as they all let it back out again. Cigar smoke swirled in tormented search for safe harbor, and the only sound now was the hoofbeats on the roof.

Mike Callahan is unflappable. He plucked his malodorous

cigar from his mouth with immense aplomb, looked up at the ceiling and shouted, ''You're early, Fatso,'' and went back to polishing the bar-top.

He received a scattered ovation, which died quickly.

I was as stunned as anyone else, but I think my strongest reaction was irritation at having my thunder stolen. There sure and hell were a lot of hooves up there. ''Eddie,'' I called out bitterly, ''someone has obviously gone to a lot of trouble to set up a gag. The least we can do is bite. Check it out, will you?''

Fast Eddie Costigan got up from his upright piano, eyes on the ceiling. ''Sure t'ing,'' he said uncertainly.

There are two openings onto the roof. One is the access hatch near the fireplace, with a ladder up to it built into the wall. On warm nights Mike lets customers take their drinks up there and stargaze, which accounts for the second opening: a big dumbwaiter at the end of the bar. It carries dollar bills down and drinks and peanuts back up. Mike built it himself, and he made it big enough for parties. Both openings would have been in use that night, of course, if it hadn't been raining. Eddie went up the ladder with a hesitancy that belied his nickname, and poked the hatch door open most gingerly. A practical joke this elaborate might have teeth in it—and Eddie, being from Brooklyn, has a horror of livestock. Prepared for anything, he hooked his head up over the coaming for a quick look.

He froze there, half out of the room, for a long moment, rain dripping in around him. Then he just *slid* down the ladder, landing hard on his butt. His monkey face was snow white.

''Well?'' Callahan asked.

''Sleigh,'' Eddie said. ''Eight tiny reindeer. Heavyset guy with a white beard.''

''Told ya,'' Callahan said.

Eddie nodded, dripping rainwater. ''Ho ho ho.''

The dumbwaiter came to life.

Callahan turned to face it and put his big hands on his hips. The room was absolutely still, absolutely quiet save for the sound of the little dumbwaiter motor being overworked. It stopped. The door opened.

Inside, a man was balanced on his head, juggling lit cherry bombs.

"*Zut alors*," he said. "God damn."

Callahan stepped back a pace.

The stranger fell forward, twisting as he fell so that he landed on his feet in front of the big barkeep, still juggling. As Mike opened his mouth, the hypnotic circle of burning fireworks opened out into a long arc whose terminus was the fireplace. All four cherry bombs exploded therein with a stupendous concussion. Broken glass sprayed outward, miraculously arranging itself on the floor to spell out the word "Al."

The stranger vaulted the bar at once and cartwheeled into the middle of the room, people scattering frantically out of his way. He landed lightly on his feet and beamed.

"Phee is the name," he cried merrily, "Al Phee, and the first one who asks me what it's all about gets a boot in the plums. Phee's my name and commission's my game—gather round like cattle and you shall be herd. I bring you the bazaar of the bizarre, the genuine Universal Pantechnicon, at a cost of just pennies! *Sacre bleu! Baise mes fesses!* Everything must go! Me stony, you savvy? Plenty bankruptcy along me."

We all stared at him.

"Come *on*," he shouted, "Look alive, get with it. This is *opportunidad muy milagroso*—act now while this offer lasts. Step right up—who'll be the first? Oh, *faddle*—" Suddenly he fell upon the room like a whirlwind, like a big mad mosquito or a horny hummingbird. He darted through the crowd, hugging people, kissing people, shaking hands, shaking feet, tugging on beards, introducing himself to the fire extinguisher and shaking its hose, grinning like Hell's PR man and talking a mile a minute. He took a scissor from his breast pocket, clipped the end off Long-Drink McGonnigle's tie and presnted it to him with a bow. He produced a white mouse from a side pocket and gave it gravely to Josie, and when she only smiled he burst into delighted laughter himself, lifted her hand to his lips and kissed the mouse. He stuck his face an inch away from mine, tousled my beard and patted my ass and danced away.

Eddie had been misleading: he didn't look much like Santa. He was not that heavyset, for one thing. The beard *was* more salt than pepper, but the neat short hair was weighted the other way—and the beard itself was not a Santa-type but something in between a spade and a van dyke. I would say that he comported himself in a manner even more dapper and elegant than Gentleman John—certainly more flamboyant.

He wore a four hundred dollar blazer over a polka-dot pajama top. He wore no trousers, and fat beaming Buddhas were printed on his shorts. He wore phosphorescent lederhosen and jester's shoes with curled up toes and bells. A propellor beanie was rakishly canted over one eyebrow. The rain had not wet him. Behind wire-rim glasses, merry eyes sparkled.

About that time Long-Drink caught up with him, roaring something about his tie. Phee spun to meet him, smiled with the enormous delight of one encountering an old and dear friend, picked three glasses of whiskey from a nearby table and began to juggle them. Not a drop did he spill. Long-Drink stopped dead in his tracks and his long jaw hung down. Phee began to clap his hands rhythmically while he juggled, then slapped his thighs.

Without taking his eyes from the glasses, the Drink felt for his tie, yanked it from his neck and tramped it into the sawdust.

Phee backed away, still juggling and clapping, until he was back in the center of the room where he had started. Suddenly the glasses were all upside down in their stately circle, their contents in motion. Each cataract ended up in Phee's mouth, and his beard was dry when he finished.

His cyclone passage among us had shattered our group stasis—the room was filled with the *rooba-rooba* of many people talking all at once. When the last of the three empty glasses hit the hearth, and the fragments had spelled "PHEE" next to the "AL," the murmur became a standing ovation.

"Mister," Long-Drink said, "that was the best goddam juggling I ever saw in my life."

Phee smiled indulgently, shook his head. "You haven't lived until you've seen it done with chainsaws, Eek! Heavy, baby."

Eddie spoke for all of us. "What de fuck is goin' on?"

"Mutual introductions, of course. I am Al Phee, and you are, in order," he ticked us off, "Marshall Artz, Boyle Deggs, Tom Foolery, Rachel Prejudice, Dee Jenrette, Miss Fortune," (pointing at Josie) "Flemming Ayniss, Manny Peeples, and Euell P. Yorpanz. Now that we know *who* we are, we may consider *what* we are: *c'est simple, non*? Shitfire, and dog my cats. I am a yoofo."

"A which?"

"Not a foe of you, but a U.F.O. And you are all Hugos. Unidentified goggling objects. What's wrong with you imbeciles *ce soir*, don't you see? *Ding an sich*: I am from outer space."

"With reindeer?" Callahan asked.

"We used to make 'em look like dishware, but believe it or not, that wasn't silly enough—people who saw us kept *reporting* it. *Nobody* reports a sleigh and eight tiny reindeer."

I think Phee expected this latest announcement to be the most stunning so far. If so, he was disappointed. Long-Drink nodded and said, "Sure, that explains it," and there was a general air of *de*mystification everywhere. I wished that Mickey Finn were around that night. (Finn is an extraterestrial himself, and I wondered what he would think of this guy. But of course it was summer, and Finn was way up north on the Gaspé Peninsula, tending his farm.)

"So what can we do for you?" Callahan asked imperturbably.

"What's a pantechnicon?" I added.

If he was disappointed at our collective sang-froid, Phee hid it well. "*Merde d'une puce*," he exclaimed, eyes flashing, "don't you know your own language?" He had one of the loudest voices I'd ever heard.

"Furniture warehouse," Gentleman John put in.

"Correct," Phee admitted, "But not the meaning I meaning."

"Oh, you must mean the 19th Century bazaars in London," John said, light dawning.

"—where arts and crafts were sold, yes," Phee said, applauding silently. "B plus. Pan plus technikos—*comme j'ai dit*, a bazaar of the bizarre."

Callahan's eyes widened. "Do you mean to tell me—?" he began, teeth clenched on his cigar.

Phee smiled like a flashbulb going off. "*Exactement*, my large. I am an Intergalactic Traveling Salesman."

People began to giggle, then laugh outright, then guffaw. Folks folded at the middle, slapped their thighs, pounded on tables with their fists, met each other's eyes and laughed anew. Even Callahan roared with gargantuan mirth, clapping his big knuckly hands together. Phee might have been excused for thinking we doubted his story—but I could see through my own tears of mirth that, after a moment's annoyance, he understood. Somehow he understood our laughter was not derision but delight.

It's like I said earlier—when you've been hanging out at Callahan's bar for a while, you begin to see a zany kind of symmetry to the way things happen there. "Hannibal's Holy Hairpiece, it's perfect!" Long-Drink crowed. "A traveling salesman has flown into Callahan's on Tall Tales Night. Sell my clothes, I'm gone to heaven!"

Phee bowed. "No fear? Marvelous; I impress. Hot damn. It is a business doing pleasure with you. I was told by blackguards that you did not civilize yet. Lies, by jiminy!"

"It just come on recent," Doc Webster said, and broke up again.

Phee waited politely until we were all finished. Then he produced a burning cigarette from out of thin air, flipped it into his face and began chewing on the filter. "To business we then progress, *jawohl*?. Groovey. Innkeeper, *gib mir getrank*—a flagon of firewater. Darn the torpedoes. Gosh.''

Callahan poured whiskey and passed it across the bar. ''How come no sample cases, brother? What's your line?''

''Oh, but I have a sample case, sweetheart. *Mais oui.*'' He reached into the inside pocket of his blazer and removed a hole. It had no edges, no boundaries, and it was no color at all. It was just . . . a *hole*, about the size of the lid on a half gallon of ice cream. He held it by the edge it didn't have, extended it to arm's length, and when he dropped his hand it stayed there, a circle of *nothing*.

There were whistles and much awed murmuring.

''Nonsense,'' Phee said airily, ''Is *nothing* sacred? *Voila le* sample case.''

''Say,'' Long-Drink began, ''how many of those would you think it'd take to fill the Alb—*ouch*!'' He glared at Doc Webster and began rubbing his shin.

''No, *compadres*,'' Phee said, ''It is not a hole-o-graph. It is a hyperpocket, a dimensional bridge to a . . . ahem . . . pocket universe. *Regardez*!''

He reached an elegantly manicured hand into the hole, and the hand failed to reappear on the other side. ''*Pardon*,'' he muttered, rummaging. ''Ah!'' His hand emerged. It was holding, by the throat, an extremely long-necked dragon, whose scaled head had barely fit through the hole. Reptilian eyes regarded us coldly, the fanged jaws opened, and a gout of flame set Phee's hair on fire.

''Damn,'' he said irritably, ''wrong drawer. One of these days I'm going to get this office organized.'' He thrust the dragon's head back into the hole with an air of embarassment. He ignored the fire on his head, and it seemed impolite to mention it, so it burned undisturbed as he rummaged, until his scalp was covered with black smoldering curls. The beanie was unaffected. ''*Boñiga de la mestizo enano* . . . aha! *Now* see.''

People edged discreetly away, and he pulled out a vaguely spherical object wrapped in soft cloth. He yanked on a corner of the cloth, and the object flew sparkling into the air; he caught it with his other hand. My first crazy thought was: "burning ice."

"My line:" he said triumphantly. "Jewels."

It looked something like a cut diamond the size of a softball, at least in physical structure. It was symmetrically faceted, very nearly transparent, and contained within it, like flies trapped in amber, perhaps a dozen splashes and streaks of liquid color, unbearably pure and lambent. The colors and shapes harmonized. It was so beautiful it hurt to look at.

"Is there anyone here who is chronically worried?" Phee asked loudly.

Slippery Joe Maser stepped forward. "I got two wives."

"Splendid! *Kommen ze hier.*"

Joe hung back.

"*Umgawa,*" Phee rapped impatiently. "Don't be such a chickenshit. Four centuries on the road this trip, and I haven't lost a customer yet. Come on, be a *mensch.*"

Joe approached uneasily.

"You *are* a worrier. Lucky I was passing by. Catch!"

He tossed the gleaming jewel to Joe, who caught it awkwardly in both hands. He stared down at the thing for a long moment.

"What do you worry about most?" Phee asked. "No, *mon vieil asperge,* don't tell me—just think about it."

Joe closed his eyes and thought about it.

From the places where his fingertips touched the jewel, streamers of a grey, milky substance began to infuse it, like milk being poured into a glass of weak tea from several points at once. Soon the entire interior of the gem was swirling grey, all the spatters of aching color hidden.

I tore my eyes from it to look at Joe. His face shone with the light that was obscured now in the jewel. Every feature was relaxed; for the first time since I've known him, his forehead was utterly smooth, no more wrinkles than a Gothic novel.

His eyes opened. "What the hell was I worryin' about?" he breathed contentedly. He worked his shoulders like a man who has just set down, at long last, a crushing burden.

"What's to worry?"

Callahan's voice was shockingly harsh. "Is that goddam thing addictive?"

"*Nyet*," Phee responded at once. "*Au contraire*. Watch."

Joe was looking at the greywashed jewel in his hands, and his expression was mournful. "Geeze," he said sadly, "did *I* do that?"

"You see?" Phee said smugly. "To despoil such a loveliness is ashaming: the *sahib* feels like a jerk. The more he uses it, the more he is conditioned not to generate worry in the first place. *Bojemoi*. One's self-indulgence is less tolerable when it is made visible as dung on a diamond, *n'est-ce pas*?"

"What's de t'ing cost?" Fast Eddie asked.

"Just pennies, I told you," Phee said, rummaging in his hyperpocket again. "Now this little sucker here is even more amazing, calculated to breed greed and fully warranteed." He produced and unwrapped a second jewel. It was similar to the first, but tinted rather than clear. The tint was the blue of a tropic lagoon before the white man came, restful to contemplate. Within it were not color impurities this time, but tiny angels. Miniature aleate females, the size of fireflies and correctly scaled. Somehow they flew slowly and gracefully to and fro within the jewel, as though it were filled with viscous fluid instead of being solid. It made my eyes sting.

"Is anyone here particularly angry?" Phee inquired.

Gentleman John looked long at Josie—who was watching Phee with rapt attention—and then at me. "Well," he said, "I'm not *generally* angry, but I suppose I am *particularly* angry. This bleeder here wrecked a perfectly good pun."

"I heard, from on high," Phee agreed sympathetically. "Monstrous. Insupportable. Tough shit. *Venez ici*."

John took the jewel from him, glanced again at me, murmured, "rat bastard," and closed his eyes.

The jewel began to suffuse with red. The tiny angels tried unsuccessfully to avoid the red, and where it touched them it congealed like quick-setting jello, imprisoning them. Soon they were invisible, and the jewel was an angry scarlet. People gasped.

John opened his eyes, blinked at the thing, and slumped. "What a vile thing anger is," he said bitterly. "I'm truly sorry, Jake." He smiled then. "Glad to be shut of it, though."

"Both jewels will clear again within an hour," Phee said brightly. "With real rage, this one becomes uncomfortably hot to the touch, in proportion to the strength of the fury. Both may be used repeatedly at hourly intervals, and will never wear out or malfunction. The Tsuris Trap and the Rage-Assuager, available only from your pal Al, *votre ami* Phee. *Sanitario e no addictivo*—"

"*Cuanto?*" Eddie said. "I mean, how *much?*"

"*C'est absurdité ou surdité*," Phee frowned. "I already *told* you, ducks: just *pennies*! *Fritz du Leiber*, twenty-three skidoo! But you ain't seen *nothin'* yet." He looked at the hyperpocket. "Well, perhaps you have—but the best is yet to come, as the bishop said to the actress. Behold, deholed:"

He produced a third jewel, and this one was untinted and contained hundreds of tiny beads of every color in the rainbow, writhing like kittens beneath the scintillant surface. It . . . wept music as he touched it, little plaintive chords and arpeggios.

"You," he said, pointing at me. "You say you play a guitar. Your face is furry, your hair abundant. You have experience of hallucinogens, *si?*"

"So?"

"*Ca.*" He tossed me the jewel.

Phantasms flickered briefly around the room as I caught it, little not-quite-seen things. My fingers tingled where they touched it.

"Think of a piece of music," Phee commanded. "Any music that you love."

I picked the first thing that came into my head. Suddenly the room filled with lush strings. I jumped and they were gone.

"Again," Phee directed. "Roll 'em, baby."

The strings returned, and when they had finished their simple eight-chord prelude, Brother Ray sang, "*Georgia . . .*"

People sat back and smiled all over Callahan's bar.

At first it was precisely like the definitive recording that everybody knows—right down to the crackle-pop surface noise of the treasured copy I own. It skipped in the same place. That told me where it was coming from, so I experimented. I have never willingly missed an opportunity to record a Ray Charles TV performance, and I have eleven different versions of "Georgia On My Mind." I concentrated, and Ray suddenly slipped smoothly into the extended bridge he has been using the last few years, where the band and the drummer just go away and let him play with it awhile. The surface noise vanished; fidelity became perfect. When the bridge was over he segued back into the original without a seam, and murmurs of appreciation came from Fast Eddie and a few others.

I glanced down at the jewel, and it seemed that all the glowing beads vanished a quarter-second after my eyes touched it. There was a collective gasp, and I looked up and The Genius himself was sitting at Eddie's beat-up piano, big black glasses and the whitest teeth God ever made, rocking from side to side in that distinctive way and caressing the keys, singing "Georgia On My Mind" for the patrons of Callahan's Place.

His finish was fabulous. I'm proud to say it was not one he has ever, to my knowledge, recorded.

As the applause died down, he modulated from G down to E and began the opening bass riff of "What I Say?" The original Raeletts appeared next to the piano, Margie Hendrix and Darlene and Pat. I shivered like a dog and threw the jewel at Phee, and artists and music vanished.

"Don't get me started," I said. "But thank you from the bottom of my heart. All my life I've wanted to do that. What *is* that thing?"

Phee did not reply vocally, but suddenly there was a flourish of trumpets and the word "VISUALIZER" was spelled out in the air in letters of cool fire, like neon without tubes, rippling in random air currents. They flared and bisected, wedged apart by a new group of letters all in gold, so that the new construct read: "VISUAL(SYNTHES)-IZER." It flared again, and the parenthetical intruder departed once more.

"'Synthes,' you've gone . . ." Phee sang, and Josie giggled. "It's a dream machine, dear boy. An hallucinator. Anything you can imagine, it gives auditory and visual substance to. *Je regrette* that at the present state of the art I cannot give you tactile—*but*, if you act *muy pronto* and because I like your face, I'm prepared to throw in olfactory for *not a dime extra*. Freebie, *kapish*?"

Make no mistake: I wanted that thing. But I reacted instinctively, with the reflex-response of a Long Islander to high-pressure sales tactics. "I don't know . . ."

"*Schlep*. Do you *know* what the olfactory mode can *do* for the porn fantasies alone?"

Eddie stared at his now-empty piano stool and shook his head. "How much?" he asked again.

Exasperated, Phee danced to the bar, grabbed up a funnel and took it back to Eddie. He stuck the business end in Eddie's left ear. "JUST PENNIES," he bellowed into it. "I'm telling you," he continued conversationally to the rest of us, "it's a steal. Good for fifteen minutes' use every four hours, an optional headphone effect for apartment use, and there's a fail safe that blows the breaker if you use it to scare people. Hoyoto! *Banzai!* Barkeep, more grog!"

"You ain't paid for the last one yet," Callahan said reasonably.

"Did I hear right through the roof earlier? On *ce soir* the teller of the tallest tale drinks *gratis*?"

"That's so," Callahan admitted.

Josie cleared her throat. "There's . . . another advantage."

Phee looked gallantly attentive.

She turned red. "Oh hell." She went up and whispered in his ear. His left eyebrow rose high, and the propellor beanie doubled its RPM.

"Hoo ha," he stated.

Josie looked around at us. "Well, it's just . . . I guess I'm grateful for a good laugh. Maybe it's an Oedipal thing: my

Dad is a brilliant jokester. And—and funny men are nicer lovers. They know about pain.''

Phee bowed magnificently. ''*Mademoiselle,*'' he said reverently, ''you are clearly the product of an advanced civilization. Furthermore you are spathic. Geologists' term: 'having good cleavage.' *Alors*, correct me now if I err: a truly great tall tale must, first, be a true story—or at least one which cannot be disproved. Second, it must be gonzo, *phweet!*, wacky, Jack. Third, it should conclude with a pun of surpassing atrocity, *nicht wahr*?''

There was murmured agreement all around. Folks ordered drinks and settled back in their chairs.

''Right. Dig it: a true story. I have witnessed this personally from my spacecraft and am prepared to document it. The toilet tanks on your commercial airliners often leak. This results in the formation of deposits of blue ice on the fuselage. The ice is composed of feces, urine, and blue liquid disinfectant. Now: occasionally, when a plane must descend very rapidly from a great height, especially near the Rocky Mountains, chunks of blue ice ranging up to two hundred pounds can—and *do*—break off and shell the countryside. *This is the truth,*'' he cried, as we began giggling. ''I have seen a UPI photo of an apartment in Denver which was pulped by a one hundred and fifty pound chunk of blue ice. The airline bought the tenants a house—and the landlord a judge.''

People were laughing helplessly, and Gentleman John's face was so red I thought he'd burst. ''My God,'' he howled, ''can you imagine them *checking in at hospital*? 'Cause of injury, please?' '' He caved in.

''Neither of them were hurt,'' Phee said. ''And for a while—until it began to thaw—they were grateful for the coolness it provided. It was summer, you see, and the impact had destroyed their electric fan . . .''

Callahan was laughing so hard his apron ripped. Doc Webster lay on his back on the floor, kicking his feet. Long-Drink laughed his bridgework loose.

''So,'' Phee concluded, sitting down on thin air and crossing his legs, "even if you live where there are no strategic military targets, you can still be attacked by an icy B.M."

Instant silence. A stunned, shuddering intake of breath, and then—the only group scream I have ever heard, a deafening howl of anguish insupportable. Somewhichway it turned, before it was done, into a standing ovation, and a barrage of glasses hit the fireplace. Josie ran over and hopped on Phee's lap, renewing the applause. John and I beat our palms bloody.

Callahan came around the bar with a huge grin, a bottle of Bushmill's and three glasses. He held the glasses up, raised an eyebrow inquiringly at Phee, and let go. They stayed there. He poured them full, took one and held it out. "Fee-free for Phee," he boomed. "Keep the bottle." He gave one to Josie, pulled up a chair and sat down next to the third glass.

Phee inclined his head in thanks. "God bless your ass. *Caramba*—is all that you? *Comment vous appelez-vous?*"

"*Je m' appelle* Mike Callahan, *señor*."

"Sure an' Gomorrah, the saints add preservatives to us, Michael, yer a foiner host than Jasus himself, and him with the free wine and all the fish you can eat. A toast, big cobber, a toast!"

"To Melba?" Callahan suggested.

"I hate Melba toasts. No. To interstellar commerce, *kemo sabe*."

Callahan raised his glass, as did several others including myself. Oddly, Josie didn't. The toast was echoed and drunk, and the glasses disposed of.

"What else you got for sale?" The big barkeep asked then.

"One more item," Phee said. "Excuse me, Mama." Josie shifted on his lap so that he could reach the nearby hyperpocket. He took out a fourth gem. This one was pink-tinted, more translucent than transparent, and within it were a spiderweb of metallic filaments that made me think of printed circuits. He tossed it to Doc Webster.

"By the bag at your feet you are a medicine man, rotund person. Have you patients in this room?"

"All of them," the fat sawbones rumbled.

"Pick one sick one. That chap there, dear Hippo-crates. Brush him with the bauble." He pointed out Chuck Samms, who all too obviously had recently suffered a bad stroke: Chuck's left side was shot. The Doc frowned down at the pink jewel, and carried it to Chuck. A couple of tiny lights went on inside it as he approached.

"His thumb," Phee suggested.

The Doc looked at Chuck. "Okay?"

Half the mouth smiled. "Sure, Sam." Chuck held out his right thumb, the Doc lifted the jewel, contact was established.

The damned thing took a blood sample, flashed a few contemplative lights, and returned it. As his own blood flowed back into him, Chuck gasped, then yelped, and pushed the jewel violently away from him.

Using both hands.

He looked down at his left hand, and began to smile the first unlopsided smile he'd had in months. Doc Webster gaped at him.

"The price for all four items," Phee said, "F.O.B., shipping and handling plus applicable tax, is pennies. Literally. Every penny in this room, and nothing else."

"You mean you want all our dough?" Eddie asked.

"No, *cochon*! All your *pennies*!"

I happened to know that Mike keeps about a hundred bucks in pennies in a sack under the bar—we pitch 'em on Friday nights. Still, it sounded like a hell of a deal. Stranger bargains have been made at Callahan's Place, and our sales resistance was smithereened. I started to check my pants—

"*No!*" Josie cried, and leaped from Phee's lap, her face white with fury.

"Why, what is it, my pigeon?" Phee asked, still sitting on nothing. "What deranges you?"

She towered over him in her wrath. "Damn it, Phee, damn you. I was going to wait until I got you home—but this is the Fourth of July, and that was the fourth jewel lie, and the lie is even more abominable than the pun. Screw you, and the reindeer you rode in on."

He blinked. "Here? Now?"

"Damn straight." She took a tube of toothpaste from an inside pocket of her vest, and before the traveling salesman could move, she had circled his knees where they crossed with a loop of toothpaste. He scrabbled at it with his fingers, and she added another loop, pinioning his hands. He began swearing fluently in several tongues—for the "toothpaste" had hardened at once into something that seemed to have the tensile strength of steel cable. Though he tried mightily, Phee could not break free. His command of obscenity was striking, and it might just have melted ordinary steel cable.

"—and may you fall into the outhouse just as a platoon of Ukrainians has finished a prune stew and six barrels of beer," he finished, and she laughed merrily.

Callahan cleared his throat. If you engage the starter on an engine that's already running, it makes a sound like that. "Josie darlin'," he began, "if you don't mind my asking?"

"Aw, you damned fools," she burst out. "My father is right: people who don't read science fiction are the most gullible people there are. *Look at him*, for God's sake: *does he look like an extraterrestrial to you*?"

Josie had no way of knowing that Noah Gonzalez and I both read sf. Of course Noah works on the Fourth—he's on the County Bomb Squad. "Well," I said, "I guess we just figured his real appearance was too horrible for us to look upon. He's obviously a master of illusions."

"Too right," she snapped, and snatched the propellor beanie from Phee's head. The propellor stopped, and Phee's invisible chair was yanked out from under him. Smiling Buddha hit the floor hard, and he howled indignantly.

We all blinked and looked around. The change was too subtle to perceive at once. All four jewels had gone opaque, and there was nothing—or rather, there *wasn't* nothing—where the hyperpocket had been, but these things took time to notice. Even when Chuck Samms cried out, the reason was not immediately apparent, for *both* sides of his mouth were turned down . . .

"This is the illusion-maker," Josie said, waving the

beanie. "All it is is a hypnotic amplifier. The illusions are gone, now—and he still looks human. Not," she snapped, "that I claim kinship with any pride!"

"Parallel evolution—?" I began.

"Don't be silly. No, *be* silly: assume he's really an alien who just happens to look human. Now explain to me why he came hundreds of light-years—past six other planets, a carload of moons and a million asteroids—to come in here and swindle you out of copper?"

There was only one other possible answer, then. I opened my mouth—and then closed it. I did not, for reasons I could not define, want Josie to know that I was a science fiction reader. You're more talkative if you think your audience doesn't understand you, sometimes.

"He's a time traveler, you idiots!" she cried, confirming my guess. "Who else would need copper as desperately as your own descendants? With the couple of thousand pennies you morons were going to give him, he could have—well, quintupled his living space at the very least. And he would have left you *nothing*, except for four prop jewels and an admittedly great tall tale to tell."

Isham Latimer is Callahan's only black regular, and he knows his cue when he hears it. "Does dis mean dat de diamonds is worthless?"

Josie giggled, losing her anger all at once, and completed the quote. "Put it dis way: he is de broker, and yo' is de brok*ee*."

All the tension in the room dissolved in laughter and cheers—leaving behind a large helping of confusion.

"So what's your angle, Josie?" Callahan asked. "Where do you come in?"

"Time travel is severely proscribed," she said. "The possible consequences of tampering with the past are too horrible to contemplate."

"Sure," Callahan said. He may not be an sf reader—but all of us at Callahan's know *that* much about time travel. We had another time-traveler in here once, who was worried considerable about that very issue—whether it was moral and/or safe to change the past of a lady he loved, to keep her from being hurt.

"And precisely because it's so tempting to 'mine the past' for all the precious things you wasted and used up on us, that is the most strictly prohibited crime on the books. Pennies are the best dodge for copper: you acquire a bunch in this era, bury them somewhere, then go back home and dig 'em up, properly aged and no way to prove it wasn't a lucky dig."

"And you—"

"Temporal agents approached my father twenty years ago, and convinced him to sign up as a kind of local way-station for authorized time-travelers, on a part-time basis. He's a science fiction writer—who *else* would they dare trust to understand the terrible dangers of time travel? He kept it from Mother and us kids—but about five years ago I found out. I blackmailed his employers into giving me a job on the Time Police."

"Why?" Callahan asked.

"Because it's the most *exciting* job I can think of, of course! You know my nature—I love jokes and paradoxes." She grinned. "I'm not *sure*, but I have a hunch I'm going to grow up to be Mom."

There was a stunned silence.

"So if I understand this," I said diffidently, "Phee here came for the coppers, and you came here for the coppers?"

She whooped with glee, and tossed the beanie into the fireplace. "Jake, are you busy tonight?"

I tingled from head to toe. "Aren't you?" I asked, indicating Phee.

I *knew* it was a silly question, but I didn't want her to know I knew. Aside from the most obvious benefits of her offer, as long as she didn't know I read sf there was a chance I could pump her for her father's name—and I was curious as hell.

"It won't take me any time at all to deal with him," she said. "Not yours, anyway." I made oh-of-course noises.

"What happens to *him*?" Chuck asked, and his voice was harsh.

"I'd like to cut him in half," Doc Webster said darkly.

"Wouldn't be the first Phee I've split."

"He will be dealt with. Not punished—punishment accomplishes nothing. Nothing desirable, anyway. He is a brilliant man, a master hypnotist: he can be of service to his own era. He will simply be surgically implanted with a tiny device. If he ever again makes an unauthorized time-jump, he will acquire a massive and permanent case of B.O."

Chuck broke up. "Fair enough."

Phee spoke for the first time since his torrent of profanity. "I apologize, sir, for what I did to you. That last lie *was* the cruelest—and perhaps unnecessary. I . . . I never *could* resist a good dazzle." He shook his head. "I'm sorry," he repeated.

Chuck was taken aback. The half of his face that could hold expression softened. "Well . . . it *was* kind of nice to be whole again there for a minute. I dunno; maybe the havin' of that minute was worth the losin' of it. I'm sorry I laughed at you, mister."

Sitting there in his shorts on the floor with his hands toothpasted to his knees, Phee managed to bow.

"I don't get it," Long-Drink complained. "If this guy wanted pennies, why not just time-travel into a bank vault and take a *million* of 'em? Why go through all this rigamarole?"

Phee looked elegantly pained. "What would be the *fun* in that? That's the only thing about being busted that really bothers me: she was here waiting for me. I *hate* being predictable."

"Don't feel bad," Josie told him. "You couldn't have known. This place is a probability nexus. Why, this was the *priori* terminus for the first-ever time-jump."

Why, sure—when I thought about it, our previous time-traveler's brother had *invented* the first time machine. His had been a bulky belt—these people were more advanced.

Phee's eyes widened. He stared around at us. "By Crom, I'm impressed. What did you do?"

"We took up a collection for him," Eddie answered truthfully.

Phee shook his head. "And I took you for yokels. Take me away, officer."

In a way it was a little saddening to see the great Al Phee bestered.

Josie picked him up effortlessly and slung him over her shoulder. With her free hand, she reached into the purse that hung from her other shoulder.

"Uh," I said, and she paused. "You'll be right back?"

She grimaced. "Soon for you. Not for me. I'll be back as quick as I can, Jake—honest! But first I've got to take him in and make out the report and do all the paperwork, and then I promised Dad I'd drop in on him for a quick visit about twenty years from now. But I'll be back before you know it."

"Why twenty years from now?"

"I hate to bother him when he's working. By then he should be done with the Riverworld ser—" She broke off. "I'll be right back," she said shortly, and fumbled in the purse. She and Phee vanished.

And I fell down howling on the floor.

What made it twice as funny was that my ethics forbade me to share the joke with everybody else—I don't think I could have stopped laughing long enough, anyhow. Gentleman John almost killed me when he understood I wasn't going to explain it.

But hell, it was so obvious! I shouldn't have needed that last hint. I didn't even need to know enough German to know what "Bauer" means. I *know* that there's a kind of delirious logic to the way things happen at Callahan's Place, a kind of artistic symmetry.

So if a traveling salesman's daughter comes into Callahan's Bar on Tall Tales Night—whose daughter is going to turn out to be his downfall?

Concerning ''Have You Heard The One . . ?'':

There's something I ought to make clear: you should not assume that I vouch for the truth of any of Jake's stories about Callahan's Place. Oh, Mike and the gang always back him up, and I've never been able to trip them up or catch them in an inconsistency (that's why I have to insert my own)—but then they are notorious and fearsome liars one and all.

But I can't be sure. I can't help noticing a kind of emotional consistency, a ''ring of truth'' in people's reactions to events described. If, for instance, someone in the situation of Kathy Saunders ever did walk into Callahan's Palce, I'm fairly sure the gang would have reacted just the way Jake described in ''Fivesight.''

As to ''Have You Heard The One . . ?'' . . .

. . . back when I was assembling the first Callahan book, I happened to meet Alfred Bester, author of The Demolished Man *and* Golem 100. *He appeared before me at a party, grabbed me by the lapels and shook me like a container of martinis (which I chanced to be at the time), patted my ass, tugged on my beard to see if it would come off, stuck a cigarette in my ear and dragged me off to a nearby bedroom, where he proceeded to extract my entire life story in five minutes without anesthesia. When he learned that I had no title for my Callahan book he swore softly in Urdu, his eyes rolled like dice and came up snake-eyes, and he intoned the words, ''Callahan's Crosstime Saloon.'' My brain reeled;* when I woke the next morning there was a ''kick me'' sign on the seat of my pajamas, and my goldfish was pregnant.*

Now, I have no reason to believe that Alfie is from the future, or that he has ever defrauded anyone in any respect, and I wasn't at Callahan's the night this story went down. But I have to admit that the resemblance, both physical and temperamental, is uncanny. Furthermore, long before I heard this story from Jake, when a second Callahan book

---

*—*Nowadays my brain cassettes.*

was only at the proposal stage, I wrote to Alfie asking if he could contribute another title—and it was he who came up Time Travelers Strictly Cash, *which is strikingly germane to the moral of this story.*

Nah—it couldn't *be.*

After all, Al Phee has, according to Jake and Josie, been returned to, and permanently contained in, his own time-frame. Whereas Alfie . . .

. . . cancelled out as Special Guest at this year's Halifax sf convention (Halcon 3) on a week's notice. And I haven't heard from him since.

Hmmmm.

And ever since the 50s, the thing most frequently said of Alfie has been that he is "decades ahead of his time" . . .

Tell you what: next time you see him at a convention, get downwind and take a sniff. Let me know.

Two more pieces of ambiguous evidence concerning this story:

Philip José Farmer insisted in a recent phone call that Josie Bauer, at least, was lying–that he is not affiliated in any way with the Time Police, and that he has no daughter named Josie.

On the other hand, his wife was listening . . .

And John (Kilian Houston) Brunner has never admitted to having commanded a submarine. But then if he'd been doing intelligence assignments he'd have to deny it, wouldn't he?

I just don't know.

LOCAL CHAMP

With a depressingly large part of his consciousness, the Warlock watched the damned fool who was trying to kill him this time.

Depressing because it rubbed his nose in the fact that he simply had nothing more pressing to think about. He had not sunk so low that assassins threatened him; rather he had risen so high that they were a welcome relief from boredom.

You must understand that he was unquestionably and indisputably the mightiest Warlock the world had ever known; for twice ten thousand years he had *owned* it. It was barely within the realm of conceivability that another *as* mighty as he *could* simultaneously exist, but they could no more have escaped each other's notice than two brontosaurs in the same pond. There had never been such a one.

Further, he was invulnerable. Not just physically, although that was nice of course, but *really*. A warlock—any sorcerer—can only be truly destroyed by a spell using his name, and it had been thrice five thousand years since the last living being who knew the Warlock's name had gone down to the final death. Since that time he had induced certain subtle mutations in the human race, so that no man now living could have pronounced his name had they known it. His most deadly secret was literally unstealable.

He suffered other minor wizards to live and work, since they kept life interesting and made tolerable servants; when they reached their two thousandth birthday he methodically killed or utterly destroyed them as indicated. He could never be seriously challenged.

In a way he was almost flattered by this latest would-be

assassin. Though the Warlock had spent centuries becoming the nastiest and most sadistic being it was within him to be (which was considerable), it had been a long time since anyone had hated him even more than they feared him. When the bugs always scurry away, you lose the fun of stepping on them. He felt something very like fondness for this gallant little bug, amused approval of its audacity. Briefly he contemplated an act of mercy: allowing the poor wretch to live out its two thousand years, in utter agony, and then simply killing it. Anyone who knows anything knows that even two thousand years of torment and physical death are preferable to the real death, the final extinction. The most unpleasant points on the Wheel of Karma are infinitely preferable to the awful emptiness within which it turns.

But even that much charity was alien to the Warlock; the impulse passed. Besides, great wizards (and the occasional especially apt sorcerer) reincarnated with their necromantic potential intact, if not mildly amplified, and there was no assurance that this young upstart would profit from the lesson. Humans seldom did. This tendency toward rebelliousness, piquant though it might be, was not after all something a prudent master of the world should encourage. From his high eyrie, the Warlock observed the pitiful pile of junk being raised up against him with perhaps a quarter of his attention, and sighed.

You may, reading between the lines, have acquired the suspicion that the mighty Warlock was something of a secret coward. Well, what kind of man did you think craves that kind of power badly enough to grasp it bare-handed, to do what must be done to get it? This was the Warlock's bane: millennia of utter security had nearly succeeded in boring the beard off him—and yet facing the problem squarely would have entailed admitting that he was too cowardly to permit any change in his circumstances. For the Warlock, millennia of boredom were preferable to even a significant *possibility* that precious irreplaceable he could be hurled from the Wheel. He preferred not to dwell on this, with any part of his consciousness.

Not that this would-be assassin even remotely alarmed him. The portion of his awareness that had absently divined its magicidal intent, and now idly watched its secret preparations for battle, felt, as has been said, some amusement, something like fondness (but not paternal, warlocks are sterile as witches)—but his overriding emotion was something more than scorn but less than true contempt.

Same old fallacies, he thought. *First they acquire a rudimentary mind shield and they get cocky. As though I needed to read their thoughts to outthink them!* He snorted. *And then they put their money on* physical *energies, three times out of five. They discover that magic, deeply rooted in the Earth, is limited to a sphere of a hundred miles around the planet, while physical energies are not, and they decide that that somehow implies a superiority of some kind. Ephemerals!*

He recalled the last really challenging duel he had ever fought, countless centuries before. He and the other had met on the highest peak on Earth, locked eyes for three and a half years, and then touched the tips of their index fingers together. The site of this meeting would one day be called the Marianas Trench, and the concussion had produced even more damage in the Other Plane.

The Warlock looked upon the massive assemblage of machineries which was supposed to threaten his—well, you couldn't say his *life*, even in jest, could you?—his peace of mind, then; and he sneered. This building full of junk was to be raised up against him? (Could you?)

Nothing but a big beam of coherent light, he complained to himself. *Surely that silly creature can deduce that I'm transparent to the entire electromagnetic spectrum? Hell knows it has clues enough; I meditate above the ionosphere for decades at a time. I've a quarter of a mind to let the impertinent little upstart shoot that thing at me before I kill it, just to see its face.*

About that much of his mind considered the question for a few months. (Meanwhile the bulk of his awareness, as it had for the last eight centuries, devoted itself to a leisurely study of how best to mutate human stock so as to increase the central nervous system's capacity to support agony. Mess with the hypothalamus? Add new senses? Subtle, satisfying stuff.)

By hell, I will, decided that quarter of his mind then. *I'll let the impudent cretin fire its toy at me, and I* won't even notice! *I'll ignore its attack completely, and it will go mad with rage. In fact, I'll be rather* nice *to it for about a hundred years, and then I'll arbitrarily destroy it for some trivial offense or other. Delicious!*

The quarter of the Warlock's mind which troubled itself with this matter savored the joy of anticipation for several months, so thoroughly in fact that he actually *did* fail to notice when the upstart wizard's harmless energy-bolt passed through the space occupied by his body. The reflex that caused his physical essence to "sidestep" into the Other Plane was so automatic, so unimportant, that it took a few weeks to come to even a quarter of his attention. He chuckled at that.

He also monitored the wizard's frustrated, impotent rage, at least on audio and video (those damned mind shields *were* a nuisance sometimes), and found it good. He invested a fortnight in devising a fiendishly offhand destruction for the fool, instructed himself to remember the affair in a century or so, and forgot the matter.

Those came to be called The Last Hundred Years Of Pain, and they were long.

At last like a child recalling a hoarded sweet the Warlock rummaged in his mental pockets and turned out the matter of the hapless wizard. Memory reported that several other shots had been fired without disturbing his peace. The mortal gave every indication of being sobbing mad. Its aim, for instance, had been going to hell for the last two or three decades; some of its shots had missed him by wide margins. He chuckled, and abandoned his century-old plan for destroying the wight without ever acknowledging its attacks.

The hell, I'll tell it. It's more *fun if it knows I've been playing with it.*

At once he was standing before the wizard in the building of futile engines, clothed in fire. In his left hand was a sword that shimmered and crackled; in his right hand was something that could not be looked upon, even by him.

Oddly, considering its displayed stupidity, the ephemeral did not seem surprised to see him. Its anger was gone, as if it had never been; it met his gaze with something absurdly like serenity.

Machines began to melt around them, and the wizard teleported outdoors, the Warlock of course following without thinking about it. They faced each other about five hundred feet above the top of the highest of many local mountains, and they locked eyes.

"You have come to destroy me," the wizard said quietly.

Of course, the Warlock sent, disdaining speech. *Lasers are harmless to me, of course, but they wouldn't be against one of you, and that makes it an insult*. He frowned. *Had you dared attempt a genuine, necromantic assault, I might have been amused enough to simply kill you hideously*. He gestured with the crackling sword at the building below them, which was also crackling now. *But* this *incompetence must be culled from the breed*.

"We all do what we can," the wizard said.

Indeed. Well, here you go:

He rummaged in his subconscious's name-file, came up with the wizard's true name, which was Jessica, incorporated that name into the thing in his right hand, and reached out toward the mortal, and "Not here!" she cried and was teleporting upward like a stone hurled by a giant, and *Why the hell not?* the Warlock thought as he pursued the creature effortlessly, intrigued enough to let a good sixty or seventy miles go by before deciding that enough was enough and hurling the thing in his right hand after her and averting his eyes.

She died the real death, then. Her soul was destroyed, instantly and forever, in a detonation so fierce that it was almost physically tangible. The Warlock grunted in satisfaction and was about to return to his eyrie, when he noted that the wizard's physical body continued to exist, an empty hulk still hurtling skyward. It chanced that the Warlock had not had lunch that decade.

Straining a bit to reach it before it passed the limits of the sphere of sorcery, he retrieved the corpse and poised there a moment with the crackling sword ready in his left hand.

And felt the mind shield he had accreted over thrice ten thousand years peeled away like the skin of an orange; felt his true name effortlessly extracted from his memory; felt himself *gripped* as though between some monstrous thumb and forefinger and *plucked* from the sphere of his power, yanked over closer to the sun where the light was better; and in the few helpless boiling-blood seconds before he died both kinds of death, the most powerful Warlock in all the history of the world had time to understand three things: that the laser beams had not been aimed at him, that lasers can carry information great distances, and that this world is only one of billions in a sea of infinity.

Then at last the end of all fear came to him, as it had come a century before to Saint Jessica.

Concerning "Local Champ":

As of even date, I have written only two fantasy stories, and this is one of them. Perhaps it explains why.

There are quite a few fantasies I've enjoyed reading; no point listing them. But at this stage in my cycle, all the wonders and enchantments and mighty magics of fantasy seem to me like pretty pale stuff compared to the scope and grandeur of the observable universe. I'm at the point where reality seems more exciting, where the puzzle of just how the hell the universe got this way fascinates me more than all of Middle-Earth. Who shaped the primal Monobloc? And exploded it so perfectly that the number of stars in any given slice of sky will be within one percent of the number in any other slice of equal size? Starting with hydrogen and gravity, how do you get heavy metal planets? Why does gravity decrease (if you didn't know that it does, go at once and buy Heinlein's Expanded Universe*), and how does that affect the Universal Escape Velocity question? What are the damned quasars anyway? What makes music so compelling, and why is a baby? What makes us all so afraid all the time, and who invented bravery? Why does pain diminish when it is shared? And underlying all, of course, how are we going to feed all these people, and power their starship?*

Show me a roc that can achieve faster-than-light speeds, and I'll be interested. Give me a warlock who can synthesize protein and you've got my attention. Tell me of a spell that has power over the heart's loneliness, and I will listen. But don't bother me with trivia about necromantic empires and zombie armies and numbskull swordsmen.

I wonder what old Sauron—or for that matter Gandalf—would have thought of Lucifer's Hammer? Or Fred Saberhagen's Berserkers?

(Say, that's a thought! Does a spell work on a sentient machine?

Hmmmm. Back to the typewriter . . .)

Concerning "The Web Of Sanity":

All Fans are crazy.

(A capital F Fan is one who actively participates in sf fandom, as opposed to those who just read a lot of the stuff.

Everybody knows that; it's like saying all oceans are moist. To read that sigh-fie stuff is crazy enough—but to spend good money and travel hundreds of miles to talk about it with a bunch of drunken strangers? Crazy squared, beyond a doubt. Even crazier are the demented masochists who volunteer (mind you) to organize and put on these conventions, at enormous expense in time, money and energy, and to no visible return. In some cities they fight for the privilege. And even among these hardcore certifiables there are certain people who command awed respect for the truly legendary extent of their brain damage.

Such as the Minicon Gang.

More formally known as the Minnesota Science Fiction Society, and sometimes (inexplicably) as Minn-STF. (No matter how many times I run that through it keeps coming out "Minnesota Science Tiction Fociety," but it's none of my business.) They pitch a ball called Minicon in Minneapolis, at no fixed interval except that there seems to be at least one a year. At this very moment they are campaigning energetically and enthusiastically for the right to hold the World Convention in Minneapolis—in 1973. They're selling advance memberships for minus one cent—write to them and they'll send you a 1973 penny for joining. Most of them are devotees (if you miss the tee, you make a divot; hence a man who's missing a few strokes is a divot-tee) of the surrealist recording group The Firesign Theater, creators of Don't Crush That Dwarf, Hand Me The Pliers *and* We're All Bozos On This Bus. *The only time in my life I was affluent enough to accompany some friends to a Minicon at my own expense, I had what I vaguely recall as a very good time, but I'll never understand how I came to wake up inside that piano (let alone how the burro got in there with me), nor what ever possessed me to have a tattoo put there.*

A year or two later the Minn-STF gonzos called me long-distance at my home in Halifax.

"We want you to come to Minicon," they said.

"Love to. Can't afford the fare."

"No problem: we'll pay."

"But I heard Chip Delany was your Pro Guest Of Honor this year."

"He is. You're our Fan Guest Of Honor."

"But I'm not a Fan. Never have been."

"That's okay. Bob Tucker's our Artist Guest Of Honor and he's not an artist."

I thought a bit. "Geeze, if I was Delany, I'd be insulted."

"Well, we wanted you three people at our convention, and we're not fussy about technicalities."

Neither was I. A free trip to anywhere is worth it, and besides, I had always wanted to meet Samuel R. Delany. I agreed to go.

But it left me with a small problem: as Fan GOH, I would have to make a speech—and as I said, I was not and had never been a Fan. So I thought about it, and the following speech resulted. What exactly is fandom? I think it may be:

THE WEB OF SANITY

Good evening, genties and ladlemen of the audio radiance, and good odding, too, for that matter. I am Spider Robinson, the Herb Varley of the Stone Age. Here I stand, a credit to my procession and a sanitary sight to see, I hope you will all agree.

We are standing in the vestibule of a new age, which, like a corporation that kicks its deadwood upstairs, can only fire us higher. Higher than the topless towers of Ilium—

Hey, do you remember when the towers first went topless?

For that matter, do any of you remember Ilium? Ilium Kuryakin, used to do a solo with a guy named Team—I mean, a team with a guy named Solo, the Man From I Surrender, who incidentally was so low he once gave a camel a hickey. I once gave a guy named Hickey a Camel, myself, when I was trying to give up smoking, but according to his father that was heir pollution too—but that's neither hither nor yon.

Excuse me for yonning, I didn't get much nest last right . . . I mean, I didn't get the next-to-last rites . . . the second serial rights went to Conde-Nast publishers. Buy all rights, they said, and by all rights I should be asleep rite now.

No, but foolishly, folks—did you ever notice that comedians always say "No, but seriously . . ." right after they've laid an egg?—the reason I'm squatting here tonight is to pass a great gasp of relief at the way we're all managing to fart at staggered intervals rather than all at once, holding it down to a tolerable level, even, if you will, helping all the candles of the world to burn a little brighter. I think it's magnificent that the Lord, in His downtown Providence, Rhode Island, saw fit to arrange things so that peristalsis runs

downward. Imagine if digestion ran in the other direction!
Toilet bowls would be placed at chin-height; tables would be
drastically *lowered;* chairs would require total redesign. All
food would have to be in suppository form, and banquets like
this one would probably pass out of existence. So would all
beards and mustaches . . . facial ones, I mean; in effect
everyone would be bearded (And I can tell you, a mustache is
hard enough to keep sanitary when it's, uh, right under your
nose as it were.) I leave the tailoring problems to your
imagination. And while you're at it, imagine young lovers
having to bend over and back up to each other . . .

And of course all the Greeks would become French and
vice-versa.

Now that I've helped you all to return your dinners (and
not a moment too soon; they're booked elsewhere), it looks
like I can't put off much longer saying something reasonably
serious and intelligent about what it feels like to be a Fan
Guest Of Honor, when you've never felt much like a Fan
before. As I said last night, for those of you who weren't here
then, I barely knew that fandom existed until I happened to
sell Ben Bova a story. Almost accidentally, he's responsible
for having exposed me to you zanies. I was too much of a
loner by nature to be more than vaguely aware of fandom's
existence, until I sold a story. This state of virginity was
ended rather quickly thereafter, and, as such things go, rather
painlessly.

The shock has not yet faded. I kind of hope it never will.

It has been said—I don't know if correctly or not—that the
ancient Chinese treated the insane with reverent fear. I believe this is an appropriate response. I have had enough
friends who worked in mental institutions and hospitals to be
certain that insanity can be more contagious than leprosy.
Hell, I'm living in New York City this month, or anyway
residing there.

And if insanity is contagious, it seems reasonable to me
therefore that so is sanity. I know this is going to dismay,
affront and offend many of you, and I apologize in advance;
but I maintain that as a group you are one of the *sanest*
collections of folks I know. I'll grant you, there's a wealth of

evidence against me on this, but I think it's true. I think of us as people who inoculate ourselves against a plague of insanity with a powerful anti-idiotic called science fiction. I think sf is a literature which by its very nature requires that you be at least a little sane, that you know at least a little something. You must abdicate the right to be ignorant in order to enjoy science fiction, which most people are unwilling to do; and you must learn, if not actually how to think things through, at least what the trick looks like when it's done. Frequent injections will keep a lot of madness away. I can tell you: I've been on sf therapy since the age of five, and here I am, I'm not even thirty years old yet and I'm a happy man, which would have surprised the hell out of me five years ago.

But even the strongest dosage of even science fiction reaches a threshold effect, and side effects start to outnumber the benefits. The inability to remember which continuum you're in at the moment, the constant necessity of reminding yourself that you're not immortal, not to mention the aching eyeballs and the good friends who cannot be persuaded or cajoled by any means to try just one little bag of science fiction, for free.

And so we gather together at frequent intervals to reinfect each other with sanity, in person. You may dispute this, but I contend that in a world like this one, gathering together to wear funny hats, sing parodies off-key, get smashed and shine lasers at each other can be—and probably is—sane behavior. The Firesign Theater, whom some of you may know, would probably consider us a subset of the group they belong to, the Bozos. ("People who get together with other Bozos to wear funny clothes and have a good time.") And the world needs all the Bozos it can get.

It seems to me that the central problem of the world today, if I may be so pretentious, is morale. Or rather, the lack thereof. I have a cousin who visited me last week, who lives in New York City, and we talked five or six hours that particular visit. At least five times in the course of conversation she said, almost like a litany, some variant of: "The whole world is going to hell, it's going to go smash in a few years and nothing can be done, so the only thing for a smart

person to do is get everything you can for yourself before the
end.''

I have heard variations on this theme for many years now,
with increasing frequency. It's not too hard to understand, I
suppose. Here on Starship Earth, after a great many thousand
years, we finally got together a reasonably efficient inter-
system—and mostly what we broadcast over it are damage
reports. Bad news and situation comedies and mock-combat
on Sunday afternoons. I can't blame anybody who's depressed. But what my cousin was talking about was *despair*,
what the Catholics call the only unforgivable sin, and that is a
different thing altogether. My cousin, I'm sorry to say, is part
of the problem, the only real problem we've got.

With so much bummer energy going around, the only way
I can stay sane, or one of the only ways I can stay sane, is to
come to Minicons, to get high and have a good time, with
people who know better than to think it's all pointless.

There's an anecdote Ben told earlier in the weekend about
one convention we both attended where the toastmaster
talked for an hour and a half and said essentially nothing.
When he was done, people applauded fairly enthusiastically
because he was done, but that was about all the enthusiasm
they had left. Nobody wanted to hear a word from anybody
else on any subject whatsoever. Poor Jay Kay Klein stepped
up to the mike next, into the hot seat. He looked around the
room and tears came into his eyes, and he said, ''Holy
smokes, just about everybody in the world I love is in this
room.'' And the whole place was his; at that moment we'd
have followed him into battle with a song.

Make no mistake: it is love, not a shared hobby, that has
brought us together here. Oh, we have as much trouble
loving our own personal selves as the mundanes do—perhaps
more trouble. But we love *each other* a great deal. Most
important, we love our species, we love the damfool human
race—or we would not be so passionately concerned with its
future.

Like it or not, I think the majority of you are sane—I think
you agree in your secret heart of hearts with what the wise
and holy Frederik Pohl said at Discon: that as a species we

have few real problems, but only complex games we have
agreed to play with ourselves.

(I have a copy of that speech, Fred, and I'm thinking
seriously of having it privately printed and selling it through
the mail. I'll talk to you about the rights later.)

The more audacious of you out there are actually working
hard on solutions for the pseudo-problems we've posed ourselves. I think nearly all of you are sane enough to know at
least that there *are* solutions, and that nothing but our best
and hardest work will provide them. The government won't
do it, the man with the white beard won't do it, not even Cal
Tech will do it—thou art God, and you cannot refuse the
nomination.

I cannot precisely echo Jay Kay—only a *lot* of the people I
love are in this room, or would even be at a Worldcon held
everywhere at once by videophone. But those of you here
whom I do know and love, and those of you here whom I
don't know and love, are a part of my family, an indispens-
able part of my life, and part of what makes it possible for me
to write my stories.

As a Johnny-Come-Lately, I am proud to be considered a
Fan. Contrary to the belief and expectation of most of you I
seem to run into, I know extremely little of Fannish legends
and rituals and famous personalities and such. I knew nothing at all about any of this until a very few years ago. I have a
particularly abominable memory for names, which cripples
me. And frankly, there are just too damned many of you for
me to keep track of, too much lore to be absorbed, too many
letters to answer more than a fraction of them. I am hampered
in convention-going by having to meet many deadlines to
stay alive, and I have no time to spare for fanac or letterhack-
ing or even keeping up with the fanzines. (I seem to get them
all—and do you have any *idea* how many fanzines there are?)
I rarely have time for more than one or two carefully-selected
conventions a year.

But this is one of them, and I've had a fabulous time so far,
and I must tell you that I have never in my life felt so at home
and so at ease with so many drunken strangers.

I really do try to do my part for fanac, but economics

require that I publish it in the prozines. I hope that is satisfactory to fandom; fandom is satisfactory to me.

In closing, I would like to thank you for your attention. But your at-ease was disgraceful, and your parade-rest was barely better than parading around *und*rest. I hope we don't fall out over this, I'm rather sensitive about face, and I'm certain that eyes right.

Nonetheless I love you all. Let's go somewhere else and put on even funnier clothes than these and have a good time.

MIRROR/ЯOЯЯIM, OFF THE WALL

I have mixed feelings about him. He was, of course, a criminal in the technical sense, but I never cared much for such. And he did have some of the finest booze I ever tasted, and was quite generous with it, which counts for a lot even if it *didn't* taste as good to *him*. Furthermore, he was the only man I know who could have performed so unlikely a miracle as taking a hundred pounds off Doc Webster.

But on the other hand, he was the kind of man who was willing to betray himself to the feds, in order to save himself from the feds—and that strikes me as selfish. Struck him that way, too, afterwards.

And so I don't feel too bad about having helped betray him to the feds myself. After all, it saved him from the feds, didn't it?

I'll tell you about it.

I generally don't get to Callahan's Place much before seven at night—but that morning my mailbox had saved my neighbor's life, so I decided noon wasn't too early for a drink or three.

Doris's Valiant had been slipping off the right shoulder, right across the street from my house, and was beginning to nose down off the twenty-foot drop to the marsh flats when it struck the mailbox. The box and the big six-by-six it stood on were of course punted some hundred yards at once, in flinders the smallest of which weighed twenty-five pounds, but they held for that millisecond necessary to lift her right front wheel and correct her angle of incidence. Instead of tumbling, the car went down like a cat, on all fours: from my point of view, across the street on my front stoop, she simply

161

disappeared. She cleared the sloping bank by inches, hit the
flats in a four-point Evel Knievel which only ruined the
suspension system, and came to rest two hundred yards later
in Stanley Butt's garden, the bumpers and crannies of the
Valiant so crammed with marsh grass, hay and lupines as to
resemble a poor attempt at camouflage. We talked about it in
my kitchen, Doris and I, and concluded that while a few
inches lefterly would have made her miss the mailbox, fall
kattycorner and explode on maybe the fourth bounce, a few
feet to starboard would have put her into the telephone pole
beside the mailbox and ended it right there. She needed a
drink and a ride home, but I keep no liquor in the house (why
would I drink *alone*?) and I'd had to leave my car keys and
car at Callahan's Place the night before, so I walked her home
and let her husband pour her a drink. I declined one, refused
to let him take my ten-gallon hat and left hastily, so that they
could collapse in each others' arms and weep while the need
was still sharp. I let my feet take me to Callahan's, while my
mind ruminated on the fragility of these bags of meat we haul
around.

Callahan and Fast Eddie were just pulling into the lot when
I got there, and it wasn't until I saw the amp, mixer and
speakers in the bed of the truck that I remembered it was
Fireside Fillmore Night, the night Eddie and I jam for Callahan's patrons. I've never tapped out on a gig before, but I
didn't feel much like playing or singing, so I told them so,
and how come. Callahan nodded and produced a flask from
the glove-box, but Eddie began offloading the equipment
anyhow—it looked like rain. While Callahan and I shared an
afternoon swallow, Eddie staggered to the door with my big
Fender Bassmaster, set it down, unlocked the door, hoisted
the amp again, took two steps into the bar and dropped the
Fender on his feet.

Curiously, I was more puzzled than dismayed—because I
was certain that Eddie had screamed a split-second *before* the
amp mashed his toes, rather than after.

He instinctively tried to cradle both wounded feet in his
hands, but this left him none to hop on, so he sat suddenly
down, raising dust from his jeans. But he wasted no time on

getting up or even on swearing—almost as he hit he was . . .
well . . . *moving* backwards, without using hands or feet.
Sort of levitating horizontally, the way Harpo used to do
when he wanted to break Groucho up in the middle of a
routine, propelling himself across the stage with his hams
alone. Eddie backed into the truck at high speed, his head
bouncing off the fuselage, and he sat there a moment, still
cradling his injured dogs, face pale.

Callahan and I exchanged a glance, and the big barkeep
shrugged. "That's Eddie for you," he said, and I nodded
judicious agreement.

Fast Eddie stared vaguely up at us, and his eyes *clicked*
into focus. All things considered, his expression was remarkable: mild indignation.

"Mechanical orangutan," he complained, and fell over
sideways, out cold.

Callahan sighed and nodded philosophically. "Probably
shat rivets all over the floor," he grumbled, and picked Eddie
up under one beefy arm, heading for the door.

I got there first. I know in my bones that *anything* can
happen at Callahan's, and the Passing of the Mailbox had
used up all the adrenalin I had in stock—but I'd never seen a
mechanical orangutan.

But I was not prepared for what I saw. As I cleared the
doorway, a tall demon with pronounced horns came at me
fast out of the gloom. Callahan and Eddie and I went down in
a heap, with me on top, and it knocked the breath back into
Eddie. He said only one word, but it killed three butterflies
and a yellowjacket. We sorted ourselves out and Eddie glared
at me accusingly.

"Demon," I explained, and backed away from the open
door.

Callahan nodded again. "Monkey demon. Probably
lookin' for Richard Farina—he usta drink here." He dusted
himself off and lumbered into the bar, receding red hair
disarrayed but otherwise undisheveled. Somehow I knew he
planned to buy the demon a drink.

He cleared the doorway, slapped the lights on with his big
left hand, and stopped dead in his tracks. I was prepared for

anything—I thought—but the two things he did then astounded me.

The first thing he did was to burst into laughter, and a good-sized whoop thereof: if the shutters hadn't been closed I'm certain dust would've come boiling out the windows. *One way to drive off a demon.* I decided dizzily, and then he did the second thing. He reached into his back pocket, produced a comb and, still looking straight ahead, put the part back into his hair. (Doc Webster once said of Mike's hair that the part is the whole.)

Then he turned back to me and Eddie, still laughing, and waved us to enter.

"It's okay, boys," he assured us. "It's only a mirror."

Only a mirror!?!

At any other bar in the world, the "only" might have been accurate—barroom mirrors are traditional. But Callahan follows his own eccentric traditions. Where most bars have a mirror, he has a blank wall on which are scribbled thirty years' worth of one-liners, twisted graffiti and pithy thayings. "Does a skinny ballerina wear a one-one?" They range from allegedly humorous to dead serious ("Shared pain is lessened; shared joy increased.") and include at least the punchline of every Punday Evening-winning stinker ever perpetrated. Callahan says he'd rather encourage folk-wisdom than narcissism. So I refused to be reassured.

I eased up to the door and peered past Callahan. Sure enough, with the lights on, it was evident that there was now an enormous mirror behind the bar, installed in the traditional manner behind the rows of firewater and the cashbox. Only if I squinted at the rolled ends of my ten-gallon hat could I make them look like horns, now, but my mind's eye could see much more clearly how Eddie might have mistaken a Fender with his face on top for a robot orangutan. A part of me wanted very much to laugh very hard, but most of me was too busy being flabbergasted.

I mean, *anything* can happen in Callahan's Place—granted. But the Place itself is supposed to be immutable, unchanging, at least in my mind. "What the hell is *that* doing there?" I yelped.

A man can live his whole life long without ever being granted a straightline like that. Callahan blinked and answered at once, "Oh, just reflecting awhile, I guess."

Eddie and I, of course, briefly lost the power of speech, but the little piano man managed to express an opinion of sorts—and, behind the bar, his spitting image did likewise.

We examined the thing together. It was held in place by four clamps that resisted our every attempt to pry them loose—Callahan bent two pry bars all to hell in the attempt. The graffiti seemed unharmed beneath the mirror, as far as we could see, but we could not uncover them. There was no clue as to who might have installed the thing, or why.

"Must have been done overnight," Callahan said. "It sure wasn't here when I left."

We kicked it around for awhile, but even a quart of Tullamore Dew failed to shed any light on the mystery. But it did kill most of the afternoon, and finally Callahan glanced up at the Counterclock over the door and tabled the subject. "Sooner or later some joker'll come 'round with a bill for it," he predicted, "and we'll use him to pry it off the wall with." And he busied himself opening up cases of glasses, barely in time. The regulars began showing up, and the glasses started hitting the fireplace. The more inventive the theory offered for the mirror's appearance, the more glasses hit the fireplace. Almost, I suspected Callahan of arranging the novelty himself in secret: for it tripled his average take and generated some fearsomely bad jokes. Nobody even missed my guitar or Eddie's piano.

Because of the commotion the mirror caused, I nearly failed to notice the newcomer. But on account of the mirror itself, I could hardly help it.

I became at least peripherally aware of any unfamiliar face in Callahan's Place. But when this guy appeared four seats down from me, next to Tommy Janssen, I heard him tell Callahan that "Dr. Webster said to say he sent me," so I knew he belonged *some* way or other. I glanced, saw no

urgent need or pain in his face, and put him out of my mind.
Things happen in their own good time at Callahan's.

And as I started to turn back to Long-Drink McGonnigle, I
did the first and only triple-take of my life.

In the mirror, the chair next to Tommy was empty.

By this point in the day, my adrenals were not only out of
stock, they were running out of room to file the back orders.
So I can't claim any credit for the fact that I kept my
composure. But I converted the triple-take into a headshake
so smoothly that Long-Drink offered to connect me with a
chiropractor and bought me a "neck-unstiffener" besides.
When Callahan delivered it, I caught his eye and winked.
One eyebrow rose a quizzical half-inch, and I nodded to the
mirror, thanking Long-Drink effusively (and sincerely) the
while. Pokerfaced, Callahan turned back to the mirror, stood
stock-still for a second, and then went back to his duties, no
more chalant than ever. But as his reflection nodded imperceptibly at mine, I noticed him take a couple cloves of garlic
out from under the bar and place them unobtrusively by the
cashbox. *As long as the guy doesn't order a Bloody Mary*, I
thought, and wondered if any of the firewood came to a
point.

By unspoken mutual consent, Mike and I restricted ourselves to watching the stranger as the night wore on. He
didn't look much like my notion of a vampire; I'd have taken
him for a Democrat. He was of medium height and weight,
with few distinguishing features: no long pointed canines, no
pointed ears—just a small keloid scar on his left cheek. And
yet somehow there was a . . . a *lopsidedness* to him, an
indefinable feeling of wrongness that nothing appeared to
justify. His hair was parted on the right, like a Jack Kirby
character, but that wasn't it. When I saw where he kept his
wallet I thought I had it: he was lefthanded. One of the
determined ones who even has his jacket cut so the inside
pocket is on the right—for from that place he soon removed a
quart-sized flask and offered it to Tommy Janssen, saying
something I couldn't hear.

Callahan clouded up—does a hooker welcome amateur

talent?—and began to descend on the stranger like the wolves upon the centerfold. But before he got there Tommy had thanked the guy and taken a hit, and as Callahan was opening his mouth Tommy suddenly let out a rebel yell that shattered all conversation.

"Waaaaaaa-A-A-A-A-*HOO*!"

Everybody turned to see, and the only sound was the lapping flames in the fireplace. Tommy's face was exalted. The stranger smiled a strangely lopsided smile and offered the flask to the nearest man, Fast Eddie. Eddie glanced from the flask to the stranger to the transfigured Tommy and took a suspicious snort from it.

Before my eyes, Eddie's forest of wrinkles began smoothing out one by one. The face revealed was undeniably human.

It smiled.

Long-Drink McGonnigle could contain himself no longer. Snagging an empty glass, he shouldered past me and held it out to the stranger, who smiled benevolently and poured an inch of amber fluid. Drink raised it dubiously to his nostrils, which flared; at once he flung the stuff into his mouth.

His eyes closed. Wax began to drip out of his ears. He screamed. Then he extended a tongue like the one on an old cork boot and began to lick the bottom and sides of the glass.

Callahan cleared his throat.

The stranger nodded, and held out the flask.

Callahan held it like a live grenade, and inspected Tommy, Eddie and Long-Drink. All three were still paralyzed, smiling oddly. He shrugged and drank.

"Say," he said. "That tastes like the Four-Eye Monongahela."

A gasp went up.

The stranger smiled again. "Exactly what I thought, the first time I had anything like it."

"Where'd you get it?" Callahan inquired eagerly.

"Liquor store."

"What *is* it?" the barkeep burst out incredulously.

"King Kong," the stranger said.

"King *Kong*?" Callahan exclaimed.

"What's that, Mike?" I asked. "I don't know it."

"I only had it once," Callahan said. "*Years* ago. It was gimme by some fellers who was camped out in a Long Island Railroad yard. One swallow convinced me not to go on the bum after all." He looked down at the flask he still held. "It is the backwards of this stuff."

"I assure you," said the stranger, "that that is King Kong. I bought it in a standard liquor store, transferred it to a flask and brought it here straightaway, unadulterated, just as it came out of the bottle. Nothing has been added or removed."

"Impossible," Callahan said flatly.

"Truth."

"But this stuff tastes *good*. In fact, 'good' ain't even the word. I never had none o' the true Four-Eye, but a feller-that-had told me if I ever did, I'd know it. And this stuff fits that description."

"De gustibus non es disputandum," the stranger observed. "The point is, I've got four quarts of this stuff out in the car, and I'm willing to trade 'em."

"*How much*?" Tommy, Fast Eddie and Long-Drink chorused, showing their first signs of life.

"Oh, not for money," the stranger demurred. "I'll swap even, for five quarts of your worst whiskey."

"Huh?" "Huh?" "Huh?"

"What's the catch?" Callahan asked.

"No catch. You line up five quarts of whiskey—and I demand pure rotgut. I'll match them with five quarts of my King Kong . . . precisely like this one," he added hastily. "Sample them all you wish. When you're satisfied, we all go home happy. Think of me as a masochist."

"It helps," Callahan admitted. "All right, bring on your sauce."

The guy excused himself and headed for the parking lot, and an excited buzz went round the room. "Whaddya think, Mike?" "Think it's really the Four-Eye?" "What was it like, Eddie?"

The last-named groped for adequate words. "Dat incestuous child is de best oral-genital-contacting booze I ever drank,'' Eddie said approximately.

"I dunno from Four-Eye," said Long-Drink reverently, "but it's for *me*."

Tommy only eyed the flask. His face was wistful.

The stranger returned with the additional four quarts, and beheaded all four flasks. "Sample up," he urged, and a stampede nearly began. Callahan filled his great lungs and bellowed, and all motion ceased at once.

"I will sample the hooch," he said flatly.

Amid a growing hush, he bent to each flask and sniffed. Then he placed his tongue over the end of one, inverted it, and put it down again.

"Yep."

He repeated the procedure with the second.

"Yep."

The third.

"Yep."

The fourth.

His face split in a huge grin. "Yes sir."

Pandemonium broke loose, a hubbub of chatter and speculation that sounded like a riot about to happen. The roar built like a cresting tsunami, and then was overridden by an enormous bellow from Callahan.

"If we can have some order in here," he roared, "there'll be drinks on the house for as long as this stuff holds out."

Sustained standing ovation.

When it had died down, the big Irishman turned to the stranger. "I don't believe I got your handle," he said.

"Bob Trevor," is what I thought he said.

"Bob," Callahan said, "I am Mike Callahan and I believe I owe you some nosepaint. What's your pleasure?"

"Oh," Trevor said judiciously, "I guess Tiger Breath'd do just fine."

Another gasp of shock ran round the room.

"*Tiger* Breath?" Callahan cried. "Why, the only use for that stuff is poison ivy of the stomach. Tiger Breath'll kill a cactus."

"Nonetheless," Trevor insisted, "it's Tiger Breath I'm

bargaining for. Have you got any?''

Callahan frowned. ''Hell yeah, I got a couple gallons in the back—I use it to unplug the cesspool. But that stuff's worse'n King . . . worse'n King Kong's *supposed* to be.''

''Whip it out,'' the stranger said.

Shaking his head, Callahan lumbered out from behind the bar and fetched a half-keg from the back. Its only markings were four Xs (a nice classical touch, I thought) and a skull and crossbones. People made way for him, and he set it on the bar.

''You're welcome to all of it,'' the barkeep declared.

Trevor unstopped the bung. A clear ten feet away, a fly intersected an imaginary circle drawn round the bunghole. The fly went down like a shot-up Stuka, raising a small cloud of sawdust from the floor when it hit. The nondescript stranger tilted the barrel, and the slosh sounded like a dangerous animal trying to get out. He poured a sip's worth into an empty glass; the drops that spilled ate smoking holes in the mahogany bartop. Tiger Breath is industrial-strength whiskey, and it tastes like rotten celery smells. It is perceptibly worse than King Kong.

He sniffed the bouquet with obvious relish, and puckered up. As the first load went past his tonsils his face lit from within with a holy light, a warm soft glow like a gaslight jack-o'-lantern. His pupils opened to their widest aperture and I saw his pulse quicken in his throat. His smile was a beatitude.

''Done,'' he said.

He and Callahan shook hands on it, and the rest of us marched as one man to the bar and held out our glasses. Callahan returned to his post and began measuring out shots of Trevor's mystery mash, and not a word was spoken nor a muscle moved until two flasks were empty and the last glass full. Then Callahan's voice rang out.

''To Bob Trevor.''

''*To Bob Trevor*!''

And we drank.

At once, my eyes (which are rated 20/20) clicked into true

focus for the first time in my life, my I.Q. rose twenty points, and my cheeks buzzed. A thin sheen of sweat broke out over every inch of my body. My powers clarified and my perceptions sharpened; my pulse rate rose high and stabilized; the universe took on a crisp, brilliant presence; and none of these things was anything more than incidental to the *TASTE*, oh god the taste . . .

There are no words. "Rich" is pitifully inadequate. "Smoky" is hopelessly ambiguous. "Full" is self-descriptive, semantically meaningless, and "smooth" is actually misleading. It felt, to the tongue and to the taste buds, like I imagine a velvet pillow must feel to the cheek—and it kicked like a Rockette. It enobled the mouth.

It was the Wonderbooze.

I gazed at my fellows—and knew them at once in a new and subtle and infinitely compassionate way, and knew that they now knew me too. We began to speak, within an empathy so profound as to be nearly telepathy, leaping a million parsecs and a hundred years of intellectual evolution with every fragmented sentence, happily explaining the alleged mysteries of life to each other and sorrowing cosmic sorrows. Men wept and laughed and embraced each other, and never a hail of more scrupulously empty glasses hit the fireplace. I found a new reason to admire Callahan's custom: it would have been sacrilegious to use those glasses again for a lesser fluid.

As the conversations gained depth and profundity, Long-Drink and I stepped up to Trevor and smiled from our earlobes. "Brother," said the Drink, "let us assist you."

"Why, thank you," he said, smiling back.

Drink and I picked up the half-keg between us and poured his glass full of Tiger Breath. Trevor drank deep, and since we already had the keg in the air it seemed foolish not to top off his glass, and then it seemed reasonable to line up some glasses for him and fill those so we wouldn't have to keep shouldering the keg, and in the end we poured six glasses full to be on the safe side, and sure enough he drank them all. So to be polite Drink and I had Callahan pour us some more of his King Kong, although it was the sort of booze that left no need for a second snort, and we sipped while Trevor gulped, and it got pretty drunk out. I remember walking over to where the fly lay dead on the sawdust, dipping my finger into my glass and letting a drop of Wonderbooze fall onto the fly. At once he rose from the floor in a series of angry spirals, spraying sawdust, and I swear he shouldered me aside on his way out the door. The conversation got a little hard to follow, then. I sort-of remember the Drink insisting that a close analysis of Stephane Grappelli's later music clearly proved that infinity is translucent; I vaguely recollect Callahan challenging us to name one single person we had ever met or heard of that wasn't a jackass; I believe I recall Fast Eddie's reasoned argument for the existence of leprechauns. But the next stretch of dialogue I retain in its entirety.

Trevor: "Who's that stepping on my fingers?"

Me: "That's you."

"Oh. That's all right then. Beer for ev'body, on me. Gotta celebrate."

Callahan nodded and began setting 'em up.

"Fren'ly place," Trevor went on. "Helpful fellas. Hardly seem backwards atall."

"Naw," I agreed. "*Strange*, yes. Backwards, no."

"Strange?"

Callahan began passing beers around, and I snagged one. "Sure. Li'l green men. Time travelers. *Anything* can happen in Callahan's joint. But not backwards. This guy here, now," I pointed at Long-Drink, "this long drink o' beer here, did you know sometimes at midnight he turns into a driveway?"

The punchline, of course, was that the Drink works as a night watchman two nights a week, and turns into the driveway of K.D.C. Chemicals at midnight on the dot. But I never delivered.

"Mmmm," mused Trevor. "Like to see that. Wha' timesit?"

And Drink and I, not thinking a thing of it, gestured with our beers at the Counterclock.

The 'Clock has always seemed to suit Callahan's Place perfectly. I don't know where Mike got it, and I've only seen one other like it, in the New York apartment of a lovely lady named Michi Stasko, and I don't know where she got hers either. What it is, it runs in reverse. I mean, the numbers are reversed— 1, 2, 3, 4, etc.—and run *counter*clockwise from 12, and the works are geared to run in reverse accordingly. It's a rather elaborate jape, but like I say it suits the Place, and if you hang out long enough at Callahan's you often have to stop and transpose in your head to make sense of a normal clock. Doc Webster has gone to the extent of having a mirror installed in the inside-cover of his pocket-watch so he can tell the time at a glance. Apparently Trevor just hadn't notice the Counterclock over the door until now, and I always enjoy observing people's first-time reactions to it. But I'd never witnessed so spectacular an effect before.

Trevor saw the clock; his eyes widened to the size of egg yolks and the blood drained out of his face. He let out a hell of a yell, backed off two paces, raced up to the bar and vaulted it, plunging headfirst into the mirror.

I mean *into* the mirror.

He had disappeared into it up to the hips and was still in headlong flight when Callahan's meaty hand trapped a flying ankle and yanked backwards, hard. Trevor came sailing back out of the mirror and into the real world like a dog jerked from a pond by its leash, and he dangled upside down from a fist the size of a catcher's mitt, swearing feebly. The big barkeep was expressionless, which is his scariest expression.

"You owe me ten bucks for them beers," he said quietly.

I don't care *how* drunk you are; if a chair bites you on the leg, you sober up at once. Your mind is perfectly capable of fighting off your own bloodstream if it must. It's an emergency system, beyond volitional control, and it doesn't *care* if it makes your head hurt. I found myself sober, at once.

But it probably didn't help Trevor any to be upside down. Clearly, his first action showed confused thought. He reached into his right hand pocket with his right hand, and pulled out and gave to Callahan a bill.

Callahan glanced at it and frowned. "Mister," he said, walking around from behind the bar, still holding Trevor by the ankle at arm's length, "up until a minute ago I liked you okay. But a man who'll try and stiff me twice running might try it a third time, and I can't be bothered." With no change in the toné or rhythm of his speech, he began during the last sentence to swing Trevor around by the ankle, in a wide circle paralleling the floor. Fast Eddie, divining the boss's intent with the supersonic uptake which has earned him his name, sprang forward and opened the front door.

Centrifugal force prevented Trevor from getting enough air into his lungs to shout, but I noticed something fluttering from his *left* hand, and read it the way you read the label on a spinning record.

"Hold it, Mike," I called out. "He's got the sawbuck he owes you."

"If it's like the last one, he'll only bounce the once," Callahan promised, but he slowed his swing, grabbed Trevor's collar with his other fist and set the hapless stranger down on the floor feet first. Trevor spun three times and collapsed into a chair.

"I don't understand at all," he said dizzily. "Which side am I on?"

"The flip side, apparently," I said, "if you really tried to cheat Callahan."

"But the mirror . . . that clock . . . I was halfway *through* the mirror, it *must* be a Bridge . . ." He shut up and looked confused.

I looked at Callahan. "The mirror must be a bridge. Because of the clock."

He nodded. "Mechanical orangutan."

Then I saw the first bill Trevor had offered Callahan, lying forgotten on the floor. It said it was a 01S bill.

It actually began to make a twisted kind of sense. I turned back to Trevor and pointed a finger at him. "I only *thought* you said 'Trevor'," I said wonderingly. "It was 'Trebor,' wasn't it? Robert Trebor?"

Trebor nodded.

"There's a mirror dimension," I went on, "one identical to our own, but mirror reversed. And you invented a dimensional bridge . . ."

He looked at it from all sides and gave up in confusion. "Yes," he admitted. "It can only be *initiated* in my continuum, because the molecules of the activating substance, thiotimoline, have different properties when they're reversed. But if the first bill I gave you looks backwards to you, then I must be in the *other* dimension, where a Bridge can't be activated. But I *did* get halfway through that mirror instead of breaking it, and there's that clock—I just don't understand this at all."

"The clock?" Long-Drink spoke up. "Why that's just ouch."

". . . just one of the many mysteries we have to consider," I finished smoothly, smiling at the Drink and rocking back off of his toes again. "So perhaps you'd better just tell us the whole thing."

Trebor looked around at us suspiciously. "You'd blow the whistle," he accused.

Callahan drew himself up to his full height (a considerable altitude). "If I understand this," he rumbled, "you ain't tried to cheat me after all, so I owe you an apology. But I'd as soon you didn't insult my friends."

It's a traditional moment at Callahan's, familiar to all of us by now. The Newcomer Examines Us and Decides Whether To Trust Us Or Not. Some take their time; some make a snap decision to open up. Nobody *ever* pressures them, one way or the other. Most of 'em cop. I had to admire Trebor at that moment. His mind must have been racing at a million miles an hour, just like mine, but he brought it under control for long enough to give his full attention to evaluating each of us one by one. Finally, as most do, he nodded. "I guess I've got to tell *some*body. And even if you wanted to cross me up, there isn't a sober witness in the lot of you. Okay."

We all settled into listening attitudes, and Callahan passed around fresh beers to them as needed 'em.

"Yes, I am an inventor," he began, "and I did invent a dimensional Bridge—which my counterpart in *this* dimensional continuum could *not* do, since as I said thiotimoline doesn't work right here."

"Then this *ain't* a perfect mirror of your world," Long-Drink interrupted.

"No, Trebor agreed. "Not a perfect mirror. There are subtle, generally unimportant differences. In my continuum, for instance, all the rock groups are different and Shakespeare wrote Bacon. Disparities like that, that make no tangible difference to the world at large. But they're essentially similar—like 'identical' twins. It's only because of their vast congruencies that the two continua lie close enough together for a Bridge to be feasible at all."

"Then you're like a time-traveler into the past," I pointed out, "At least in a sense. If you change *this* world in any significant way, you'll never be able to return to your own."

"Precisely what I'm afraid of," Trebor agreed. "Which is why this Bridge-mirror of yours disturbs me so much. Because I didn't build it, which means someone else did, which means the chances of some accident making the two continua diverge have just effectively doubled. At *least*. I ought to get home at once . . . but I *can't*."

Because his Bridge couldn't be activated from this side? Surely he must have planned for such a contingency. *I* always buy a round-trip ticket.

Unless I'm rushed . . .

"What about your counterpart?" I asked, breaking his train of thought. "The Robert Trebor of *this* world, I mean?"

"Oh, I swapped places with him," Trebor said absently.

"Where's he now?"

"In jail, I should exp . . . uh, I don't know."

"I don't get this," Callahan growled, "but I don't think I like it."

I was still enough under the influence of the Wonderbooze to be capable of positively Sherlockean flights of deduction. "I think I get it, Mike. Trebor here invents a dimension-Bridge to our world, right? What does he do? Collect samples of our 'reversed' artifacts as proof of where he's been. Then when he gets home, he gets cagey and decides to keep his mouth shut. That makes sense: if too many people hear about the Bridge, it becomes useless.

"But he makes a fatal error. Through some mix-up, just

like the one he pulled here tonight, he spends some of *our* money over *there*. This puts the feds onto him, and he finds it necessary to change neighborhoods in a hurry. So he steps through the Bridge to *our* world again, somehow suckers his mirror-twin into trading places with him, and burns his Bridge behind him. He probably has a second Bridge hidden somewhere, set to activate itself whenever the heat has died down—all he has to do is wait. His twin takes a fall on a bad-paper rap, and he walks away clean. Pretty slick.''

There was a pistol in Trebor's hand. I noted absently that the safety was on the wrong side, and that it was off.

''Very astute,'' he said quietly.

''Listen Trebor,'' I called, ''don't be a jerk! Right now you're wanted by the cops in one dimension only—in *this* one your biggest problem is that a barfull of guys think you stink. Don't blow it.'' I spoke with great haste, but my mind was racing even faster.

''You have a point,'' he allowed. ''As long as no one is foolish enough to get in my way, I believe I'll just take my Tiger Breath and toddle off.'' He picked up the half-keg in his right arm and started edging toward the door.

The deductions were coming like clusters of grapeshot now. I glanced up at the mirror, and what I saw there confirmed all speculation. Trebor *had* a reflection in the mirror, now, and the image looked straight at me with pleading eyes.

''Hold on, buddy,'' I barked. ''The least you can do is tell us why you went through all this.''

He stopped, about three feet out of position. I wanted him right on the chalk line from which one addresses the fireplace. ''I don't expect you'll believe me, at this point, but I sincerely want to improve both worlds,'' he said.

''How? By swapping your booze for ours?''

''That's one small way,'' he agreed. ''Alcohol has a symmetrical molecule, so either one gets you loaded. It's the congeners, the asymmetrical esters which produce the taste and the impact, that make one world's mead another world's poison.'' He paused, and giggled. To my annoyance, so did I. ''But there are infinite possibilities. That's what I've been

doing for the last week: walking around your world thinking
of all the splendid possibilities. Once it's safe to use my
auxiliary Bridge, I could . . . well, figure it out for yourself.
Suppose I swapped our smog for yours, molecule by
molecule, in bulk? The reversed ozone wouldn't be an irri-
tant any more . . .''

"Brilliant," I said sarcastically. "It'd still block sunlight
and foul our lungs, but it wouldn't be irritating enough to
remind us to clean up the source any more. Remove the
nuisance value and leave the menace intact, that's a *great*
idea, Trebor.'' I was frantically trying to catch Callahan's
eye without alerting Trebor, and at last I succeeded. I
motioned imperceptibly toward the mirror, and Callahan
casually turned to it. The mirror-image of Trebor gesticu-
lated at him, and I prayed that Mike would dope it out in time.
Just like Doris's Valiant and my mailbox: the only thing that
could help Trebor now was an unexpected collision.

Trebor failed to notice. "Well," he said, plainly crest-
fallen, "then suppose I imported food from my dimension,
and exported yours? Really fattening items, I mean. Tarts,
creampuffs, banana splits. The stereisomer of a strawberry
shortcake would taste as good as the real thing—I know, I've
tested it—but your digestive system would ignore it entirely.
All the fat people could get thin!''

Callahan answered this time, coming around the bar with
an air of total innocence, plainly involved in the intellectual
exercise of talking to this nice man with the pistol. Trebor
moved to let him by, covering him carefully with the pistol,
placing himself just where I wanted him to be. I hoped Mike
understood his part.

"Nope, I'm afraid that's no good either, pal," he boomed.
"Glandular cases aside, the only genuine cure for fat is to not
be a hog. Your method would encourage fat people to keep
on being hogs—so, they'll keep on being fat people, regardless of what they happen to weigh. You'd know one anywhere. That's the third time you've proposed to treat the
symptoms instead of the disease.''

"*Third* time?'' Trebor said, puzzled.

"Yeah. The first was when you decided you could get

yourself out of a jam by throwing your mirror-twin to the wolves. They used to say when I was a kid that that kinda stuff'd grow hair on your palms. Self-abuse, I mean. And just like the last two 'cures' you proposed, it didn't cure a thing. *Look*!''

He pointed over Trebor's shoulder at the mirror, and Trebor smiled.

''That's an *old* old gag,'' he said reprovingly.

And then Fast Eddie caught sight of the mirror and yelped, and Trebor must have known the runty little piano man was no actor, for he whirled then, gun ready, and—

—froze. In the mirror, he saw himself, keg and all, but the ''right'' hand held no pistol, and it was upraised in a ritual gesture that loses nothing by mirror-reversal. Trebor's jaw dropped, he raised the pistol . . .

And Callahan kicked him square in the ass.

No other man among us could have pulled it off—but Callahan is built along the lines of Mount Washington, and I've seen him carry a full keg in each hand. His big size-twelve impacted behind Trebor's lap with the speed and power of a cannonball, lofting the inventor into the air, clean over the bar and into the mirror. As he struck it, he seemed to reverse direction and bounce back into the room, landing in a heap on the sawdust.

But when he landed, his hand was empty.

''Thanks,'' he gasped to Callahan. ''I *needed* that.''

And in the mirror, a man in a grey flannel suit stepped up to *that* Trebor, took away his pistol, and slapped handcuffs on him. The grey man turned to the mirror, aimed the pistol at it and pulled the trigger. There was no bang, but the mirror exploded in a million shards, which fell to the floor of Callahan's Place with the multiple crashes you'd expect.

Fifteen minutes later, Bob Trebor—the one who *belonged* here—was sitting by the fireplace with his feet up, sipping at some Wonderbooze and rounding up the story of his exploits in Mirrorland.

''If the local police had apprehended me, it might have

been a sadder story. But the .I.B.Ⅎ has some people bright enough to add together my story plus the fact that my fingerprints were mirror-reversed plus the scar on the wrong cheek plus what the X-rays showed and come up with the plain truth—and tough-minded enough to believe their own eyes. Pretty soon everybody I was talking to was named Smith, and they cooked up a plan to trap the other Trebor and send me home again. They put a top .I.B.Ⅎ computer onto predicting Trebor's movements, using data I supplied them as well as their own dossiers. Then, with access to *his* lab and notes, I used my similar background and skills to build another Bridge. It took me a week. By that time computer analysis indicated that he was 89% liable to come in here, tonight, so we had the Bridge installed. I hope you didn't mind?''

''Not at all,'' Callahan assured him. ''Livened up a dull night.''

''I don't get it,'' Eddie complained. ''Why din't the feds just come t'ru de Bridge an' bust 'im?''

''They couldn't, Eddie,'' Trebor said patiently. ''Jurisdictional questions aside, the more changes they caused in *this* continuum, the greater the chance of separating the two forever. They were nervous about doing anything at all.''

''So you worked it out with the folks at Callahan's Place—the *other* Callahan's—and they agreed to stage as perfect an exchange as possible,'' I said wonderingly. It was kinda nice to know that each world had a Callahan's—but I wondered if the other me still had his wife and kids. Probably not, or he wouldn't be there . . . but I wonder.

''Yes,'' Trebor agreed. ''And fortunately for me, you were as quick on the uptake as your counterparts assured me you'd be. You followed my cues beautifully.''

''The Wonderbooze helped,'' Callahan observed, sweeping the last of the mirror into the fireplace.

''That it did. Amazing what molecular reversal will do for liquor.'' He gazed meditatively at his glass.

''That's what *I* don't get,'' I admitted. ''Most of our food must have been wrong for his digestive system—and theirs must've been mostly useless to you. How come neither of you came down with malnutrition?''

"We were both starting to," Trebor said drily. "That's what brought *him* to Dr. Webster, which in turn brought him here. He must have planned to use his alternate Bridge to bring food across eventually, and he must have had a cache of food *with* him that he could ration out 'til then. If I find it at my house I'll bring it around." That, by the way, is how Doc Webster came to lose a hundred pounds. For awhile, anyway—the hog. Don't tip him off, okay? "I guess he simply expected me to starve—if he thought about it. He couldn't have been very imaginative, or he'd have realized that I had enough evidence to sell the truth to the ꟻ.B.I."

"That kinda bothers me too," I said. "The feds are not, for one reason and another, my favorite people—and I don't imagine a mirror-fed is any better. I have to admit I don't find it reassuring that men analagous to our F.B.I. possess a secret bridge to our world."

"True," said Callahan "But what do we do? Tell *our* feds? With no sober witnesses and no way to make a working Bridge in *this* world? If we *could* put it over, would it help—or make things worse?"

"Forget it," Trebor advised. "Whatever their intentions, there isn't a lot they can do, for good *or* ill. If they take any action benefiting their continuum at the expense of ours, the two continua become too dissimilar and the Bridge is useless."

Callahan burst into gargantuan laughter. "I'll bet they're sittin' around a table right now, quiet as mice, wonderin' what the hell they can possibly *do* with the goddam thing," he whooped, and slapped the bar.

The picture of a dozen top government thinkers staring in silent frustration at a device more awesome than the atomic bomb—with no known use—was so lovely that we all broke up, and Eddie struck up Stevie Wonder's "It Ain't No Use."

"At least they got a half-keg o' Wonderbooze out of it," Long-Drink yelled, and we laughed louder; and then Eddie yelled, "An' so did *we*!" and a cheer went up that rattled the rafters.

But I noticed that Trebor wasn't smiling. "What's wrong, Bob?"

He sighed moodily and sipped of the Wonderbooze. "It's not fair," he said.

"How do you mean?" Callahan asked. "You're home free and your rotten twin is in Leavenworth—what's your beef?"

"That's it precisely," Trebor said exasperatedly. "My counterpart is, I agree with you, rotten. I knew him only for the half hour it took him to shanghai me into stepping through his damned Bridge, but in retrospect I don't believe I've ever met a more classic sociopath. I, on the other hand, like to think of myself as . . . well, as one of the good guys, and I believe I've conducted myself honorably throughout this affair. I even took a kick in the pants that I'm not certain I deserved. That's why I think it's unfair."

He emptied his glass, tossed it into the fire, and sighed again.

"Why is it," he mourned, "that *I* will never again see my face in the shaving mirror without wincing?"

Concerning ''Mirror/ꓤoꓕꓤiM, Off The Wall'':

As I say, I've never actually caught Jake in a flat lie. But often his earns are built on elements I find oddly familiar—perhaps because both Jake and I are regular readers of sf. (We take prunes to keep it that way.)

The mirror-reversal business in this story, for instance, bears a remarkable resemblance to ideas put forth in Roger Zelazny's demonically inventive novel, Doorways In The Sand *(although the two stories in no other way resemble each other).*

Similarly, Isaac Asimov has written extensively about thiotimoline—which in this continuum has the odd property of reacting a split second before it contacts the reagent. Interested readers are directed to the Good Doctor's (Is he a good doctor? Does he make house calls?) autobiography; specifically to Volume One, In Memory Almost Ripe.*

Finally, the Four-Eye Monogahela made its first appearance (as did a variant of Tiger Breath called ''Tiger Bone'') in a magnificent Oliver La Farge story called ''Spud And Cochise''—which happens, by happy coincidence, to be reprinted in my current anthology, The Best Of All Possible Worlds, *Volume One. (Ace Books, another coincidence.)*

Does all this mean that Jake is putting us on?

I don't think so. I might have thought so—if Jake hadn't shown me the 01Ձ bill that Trebor left behind. And if Mike hadn't privately slipped me a snort of the Wonderbooze . . .

Instead I find myself wondering whether Zelazny, Asimov or La Farge ever owned unusual mirrors . . . . . .

—All right, all right, Isaac: the real title is In Memory Yet Green.

SERPENTS' TEETH

LOOKOVER LOUNGE

House Rules, Age 16 And Up:

IF THERE'S A BEEF, IT'S YOUR FAULT. IF YOU
BREAK IT, YOU PAY FOR IT, PLUS SALES TAX AND
INSTALLATION. NO RESTRICTED DRUGS. IF YOU
ATTEMPT TO REMOVE ANY PERSON OR PERSONS
FROM THESE PREMISES INVOLUNTARILY, BY
FORCE OR COERCION AS DEFINED BY THE HOUSE,
YOU WILL BE SURRENDERED TO THE POLICE IN
DAMAGED CONDITION. THE DECISIONS OF YOUR
BARTENDER ARE FINAL, AND THE MANAGEMENT
DOESN'T WANT TO KNOW YOU. THE FIRST ONE'S
ON THE HOUSE; HAVE A GOOD TIME.

Teddy and Freddy both finished reading with slightly
raised eyebrows. Any bar in their own home town might well
have had nearly identical—unofficial—house rules. But
their small town was not sophisticated enough for such rules
to be so boldly committed to printout.

"*You can surrender those sheets at the bar for your
complimentary drink,*" the door-terminal advised them.
"*Good luck to you both.*"

Freddy said "Thank you." Teddy said nothing.

The soft music cut off; a door slid open. New music spilled
out, a processor group working the lower register, leaving

the higher frequencies free for a general hubbub of conversation. Smells spilled out as well: beer, mostly, with overlays of pot, tobacco, sweat, old vomit, badly burned coffee and cheap canned air. It was darker in there; Teddy and Freddy could not see much. They exchanged a glance, shared a quick nervous grin.

"Break a leg, kid," Teddy said, and entered the Lounge, Freddy at her heels.

Teddy's first impression was that it was just what she had been expecting. The crowd was sizable for this time of night, perhaps four or five dozen souls, roughly evenly divided between hunters and hunted. While the general mood seemed hearty and cheerful, quiet desperation could be seen in any direction, invariably on the faces of the hunters.

Teddy and Freddy had certainly been highlighted when the door first slid back, but by the time their eyes had adjusted to the dimmer light no one was looking at them. They located the bar and went there. They strove to move synchronously, complementarily, as though they were old dance partners or old cop partners, as though they were married enough to be telepathic. In point of fact they were all these things, but you could never have convinced anyone watching them now.

The bartender was a wiry, wizened old man whose hair had once been red, and whose eyes had once been innocent—perhaps a century before. He displayed teeth half that age and took their chits. "Welcome to the Big Fruit, folks."

Freddy's eyebrows rose. "How did you know we're not from New York?"

"I'm awake at the moment. What'll it be?"

Teddy and Freddy described their liquid requirements. The old man took his time, punched in their order with one finger, brought the drinks to them with his pinkies extended. As they accepted the drinks, he leaned forward confidentially. "None o' my business, but . . . you might could do all right here tonight. There's good ones in just now, one or two anyways. Don't push is the thing. Don't try quite so hard. Get me?"

They stared at him. "Thanks, uh—"

"Pop, everybody calls me. Let them do the talking."

"We will," Freddy said. "Thank you, Pop."

"Whups! 'Scuse me." He spun and darted off at surprising speed toward the far end of the bar, where a patron was in danger of falling off his stool; Pop caught him in time. Teddy would have sworn that Pop had never taken his eyes from them until he had moved. She had smuggled a small weapon past the door-scanner, chiefly to build her morale, but she resolved now not to try it on Pop even in extremis. "Come on, Freddy."

Teddy found them a table near one of the air-circulators, with a good view of the rest of the room. "Freddy, for God's sake quit staring! You heard what the old fart said: lighten up."

"Teddy!"

"I like him too; I was trying to get your attention. Try to look like there isn't shit on your shoes, will you?"

"How about that one?"

"Where?"

"There."

"In the blue and red?" Teddy composed her features with a visible effort. "Look, my love: apparently we have 'HICK' written across our foreheads in big black letters. All right. Let's not make it 'DUMB HICK,' all right? Look at her arms, for God's sake."

"Oh." Freddy's candidate was brazenly wearing a sleeveless shirt—and a cop should not miss track marks.

"I'm telling you, slow down. Look, let's make an agreement: we're not going to hit on anybody for the first hour, all right? We're just out for an evening of quiet conversation."

"I see. We spent three hundred and sixty-seven New dollars to come to New York and have a few drinks."

Teddy smiled as though Freddy had said something touching and funny, and murmured, "God damn it, Freddy, you promised."

"All right, but I think these people can spot a phony a mile away. The one in pink and yellow, on your left."

"I'm not saying we should be phony, I'm—" Teddy made

an elaborate hair-adjusting gesture, sneaked a look, then frankly stared. "Wow. That's more like it. Dancing with the brunette, right?"

"Yes."

Freddy's new choice was golden-haired and heartbreakingly beautiful, dressed daringly by their standards but not shockingly. Ribs showed, and pathetically slender arms, and long smooth legs. Intelligence showed in the eyes, above lips slightly curled in boredom.

"Too good to be true," Teddy said sadly. "All these regulars here, and we walk in our first night and score that?"

"I *like* wishful thinking. You shoot for the moon, once in a while you get it."

"And end up wishing you'd settled for a space station. I'd settle for that redhead in the corner with the ventilated shoes."

Freddy followed her glance, winced, and made a small sound of pity. "Don't mock the funny-looking."

"Me? I grew *up* funny looking. I worked four summers selling greaseburgers for this chin and nose. I'll settle for anyone halfway pleasant." She lowered her voice; the musicians were taking a break.

"I love your chin and nose. I don't like him anyway. He looks like the secretive type."

"And you aren't? This drink is terrible."

"So's this—"

The voice was startlingly close. "Hey! You're in my seat, Atlas."

It was the stunning golden-haired youngman. Alone.

Freddy began to move and speak at the same time, but Teddy kicked him hard in the shin and he subsided.

"No we're not," she said firmly.

There was nothing especially grudging about the respect that came into the youngman's eyes, but there was nothing especially submissive about it either. "I always sit by a circulator. I don't like breathing garbage." He made no move to go.

Teddy refused her eyes permission to drop from his. "We

would be pleased if you'd join us.''

"I accept.''

Before Teddy could stop him, Freddy was up after a chair. He placed it beside the youngman, who moved it slightly to give himself a better view of the room than of them, and sat without thanks.

"You're welcome,'' Freddy said quietly, slouching down in his own chair, and Teddy suppressed a grin. When she led firmly, her husband always followed well. For the first time Teddy became aware that she was enjoying herself.

The youngman glanced sharply at Freddy. "Thanks,'' he said belatedly.

"Buy you a drink?'' Teddy asked.

"Sure. Beer.''

Teddy signaled a waiter. "Tell Pop we'd like a couple of horses over here,'' she said, watching the youngman. The pacification of Mexico had made Dos Equis quite expensive, but his expression did not change. She glanced down at her own glass. "In fact, make it three pair.''

"Tab?'' asked the waiter.

"Richards Richards, Ted Fred.''

When the waiter had left, the blond said, "You people always know how to do that. Get a waiter to come. What is that, how do you do that?''

"Well,'' Freddy began, "I—''

"Which one of you is which?''

"I'm Freddy.''

"Oh God, and you're Teddy, huh?'' He sighed. "I hope I die before I get cute. I'm Davy Pangborn.''

Teddy wondered if it were his legal name, but did not ask. It would not have been polite; Davy had not asked them. "Hello, Davy.''

"How long have you been in the city?''

Teddy grinned broadly, annoyed. "Is there hay in my hair or something? Honest to God, I feel like there's a fly unzipped on my forehead.''

"There is,'' Davy said briefly, and turned his attention to the room.

Teddy and Freddy exchanged a glance. Teddy shrugged.

"How old are you, Davy?" Freddy asked.

Davy turned very slowly, looked Freddy over with insolent thoroughness. "How many times a week do you folks do the hump?" he asked.

Teddy kept her voice even with some effort. "See here, we're willing to swap data, but if you get to ask questions that personal, so do we."

"You just did."

Teddy considered that. "Okay," she said finally. "I guess I understand. We're new at this."

"Is that so?" Davy said disgustedly and turned back to face the room.

"We make love about three times a week," Freddy said.

"I'm nine," Davy said without turning.

The beer arrived, along with a plate of soy crunchies garnished with real peanuts. "Compliments of the house," the waiter said, and rolled away.

Teddy glanced up, craned her head until she could see through the crowd to the bar. Pop's eyes were waiting for hers; he shook his head slightly, winked, and turned away. Total elapsed time was less than a second; she was not sure she had not imagined it. She glanced at Freddy, could not tell from his expression whether he had seen it too.

She examined Davy more carefully. He was obviously bright and quick; his vocabulary and grammar were excellent; his education could not have been too badly neglected. He was clean, his clothes were exotic but neat and well-kept. He didn't look like a welfare type; she would have given long odds that he had some kind of job or occupation, perhaps even a legal one. He was insolent, but she decided that in his position he could hardly be otherwise. He was breathtakingly beautiful, and must know it. She was sure he was not and had never been a prostitute, he didn't have that chickie look.

Her cop-sense told her that Davy had potential.

Did Pop know something she didn't? How honest was Davy? How many scars were drawn how deep across his soul, how much garbage had society poured into his subconscious? Would he grow up to be Maker, Taker, or Faker?

Everyone in this room was walking wounded; how severe were Davy's wounds?

"How long have you been single, Davy?"

He still watched the roomful of hunters and hunted, face impassive. "How long since *your* kid divorced *you*?"

"Why do you assume we're divorced?"

Davy drank deeply from his beer, turned to face her. "Okay, let's run it down. You're not sterile, or if you are it was postnatal complications. You've had it before, I can see it in your eyes. Maybe you worked in a power plant, or maybe Freddy here got the measles, but once upon a time someone called you Mommy. It's unmistakable. And you're here, so the kid walked out on you."

"Or died," she suggested. "Or got sent up, or institutionalized."

"No." He shook his head. "You're hurting, but you're not hurting that bad."

She smiled. "All right. We've been divorced a year last week. And you?"

"Three years."

Teddy blinked. If Davy was telling the truth—and a lie seemed pointless—he had opted out the moment he could, and was in no hurry to remarry. Well, with his advantages he could afford to be independent.

On the other hand—Teddy looked around the room herself, studying only the hunters, the adults, and saw no one who made her feel inferior. *He never met a couple like us before*, she told herself, and she made herself promise not to offer him notarized resumé and net-worth sheets unless and until he offered them his.

"What was your kid like, Atlas?" Davy sipped beer and watched her over the rim of the glass.

"Why do you call us that?" Freddy asked.

Teddy frowned. "It's pretty obvious, darling. Atlas was a giant."

Davy grinned through his glass. "Only half the answer. The least important half. Tell me about your kid—your ex-kid—and I'll tell you the other half."

Teddy nodded. "Done. Well, his name is Eddie, and he's—"

" *'Eddie'*?" the youngman exclaimed. "Oh my God you people are too much!" He began to laugh. "If it'd been a girl it would've been Hedy, right?"

Teddy reddened but held her temper. She waited until he was done laughing, and then two seconds more, and continued, "And he's got dark brown hair and hazel eyes. He's short for his age, and he'll probably turn out stocky. He has . . . beautiful hands. He's got my temper, and Freddy's hands. And he's bright and quick, like you. He'll go far. About the divorce . . ." Teddy paused. She and Freddy had rehearsed this next part for so long that they could make it sound unrehearsed. But Davy had a Bullshit-Detector of high sensitivity. Mentally Teddy discarded her lines and just let the words come. "We . . . I guess we were slow in getting our consciousness raised. Faster than some, slower than most. We, we just didn't realize how misguided our own conditioning had been . . . until it was too late. Until we had our noses rubbed in it." Teddy sipped her beer without tasting it.

Although he had not been fed proper cues, Freddy picked it up. "I guess we had our attention on other things. I don't mean that we fell into parenting. We thought it through—we thought we thought it through—before we decided to conceive. But some of our axioms were wrong. We . . ." He paused, blushed, and blurted it out: "We had plans for Eddie."

"Don't say another word," Davy ordered.

Freddy blinked. Teddy frowned; she was studying Davy's expression.

He finished his beer on one long slow draught, stretching the silence. He set the glass down, put both hands on the table and smiled. The smile shocked Teddy: she had never, not in the worst of the divorce, not in the worst of her work in the streets, seen such naked malice on so young a face. She ordered her own face to be inscrutable. And she took Freddy's hand under the table.

"Let me finish, it'll save time," Davy said. "And I'll still tell you why you're an Atlas." He looked them both up and down with care. "Let's see. You're hicks. Some kind of civil service or social work or both, both of you. Very committed, very concerned. I can tell you what grounds Eddie cited at the hearing, want to hear me?"

"You're doing okay so far," Teddy said tightly.

"On the decree absolute it says 'Conceptual Conditioning, Restraint of Personality, and Authoritarianism.' Guaranteed, sure as God made little green boogers. But it won't have the main reason on it: Delusions of Ownership."

They had not quite visibly flinched on the first three charges, but the fourth got to them both. Davy grinned wickedly.

"Now, the key word for both of you, the word that unlocks you both, is the word *future*. I can even sort of see why. Both of you are the kind that wants to *change* things, to make a better world. You figure like this: the past is gone, unchangeable. The present is here *right now* and it's too late. So the only part you can change is the future. You're both heavy into politics, am I right? Right?"

He knew that he was getting to them both; his grin got bigger. Teddy and Freddy were rigid in their chairs.

"So one day," the youngman went on, "it dawned on you that the best way to change the future is to colonize it. With little xeroxes of yourselves. Of course one of the first concerns of a colonizing country is to properly *condition* the colonists. To ensure their loyalty. Because a colonist is supposed to give you the things *you* want to have in exchange for the things *you* want *him* to have, and for this golden opportunity he is supposed to be properly grateful. It wouldn't do for him to get any treasonous ideas about his own destiny, his own goals." He popped a handful of soy crunchies into his mouth. "In your case, the world needed saving, and Eddie was elected. Like it or not." He chewed the mouthful, washed it down. "Let me see. Don't tell me, now. I see the basic program this way: first a solid grounding in math, history and languages—I'd guess Japanese Immersion followed by French. Then by high school begin working toward law, maybe with a minor in Biz Ecch. Then some military service, police probably, and then law school if he survived. With any luck at all old Eddie would have been governor of wherever the hell you live—one of the Dakotas, isn't it?—by the time he was thirty-five. Then Senator Richards by forty or so.''

"Jesus," Teddy croaked.

"I even know what Eddie wants to be instead. A musician. And not even a respectable musician, piano or electric guitar or something cubical like that, right? He wants to play that flash stuff, that isn't even proper music, he wants to be in a processor group, right? I saw the way you looked at the band when you came in. There can't be many things on earth that are as little use to the future as flash. It doesn't even get recorded. It's not supposed to be: it's for the *present*. I wonder if Eddie's any good.''

"What are you trying to do to us?"

"Now: about why you're Atlases. Atlas isn't just a giant. He's the very worst kind of giant. The one to avoid at all costs. Because he's got the weight of the whole world on his shoulders. And he wants you to take it over for him as soon as you're big enough.'' Suddenly, finally, the grin was gone. "Well stuff you, Atlas! You're not even cured *yet*, are you? You're still looking for a Nice Young Kid Who Wants To Make Something Of Himself, you want a god damned volunteer! You're suddenly-childless, and you're so fucking lonely you tell each other you'll settle for anything just to have a kid around the house again. But in your secret hearts you can't help hoping you'll find one with some *ambition*, can you?''

He sat back. He was done. "Well," he said in a different voice, knowing the answer, "how'd I do?" and he began eating peanuts.

Teddy and Freddy were speechless for a long time. The blood had drained from both their faces; garish bar lighting made them look like wax mannequins, save that Teddy was swaying slightly from side to side. Her hand crushed Freddy's hand; neither noticed.

It was Teddy who found her voice first, and to her horror it trembled, and would not stop trembling. "You did very damned well. Two insignificant errors. It was going to be Swahili Immersion after the Japanese. Not French."

"And . . .?"

"Our mutual occupation. You bracketed it, but no direct hit."

"So? All right, surprise me."

"We're cops."

It was Davy's turn to be speechless. He recovered faster. "*Pigs.*"

Teddy could *not* get the quaver out of her voice. "Davy, how do you feel when some Atlas calls you 'punk,' or 'kid,' or 'baby'?"

Davy's eyes flashed.

The quaver was lengthening its period. Soon she would be speaking in sing-song ululation, and shortly after that (she knew) she would lose the power to form words and simply weep. She pressed on.

"Well, that's how we feel when some punk kid baby calls us 'pigs'."

He raised his eyebrows, looked impressed for the first time. "Good shot. Fair is fair. Except that you *chose* to be pigs."

"Not at first. We were drafted at the same time, worked together in a black and white. After the Troubles when our hitch was up we got married and went career."

"Huh. Either of you ever work Juvenile?"

Teddy nodded. "I had a year. Freddy three."

Davy looked thoughtful. "So. Sometimes Juvie cops are all right. Sometimes they get to see things most Atlases don't. And hick cops aren't as bad as New York cops, I guess." He nodded. "Okay, I grant you the provisional status of human beings. Let's deal. I've got no eyes for anything lengthy right at the moment, but I could flash on, say, a weekend in the country or two. If we're compatible, I like your place and all, maybe we could talk something a little more substantial—*maybe*. So what's your offer?"

Teddy groped for words. "Offer?"

"What *terms* are you offering? We might as well start with your resumés and stuff, that'll give us parameters."

She stared.

"Oh, my God," he said, "don't tell me you came *here* looking for something *permanent*? On a first date? Oh, you people are the Schwartzchild Limit!" He began to laugh. "I'll bet your own contract with each other is permanent. Not even ten-year-renewable." When that sank home he laughed even harder. "Unbelievable!" He stopped laughing suddenly. "Oh Momma, you have a *lot* to learn. Now how about those resumés?"

"Shut up," Freddy said quietly.

Davy stared at him. *"What did you say?"*

"Shut up. You may not call her that."

Teddy stared as well.

Freddy's voice did not rise in volume, but suddenly there was steel in it. "You just granted us the provisional status of human beings. We do not reciprocate. You are cruel, and we would not inflict you on our town, much less our home. You can go now."

The enormity of the affront left Davy momentarily at a loss for words, but he soon found some. "How'd you like to wake up in the alley with a broken face, old man? You read the house-rules, your badges are shit in here. All I have to do is poke you right in the eye, and let the bouncers do the rest."

Freddy had the habit of sitting slouched low, curled in on himself. He sat up straight now, and for the first time Davy realized that the man topped one hundred and eighty-five centimeters and massed well over ninety kilos. Freddy's shoulders seemed to have swollen, and his eyes were burning with a cold fire. Teddy stared at him round-eyed, not knowing him. Suddenly it registered on Davy that both of her hands were now visible on the table, and that neither of Freddy's were.

"They'll put us in the same emergency Room," Freddy said dreamily. "You're a lot younger than I am. But I'm *still* faster. Leave this table."

Shortly Davy realized that his face was blank with shock,

and hastily hung a sneer on it. "Hah." He got to his feet. "My pleasure." Standing beside them he was nearly at eye-level. "Just another couple of dumb Atlases." He left.

Freddy turned to his wife, found her gaping at him. The fire went out in him; he slumped again in his chair, and finished off his beer. "Stay here, darling," he said, his voice soft again. "I'll get us another round."

Her eyes followed him as he walked to the bar.

Pop had two more beers waiting for him. "Thanks for the munchies, Pop. And the wink."

"My pleasure," Pop said, smiling.

"Can I buy you a drink, Pop?"

The old man's smile broadened. "Thank you." He punched himself up an apricot sour. "You're well shut of that one. Little vampire."

Freddy's eye was caught by graffiti crudely spray-painted on a nearby wall. It said: "TAKE OUT YOUR OWN FUCKIN GARBAGE." On the opposite wall a neater hand had thoughtfully misquoted, "HOW SHARPER THAN A SERPENT'S TOOTH IS A THANKLESS CHILD."

"Why is it that the word 'another' is the cruelest word in the language, Pop?"

"How d'ya mean?"

"Well, when he's alone with himself a man may get real honest and acknowledge—and accept—that he is a fool. But nobody wants to be 'just' *another* fool. 'Another couple of dumb Atlases,' he called us, and of all the things he said that hurt the most."

"Here now—easy! Here, use this here bar rag. Be right back." While Freddy wiped his eyes, the old man quickly filled a tray of orders for the waiter. By the time he returned Freddy was under control and had begun repairing his makeup with a hand mirror. "See here," Pop said, "if you're hip deep in used food, well, maybe you could climb out. But if you see a whole other bunch of people hip deep too, then the chances of you becoming the rare one to climb out seem to go down drastic. But you see, that's a kind of optical illusion. All those others don't affect *your* odds atall.

What matters is how bad *you* want to get up out of the shit, and what purchase you can find for your feet.''

Freddy took a sip of his new beer, and sighed. ''Thanks, Pop. I think you're into something.''

''Sure. Don't let that kid throw you. Did he tell you his parents divorced *him*? Mental cruelty, by the Jesus.''

Freddy blinked, then roared with laughter.

''Now take that beer on back to your wife, she's looking kind o' shell-shocked. Oh, and I would recommend the redhead over in the corner, the funny-looking boy with the holes in his shoes. He's worth getting to know better, he's got some stuff.''

Freddy stared at him, then raised his glass and drank deep. ''Thanks again, Pop.''

''Any time, son,'' the old man said easily, and went off to punch up two scotches and a chocolate ice cream soda.

Concerning "Serpents' Teeth":

This is the Age of the Minority Group. Women's rights, Indians' rights, writers' rights, left-handed people's rights (motto: "Left is right; right is wrong.")—name a group and you'll find it lobbying for its legal and societal rights. What more logical minority group than minors?

It has been shown that a minority group need not even have the franchise to achieve its aims (women's suffrage, ex-cons' rights, wetbacks, etc.), although it helps. All you really need are the sympathies of enough liberals who do have the vote, and you're in. My own experience has been that liberals tend to have few or no children, while conservatives tend to have a lot. (There's nothing like having a bunch of kids to make you conservative, I guess.) So perhaps Kid's Lib will make the great strides postulated by this story.

But even if it doesn't, the issues raised by "Serpents' Teeth" remain.

It is, at this writing, my most recent story. It reflects some of the ambiguity I feel about being a parent, about having become somehow my own Natural Enemy of old. Jeanne and I have a five-year-old, Luanna Mountainborne, and we often wonder what our daughter is going to come up with that will shock us as badly as we shocked our parents. (It'll have to be a pip; we're hard to shock. Ritual murder? Senior Prom suicide pacts? Celibacy?) In the meantime, Luanna has reached the age/stage where she's getting feisty, constantly challenging our authority, working hard to define and expand the limits of what she can get away with. This is as it should be, and delights me—but it forces me to constantly re-evaluate those limits myself, and then enforce them, and frankly limit-enforcer is not a role I enjoy a whole lot. Especially when the limits are so hard to pin down fairly.

Luanna feels she is old enough to cross the street by herself. I disagree. In case of a tie, I win. But why? Why does my opinion control? Is it because of my extensive experience with children crossing streets? Hell, no—this is the first time I ever considered the matter. I have no data to offer, no observations to cite. I've never known a kid who was killed crossing a street—how do I know what a kid-who-is-too-young-to-cross-the-street looks or acts like? I'm frankly guessing—and my guess controls her freedom of action.

It has to be that way: a wrong guess could be fatal, and it will be many years before Luanna has any conception of what "fatal" means. But how many years? At what age is she allowed to make her own mistakes, even if it kills her? (If she reaches breeding age without ever having had a chance to demonstrate survival-fitness or -unfitness, does that improve the gene-pool or harm it?) At what age do Jeanne and I change from absolute (hopefully benevolent) despots to advisors—and who decides? Society? It seems to me that my authority over my child is both necessary and inevitable— but that is what tyrants always say. It sure didn't seem fair to me when I was a kid.

Whenever I expressed this resentment, my father offered a simple solution, the same one rotten husbands offer oppressed wives: if you don't like it here, leave. Of course, this was a bad joke and we both knew it. Like those unhappy wives before feminism got going, I could not leave; there existed no societal means which would allow me to survive as an unattached child; I could not work, own property, obtain credit or in any way supply my own needs. The child's second-class status is a result of his or her utter dependence on elders.

So I stayed. And now—at the vantage point of age thirty-one—I see that it was a good deal, the best I've ever gotten. In exchange for absolutely minimal cooperation and politeness my father and mother gave me a solid upbringing, wise counsel, constant financial and emotional support, and advantages and opportunities which they as children could never have dreamed of.

But at seventeen I was convinced I was being ripped off, and yearned for my emancipation.

As long as kids have no choice, no genuine alternative, perhaps they will always be sharper than serpents' teeth.

And yet now I'm honestly glad I didn't have that choice. I'd have knocked up some twelve-year-old and today I'd be working nights in a gas station to meet the alimony and child-support, dreaming of going back to junior high school some day.

I don't welcome Kids' Lib, the way I yearned for it when I was a kid.

But I suspect something like it is coming . . . and if you're not careful, you could find yourself in the Lookover Lounge some day.

Thanks, Dad. Thanks, Mom. I'm just beginning to understand how much I owe you.

I think I even understand that the debt reads: "Pay to the order of Luanna Mountainborne Robinson." Isn't that right?

I'll try to make the payments.

As for the rest of you: perhaps I'll see you at Callahan's Place!